MW00623535

LIFE AND DEATH
AT ZOO ARROYO

Life and Death at Zoo Arroyo

A Witherston Murder Mystery

BETTY JEAN CRAIGE

LUMINARE PRESS
WWW.LUMINAREPRESS.COM

Life and Death at Zoo Arroyo: A Witherston Murder Mystery
Copyright © 2022 by Betty Jean Craige

All rights reserved. This book or any portion thereof may not be reproduced
or used in any manner whatsoever without the express written permission
of the publisher, except for the use of brief quotations in a book review.

Printed in the United States of America

Luminare Press
442 Charnelton St.
Eugene, OR 97401
www.luminarepress.com

LCCN: 2022901308
ISBN: 978-1-64388-927-6

To Branch, Siobhan, and Keelin Craige

Acknowledgments

A murder-mystery resembles an ecosystem: Its parts are interrelated. When the writer makes a mistake—such as giving a sleuth information the sleuth could not logically acquire until later in the narrative—the mistake affects the whole narrative. When the writer fixes the mistake, the fix affects the whole narrative. Fixes take time more time than mistakes, as any mystery writer knows.

I am grateful to Susan Tate, Margaret Anderson, and Lynn Beckmann for reading my manuscript and giving me multiple opportunities to fix the narrative.

I am indebted to Susan in particular for acquainting me with the wondrous Appalachian mountains of north Georgia and western North Carolina, where I have set all my mysteries.

I owe much to John Avise, author of *The Hope, Hype, and Reality of Genetic Engineering*, for introducing me to the possibilities of genome modification.

I thank Chuck Murphy, photographer extraordinaire and lover of all wildlife, for the image of the raccoon on the cover of this book. I modeled my character Benito Montoya after Chuck.

Finally, I thank Cosmo, my beloved twenty-year-old smart, talkative, witty, mischievous, affectionate African Grey parrot, for entertaining me every waking hour during the pandemic year of 2020.

I dedicate the book to Branch and Siobhan Craige, both of them scientists, and their daughter Keelin, who are dear to my heart.

If possessing a higher degree of intelligence does not entitle one human to use another for his or her own ends, how can it entitle humans to exploit non-humans?
—Peter Singer, *Animal Liberation*, 1975

Nature in the twenty-first century will be a nature that we make; the question is the degree to which this molding will be intentional or unintentional, desirable or undesirable.
—Daniel B. Botkin, *Discordant Harmonies*, 1990

. . . the weight of evidence indicates that humans are not unique in possessing the neurological substrates that generate consciousness. Nonhuman animals, including all mammals and birds, and many other creatures, including octopuses, also possess these neurological substrates.
—*The Cambridge Declaration on Consciousness*, 2012

PROLOGUE

The New York Times

AMERICAN SCIENTISTS
WIN APEX PRIZE

*October 31, 2029—The 2029 Apex Prize for Bio-
logical Innovation will be awarded to two American
scientists for genetically editing a chimpanzee's reproductive cells to create offspring whose organs may be
successfully transplanted into humans. The human
immune system will not reject the organs of the bioengineered chimp's descendants because it will not
recognize the organs as foreign. The genetic changes
are passed on to succeeding generations of chimps.*

*Drs. Hernando Ibarra and Olivia Wong, of the
Taxon Institute for Advanced Biological Studies in San
Francisco, will accept the $5 million international prize
at the American Academy of Scientific Research in New
York City on Saturday, January 26, 2030.*

*The bioengineered chimpanzees constitute a new
species, which Ibarra and Wong have named "the
Ibarra-Wong chimpanzee." The Ibarra-Wong chimpanzees physically resemble their African cousins
but are genetically distinct. The two species are not
reproductively compatible.*

*Dr. Ibarra said, "Dr. Wong and I have unveiled
the future of gene editing: that we humans can create*

new species for whatever purposes we imagine."

The Apex Prize recognizes pioneering achievements in the biological sciences.

The application deadline for the 2030 Apex Prize is October 1, 2031. The application should include executive summary, full report, and project data.

See: www.apexbiologicalinnovationprize.com.

PART I

Jorge

CHAPTER ONE

Friday, March 8, 2030

"Jorge! You here?"

"I'm in the clinic, Zell."

Zookeeper Zell rushed into the veterinary clinic. "Jorge, Marco's been shot!"

"What?" Dr. Jorge Arroyo looked up from his microscope.

"Shot! Almost killed. I called nine-one-one."

"Oh, no! Where is he?"

"At the otter pond," Zell Larson said. "He's barely conscious. He's lost a lot of blood. Nick and Bernie are with him."

"Nick? Isn't he in school?"

"Nick's on spring break."

Jorge arose from his chair, adjusted his prosthetic leg, grabbed his cane, a first aid kit, and a blanket, and climbed into Zell's pickup. They drove up the lane to the mink and otter enclosure. Nine-year-old Nick Crane and nine-month-old Bernie, Nick's Bernese Mountain dog, ran to the the gate.

"Marco got shot, Jorge!" Nick shouted. "He might die!"

Jorge spotted Marco immediately. The young scientist, his pajama top covered in blood under his unzipped yellow slicker, was lying face-up on the muddy ground. A flashlight, its beam weak, lay a few feet away.

"Hey there, Marco. Can you hear me?"

"Hi, Jorge." Marco opened his eyes.

Jorge opened Marco's shirt and listened to his heart. "Breathing is normal."

"Will he survive?" Nick asked.

"Looks like a bullet lodged in his left shoulder, near his heart," Jorge said after examining Marco. "But not in his heart, and not in his lungs. Yes, Nick, he'll survive."

Jorge held up Marco's head and gave him water.

"I'm cold," Marco said.

Jorge covered him with a blanket.

"Thanks, Jorge," Marco said. "You're a good vet."

"Marco must have been trying to stop a burglar," Nick said. "The minks are gone. Someone stole the minks."

"What? Nobody even knows we have minks," Jorge said.

"You haven't told anybody about the minks?" Zell asked him. "What about your brother?"

"Jaime would not have told anybody."

"What about that pretty lady who photographed the wolves for a magazine? Did you tell her about the minks?"

"Oh, you mean Lola Montoya. I guess I may have told her, but no way would she have shot Marco," Jorge said, "or stolen the minks."

"She could have told somebody about them," Zell said. "Was the shooter alone, Marco?"

"I think so," Marco murmured.

"What time did this happen, Marco?" Jorge asked.

"About one or two in the morning. Thunder woke me up after midnight. I couldn't get back to sleep. I heard a vehicle go up the lane, so I went out to see who it was. Next thing I knew I got shot."

"Marco, what did the shooter look like?" Jorge asked.

"I couldn't tell. The rain was coming down hard," Marco said.

"I hear a siren," Zell said. "Must be the ambulance."

AS THE MEDICS MOVED MARCO ONTO A GURNEY AND into the ambulance, Jorge got a call from Detective Mira Dunning of the Witherston Police.

"The victim's name is Marco Ramos," Jorge told her. "Marco is an intern at Zoo Arroyo. He assists my brother Jaime in artificial insemination, and he helps our zookeeper and me take care of the animals. He's from Perú, but he speaks English perfectly. He lives alone in an A-frame near the bison pasture."

After listening for a few moments, Jorge said, "Jaime and I have known Marco for almost two years. We trust him completely."

Jorge disconnected. "Detective Dunning will take the case. She'll be here in thirty minutes," he said to Zell and Nick. "She recommended that we lock the enclosures. I'll get a locksmith out this afternoon to put padlocks on the enclosure gates. Also on the zoo's entrance."

"Could all the padlocks open with the same key?" Zell asked. "That would make my job easier."

"Good idea. And I'll get keys for all of us."

JORGE AWAITED MIRA'S ARRIVAL IN HIS FRONT PORCH rocker. Poe the Crow perched on his shoulder. The day was warm for early March in the north Georgia mountains. Sixty degrees. The trees had not yet leafed out, but the forsythia, the daffodils, the crocuses, and the irises were blooming. They covered the hillside with purples and yellows.

Jorge remembered the day Marco came to the zoo seeking a job. It was early May, almost two years ago. After he and Jaime had completed their formal interview, Jaime asked Marco what he did for fun.

Marco replied, "I carve. I turn Rosewood and Mahogany and other Peruvian wood into furniture and musical instruments. And I play the flute."

"And you like poetry, I understand," Jaime said.

"I do. I like Federico García Lorca, Edgar Allen Poe, Walt Whitman, and Henry Wadsworth Longfellow."

"You favor poets who rhyme," Jaime said.

"I do."

"Marco has the makings for a good scientist," Jaime said after Marco had left, "because he has a heart."

Marco was only twenty-four years old at the time, four years younger than Jorge and Jaime.

If Marco had been killed he and Jaime—and Nick—would have been devastated.

Jorge watched Mira drive slowly into the zoo, park on the grass in front of the farmhouse, and jump out of the patrol car, an all-wheel drive Tesla wagon. He noticed that Mira now wore her wavy blond hair long. On a sunny day like this a few years ago, Jorge and Mira had bade farewell to each other. He had not seen her since.

"Hey there, Jorge!" Mira removed her officer's cap and gave him a hug.

"Hey there, Mira. Good to see you! Congratulations on your promotion to detective. Welcome to Zoo Arroyo."

"How have you been?"

"I've been well, Mira. And I understand your family has grown."

"We have two dogs, two cats, two cockatiels, two rabbits, and two little boys, ages seven and five."

"You all could fill an ark," Jorge said.

"Who's your bird, Jorge?"

"This is Poe. I rescued him when he fell out of his nest a year ago. He's pretty attached to me."

"I see. How do you know Poe is a male?"

"DNA test. Would you like water?" Jorge handed Mira a bottle of spring water.

"Thanks. Now take me to the crime scene."

Poe clung to Jorge's shoulder as Jorge walked with Mira up the lane and into the enclosure belonging to the minks and the otters, and a raccoon that came to visit and stayed. The ground was still muddy.

"No tire tracks here," Mira said. "Tell me, do you think that Marco Ramos interrupted a robbery and that he was an innocent victim? Or could he have recognized the intruder?"

"Marco was an innocent victim, Mira. He would have told me if he'd recognized the intruder. You have to meet Marco. He is as honest as they come."

"Another question: Why would anybody steal the minks?"

"American minks fetch a high price in the marketplace. Otters don't. That's why the intruder left the otters."

"Who knew that you had minks, Jorge?"

"Almost nobody. We've been keeping the minks a secret because of their rarity. So many minks died of COVID-19 that the species is endangered. My brother Jaime intends to rebuild their population in the Appalachians."

"Somebody had to know about them. You're sure you and Jaime told nobody?"

"Other than our staff? Possibly Lola Montoya, a photographer for *Wild Beasts Magazine.* She interviewed me on Tuesday. I may have told her."

"Did she record the interview?"

"Yes."

"Give me her email address and I'll get the recording."

As Mira drove away Jorge received a call from the editor of OnlineWitherston, the local news source.

"I understand you've had a shooting, Jorge."

"How did you find out about it, Beverly?"

"Police scanner. Can you talk?"

"Yes."

Jorge told Beverly what he knew.

"I'll post my article this afternoon, Jorge."

BIOLOGIST SHOT AT ZOO ARROYO
By Beverly Everett

3:00 pm, March 8, 2030. Marco Ramos, an employee of Zoo Arroyo in Rabun County, Georgia, was shot after midnight this morning by an intruder. He could not identify his assailant because of the heavy rain.

Mr. Ramos, age 26, was taken by ambulance to the Dahlonega Medical Center, where Dr. Reginald Mayfield removed a 9mm bullet from his left shoulder. Dr. Mayfield said that Mr. Ramos would suffer no long-term ill effects.

Mr. Ramos is a genetic engineer with a Master's degree from Georgia Tech. He assisted Zoo Arroyo in artificial insemination.

According to Dr. Jorge Arroyo, the zoo's director, Mr. Ramos must have interrupted a robbery. The intruder apparently stole a pair of American minks named Mickie and Minkie.

"The American mink is an endangered species," Dr. Arroyo said. "Zoo Arroyo obtained the pair to help increase their numbers in the Blue Ridge Mountains. The minks have reached reproductive age, and Minkie may be pregnant."

Zoo Arroyo is located at 1200 Bison Highway, twenty miles north of Witherston. Dr. Jorge Arroyo, a veterinarian, co-founded the zoo in 2027 with his twin brother Dr. Jaime Arroyo, a geneticist at the University of North Georgia in Dahlonega.

Detective Mira Dunning of the Witherston Police Department is investigating the case.

Jorge called Jaime, brought him up to date on the shooting, and read him Beverly's article.

"Now the shooter has the name of his victim," Jaime said. "I wonder if that puts Marco in danger."

⸻

AT FOUR THIRTY, MIRA CALLED. "HEY, JORGE. WOULD you like to listen to Lola Montoya's recording? I can play it to you on the phone."

Jorge could hear Mira's children laughing. Mira must be at home. He remembered the fun he and Mira had had together before the accident.

"Yes, Mira, please play it."

This is Lola Montoya, photographer for Wild Beasts Magazine. I am speaking with Dr. Jorge Arroyo, director of Zoo Arroyo. The date is March fourth, 2030. Dr. Arroyo, what is the zoo's mission?

Call me Jorge. The mission of Zoo Arroyo is two-fold. Wildlife rehabilitation and captive breeding of rare and endangered species.

You're a wildlife veterinarian.

Yes, and my twin brother Jaime is a wildlife biologist. I focus on wildlife rescue and rehabilitation, which means rescuing injured animals and treating them. If they can survive in the wild, we release them. If they cannot, we keep them. Jaime focuses on breeding to save a species from extinction.

So Zoo Arroyo is not really a zoo, Jorge.

Zoo Arroyo is a petting zoo for children on Saturdays. But it's primarily a rescue zoo. I have an exhibitor's license and a wildlife rehabilitator's license.

Who lives in this enclosure?

Look beyond the pond and you'll see a female American mink named Minkie, who lost a foot in a trap, and her mate Mickie. They have just reached sexual maturity, so they will probably breed soon if they haven't already. It's the season for mink love.

I'll take their pictures.

Please don't, Lola. We are not publicizing the minks. They are the zoo's most valuable animals. Monetarily, that is. COVID-19 drastically reduced the mink population in the Appalachian mountains. That's why we're hoping that Minkie will be fertile and fecund.

Who else lives here?

Two otters, Slippy and Slidey, who are playing in the pond. A raccoon named Bandit. A Red-shouldered hawk named Quill, and a Barred owl named Hoot. Quill has a broken wing. Hoot flies all over the zoo, but he seems to prefer this place. The fence encloses seven acres.

Does Hoot hoot?

At night Hoot hoots a lot. You can remember a Barred owl's hoot by saying, Who cooks for you? Who cooks for you all?

Okay. And the bears live next door?

Yes. The three bears: Romeo, Juliet, and Jackie. The bears' enclosure covers seventeen acres. So we don't see them every day. But they are fond of Zookeeper Zell and me, so they often greet us at the fence. I'll give them some beef knuckles. We got the bears last October, when the fire destroyed their habitat. Juliet gave birth to Jackie in January.

Here they come, all three of them. Let me get a picture.

Hey bears, here's dinner for you.

Oh, look. There's somebody in the tree.

That's Bob the bobcat. He's lame. He can't run, but he can still climb. He likes the bears too.

How big is your property, Jorge?

A hundred and ten acres, not counting the stream that runs through the zoo and feeds the larger pond in the pasture. The fifteen-acre pasture is the home of two American bison.

Where do the wolves live?

Sol, Luna, and their pack live over yonder in a sixty-acre fenced area of the forest that we call Sol's Woods.

How big is the pack?

Eight wolves in total. Sol and Luna are Gray wolves who came to us in February of 2028. The younger ones are Red wolves. The Red wolf is extinct in the wild, but we hope to bring it back. We want to restore the Appalachian mountains to their natural state when wolves kept the forest ecosystems in balance.

How are you getting Red wolves out of Gray wolves?

My brother Jaime and his colleagues clone captive Red wolves at a North Carolina facility, vitrify the embryos, transport them here in a freezer, thaw them, and implant them in the uterus of female Gray wolves. Last fall Jaime won the Benningham Prize for Young Scientists for inventing a new cloning technique.

When will he implant the embryos?

In late April, when wolves naturally mate. On April twenty-second, to be exact. But don't put that into the article.

"Next comes the personal part, Jorge. I must ask you, why did you speak so freely to Lola?"

"I confess I liked her, Mira. I actually want to see her again."

"That's obvious. Shall I play the rest of the recording?"

"Actually, I'd prefer to listen to it when I have more time. Could you email the recording to me?"

"Sure, Jorge. And I'll keep you informed."

AFTER DINNER JORGE CALLED LOLA AND TOLD HER THAT an intruder had shot Marco.

"*Por dios*, Jorge. What happened?"

"I think that Marco's shooter was after the minks, not Marco. Marco must have surprised him."

Will Marco be alright?"

"The bullet lodged in his shoulder, his left shoulder. The surgeon got it out. So Marco will be fine in a few days."

"Did Marco identify the shooter?"

"No. It was too dark for him to see clearly, even though he had a flashlight. The intruder stole our pair of minks.

You saw them. Minkie and Mickie."

"I wonder who could have wanted your minks enough to enter your zoo in the middle of a storm."

"I wonder too. I wonder who could have known about the minks."

"I hope you'll be fine, Jorge. I told my son Benito about you. He wants to meet you. He is a photographer like me, but maybe better."

"We'll arrange it. I would like to meet Benito. How old is he?"

"He will be thirteen on April twenty-second. I appreciate your call, Jorge. I look forward to seeing you again."

"Before you disconnect, Lola, I have one request: Would you please not mention in the *Wild Beasts* article that Zoo Arroyo is involved in cloning."

"I won't be writing the article, Jorge, but I'll convey your wishes to the editor. That's Willard Tavis."

"I have really enjoyed meeting you, Lola."

"I have enjoyed meeting you too, Jorge."

"Lola, I have to ask you. Why do you carry a gun?"

"You saw my gun?"

"Yes. I saw it in your bag when you took out your camera."

"My uncle Juan gave it to me a week ago. He said that I might need it for protection. I do a lot of driving at night."

"Have you ever used it?"

"Heavens no! I've never shot a gun in my life. My uncle says he will teach me soon."

"You'll have to tell me more about what you do, Lola."

"I will, Jorge, next time we get together."

"*Buenas noches*, Lola."

"*Buenas noches*, Jorge."

Jorge poured himself a glass of Chardonnay, removed his prosthesis, settled into his wheelchair, and opened the recording on his phone. He enjoyed listening to Lola's voice. Apparently Poe did too. Poe flew from the top of his cage to Jorge's shoulder.

> *Now let's go see the wolves, Lola. It's a bit of a walk. Okay with you?*
>
> *Sure.*
>
> *The wolves were the zoo's first residents.*
>
> *How did you come to have a zoo, Jorge?*
>
> *I owe the zoo to an automobile accident that took my leg. A decade ago, on Valentine's Day, Jaime and I drove up to Witherston in a snow storm. We shouldn't have gone, given the weather conditions, but Jaime wanted to see his girlfriend Annie. Jaime was driving. The mountain road was icy. A deer jumped out in front of the car, and Jaime swerved. The car skidded off the road and down a steep bank. Jaime got a concussion and a broken arm. I lost my left leg below the knee.*
>
> *Oh, no. How did that change your lives?*
>
> *The truth is, Jaime was more devastated than I. I do fine, but I don't think Jaime will ever get over feeling guilty. Anyway, after we recovered we made a pact to do something with our lives that would keep us together.*
>
> *You all were smart.*
>
> *I thought of wildlife rehabilitation, and Jaime, who was majoring in genetics, thought of species*

preservation. I got a doctorate in veterinary medicine, and Jaime got a PhD in wildlife genetics. We heard about this old farmhouse on a large plot of mostly forested land and we bought it with our inheritance. Our first goal was to reinstate the wolf population in the southern Appalachian mountains.

Your inheritance?

From our parents. They died of COVID-19 the summer after the accident.

I'm so sorry!

Anyway, when we announced we were creating a wildlife sanctuary, our family friend Rhonda Rather surprised us with a five-million-dollar endowment gift to enable us to become a non-profit.

Jorge paused the recording. He looked at the framed family photograph of himself and his identical twin Jaime standing behind their seated parents. With their dark eyes and curly black hair they resembled their mother. But when smiling they resembled their father. In the picture they were smiling. The picture was taken in 2019, at Thanksgiving, when he and Jaime were nineteen years old and their lives were uncomplicated.

Jorge poured himself another glass of wine and resumed listening. He heard Zookeeper Zell's baritone voice.

Hey, Jorge. You all need a ride anywhere?

Hello, Zell. Let me introduce you to Lola Montoya. She's doing a story on our zoo for Wild Beasts Magazine. Lola, this is Zell Larson, our zookeeper.

Pleased to meet you, Ms. Montoya. I'm Zookeeper Zell. I'm headed out to feed the wolves.

Want to come along?

Sure, thanks.

Hop in. Nice camera.

Oh, my god. I've never been so close to wolves before. I'm getting some great shots of them.

That's Sol with the red collar, and Luna with the pink collar. The younger wolves are coming now. They smell the meat.

Jorge, I can take you all back to the farmhouse now.

Thanks, Zell. But Lola and I will enjoy the walk.

See you later, Jorge. You too, Ms. Montoya.

Who else works here, Jorge?

Marco Ramos, our intern, Eddie Crane, our handyman and builder, Eddie's wife Emma, our computer geek, and their son Nick. You can see Marco's house from here. It's the A-frame on the other side of the bison pond. Marco is from Perú. He is teaching Nick to play the Andean flute.

I have an ecological question for you, Jorge. If you stock forests with wolves, are the forests still natural? Aren't you artificially re-creating the forests the way you imagine they were two hundred years ago?

Wow, Lola. You're asking, Are we making a designer forest? Let me think about it.

Maybe there's no right answer, Jorge. Anyway, thanks so much for the tour. I enjoyed meeting you.

Do you have to go now? Could you stay for dinner? I could open a bottle of wine and grill us a Rainbow trout I caught.

I wish I could, but I have to get on the road. Charleston is five hours away. My son is expecting me home by nine.

We have much to talk about, Lola. Where do you come from? Originally, I mean.

I am from Juárez, on the Mexican border across from El Paso. I am a naturalized citizen of the United States.

My father was from Madrid. He was a naturalized citizen.

It's a pleasure to meet you, Jorge.

The pleasure is mine. Do you have enough material, Lola?

I have enough pictures, Jorge. Oops, I forgot to turn off the recorder. I'll turn it off.

Jorge wrote Lola an email.

From: Jorge Arroyo (JorgeArroyo@zmail.com)
To: Lola Montoya (LolaMontoya@zmail.com)
9:44 pm, Friday, March 8, 2030
OUR INTERVIEW
    Hi, Lola.
    I just listened to the recording.
    I hope that I can persuade you (and your son) to share a meal with me.
    Hasta la vista,
    Jorge

Lola wrote back.

From: Lola Montoya (LolaMontoya@zmail.com)
To: Jorge Arroyo (JorgeArroyo@zmail.com)
9:52 pm, Friday, March 8, 2030
Re: OUR INTERVIEW
   Hi, Jorge.
   Do try.
   Hasta la vista,
   Lola

CHAPTER TWO

Saturday, March 9, 2030

O n his way to the Dahlonega Medical Center Jorge took a call from Mira.

"Mr. Ramos is awake and talking, Jorge. I interviewed him at nine o'clock this morning. He said his assailant drove a big, loud truck, black or navy blue. Do you know anybody who drives a dark-colored big, loud truck?"

"No, I don't. Zell Larson drives a small Ford Ranger, single cab. It's white. And my brother drives a silver Toyota Tacoma, double cab. You wouldn't call those trucks big. Certainly not dark-colored. Eddie drives a white Honda CRV. I drive a red jeep."

"Just checking. I have another question. Do you or any of your employees own a nine millimeter pistol?"

"No, Mira. The only guns we have at the zoo are stun guns. I have four employees. Zell Larson, Eddie Crane, Emma Crane, and Marco. Oh, and also Eddie and Emma's son Nick, whom I pay fifty dollars a week to assist me. None of them has ever mentioned owning a real gun."

"I find it hard to believe that a complete stranger entered the zoo in a thunderstorm to steal your minks. I just wondered whether it could be an inside job."

"Let me assure you, Mira. It could not have been an inside job. Zell, Eddie, Emma, and Marco are my best friends. They are loyal to me and devoted to the zoo's animals."

"I hope you're right Jorge. Anyway, I have one clue—the nine millimeter bullet Dr. Mayfield extracted from Marco's shoulder."

JORGE MET DR. MAYFIELD IN MARCO'S HOSPITAL ROOM. Dr. Mayfield finished signing the discharge papers.

"Your friend will recover quickly," Dr. Mayfield said to Jorge. "Watch him carefully today. No alcohol till he's off these pain meds." Dr. Mayfield handed Jorge a bottle of pills. "You can remove the bandages on Monday, but make sure he wears the sling for ten days."

"I'll treat him with the care I give all my patients," Jorge said.

"His patients are wolves and foxes and bears," Marco said. "But I'll be grateful if he treats me as kindly as he treats them.

"JORGE, HAVE YOU EVER HEARD OF THE GENETIC ENGI-neers Hernando Ibarra and Olivia Wong?"

"Can't say that I have, Marco."

Jorge and Marco were on their way back to the zoo when Marco opened his eyes and asked Jorge the question.

"Ibarra and Wong created a species of chimpanzee whose organs can be transplanted into humans. Do you think that's ethical?"

"Is that what you've been thinking about, Marco? Xenotransplantation? I figured you were thinking about your shooter."

"Ethics has been on my mind lately. I'd hoped we could talk this weekend. But maybe I don't feel up to it now."

Marco closed his eyes again.

Jorge nudged him awake when they got to the farmhouse.

"How about staying in my guest room for a couple of days, Marco? I'd make sure you got good food and rest. We could even play a game or two of chess."

"Thanks, but I'd like to sleep in my own bed tonight. Besides, Bonita must be waiting for me."

"Will you have dinner with me? I'll fix us a fish soup."

"Sure, Jorge. Thank you. But first please drop me off at my place. I need to send some texts."

Nick ran up to the passenger side of the jeep. "Hey, Marco! Are you gonna be okay? I took care of Bonita while you were gone."

"Thanks, Nick," Marco said.

"Would you like to join us for supper, Nick?"

"Yes! Thanks, Jorge. I'll go tell my mom right now."

CHAPTER THREE

Wednesday, March 20, 2030

At four in the afternoon Jorge's phone rang.

"Hello, Jorge. This is Lola Montoya. I've just finished a photo shoot about an hour's drive from Zoo Arroyo. Would you like me to drop by on my way home?"

"Sure, Lola! That would be terrific. Can you stay for an early dinner?"

"I'd love to."

"Do you eat chicken?"

"I eat chicken and fish and seafood. No red meat. I'll see you at five."

"I'll unlock the gate."

Jorge prepared a spicy chicken stew and a big tossed salad. He uncorked a bottle of Rioja.

At five o'clock Jorge heard Lola's Range Rover roll down the gravel road and stop in front of the farmhouse. With his cane in his right hand and Poe on his left shoulder Jorge walked down the steps to greet her.

"*Hola*, Jorge." Lola said. She gave him a hug.

Lola was dressed in tight jeans, a bright red shirt, and a black leather jacket. She had pulled her black hair into a pony tail. Her red lipstick set off her brown skin. She looked younger than her thirty-two years.

"Thanks for stopping by, Lola."

"Good to see you again, Jorge. And Poe too." Lola allowed Poe to peck her hand. "Aren't you afraid Poe will fly away?"

"Poe injured his wing when he was a hatchling, so he can fly over short distances only."

"I'll take a picture of you and Poe for my son Benito."

"Would you like to have Billy Bear in the picture too?" Jorge put his hand on the shoulder of a six-foot-tall chain-saw carving of a Black bear on the porch.

"I would." Lola extracted her late-model Nikon from her red satchel and took several pictures of Jorge and Poe by the standing bear. Jorge again glimpsed the small handgun.

"A peacock!" Lola exclaimed.

"Meet Narcissus, our affectionate and noisy Indian Blue peacock. He wants to touch your hand."

Lola extended her hand to Narcissus. Narcissus spread his tail feathers.

"Let's go inside," Jorge opened the farmhouse door for Lola. Poe flew onto his perch.

"Your home tells me a lot about you, Jorge. For one thing you like art. You have a wonderful collection."

"Thank you. I collect Native American art and chainsaw bears. Look around while I get our wine."

Native American paintings covered one wall of the farmhouse living room. Small wood carvings of eagles, owls, and deer filled the glass shelves of a curio cabinet. A large framed charcoal drawing of two foxes hung over the mantle. A chain-saw Black bear cub occupied the rocking chair. Another one sat on the hearth. A six-foot-tall bird cage took up the corner. Sunshine flowing through a skylight illuminated the stone fireplace.

Lola sat down on the leather couch and picked up the family photograph on the end table. "So these are your parents?"

"Yes. I still miss them."

Poe flew to Lola's shoulder. Jorge took the recliner across from her.

"I hope you like birds, Lola," Jorge said, filling her glass.

"I do. I grew up with a Mexican Red-headed Amazon parrot named Conchita, and now Benito and I live with a Yellow-headed Amazon named Cha Cha. I love birds."

"How big is your family, Lola?"

"My immediate family is small. Only Benito and me. Benito's father and I divorced when Benito was a toddler. My mother resides in Juárez and has a good job at the autonomous university there. My uncle Juan, who is my mother's brother, brought me to Charleston nine years ago to work with him waiting tables at La Fiesta. Now he works for Willard Tavis with a man he calls Gordo. Juan lives on Mr. Tavis's property."

"What's Willard Tavis like?"

"I don't know much about him, actually. Juan tells me that Mr. Tavis makes a lot of money. He has a niece but no children. He's divorced."

"And he edits *Wild Beasts Magazine*."

"Right, Jorge. Now tell me about Jaime."

"Jaime is my twin brother, my best friend, and my soul mate. He's my other half. Jaime, his wife Annie, their twin daughters, and their Golden retriever Amigo, live in Dahlonega. Jaime teaches genetics at the University of North Georgia. And he plays the guitar really well."

"Do you play the guitar?"

"No. I am better at writing and drawing."

"Did you do that charcoal drawing of the foxes?"

"I did."

"It's remarkable. So you must have done the zoo's logo of the wolf baying at the moon."

"I did."

"You're also good at interviewing environmentalists on your radio show."

"Yes! 'People for the Planet.' How did you know about it?"

"I googled you and listened to a program on the Zoo Arroyo website."

"Now tell me what you do, Lola."

"I sing, play the guitar, and cook."

"You're a photographer. What do you shoot besides animals?"

"I shoot weddings, graduations, corporate events, banquets, even birthday parties. It's only once or twice a month that I take pictures for Mr. Tavis."

"Is photography your passion?"

"My passion, Jorge, is protecting the environment. I was just elected president of Green Earth Charleston. Our big project for 2030 is to document the effect of climate change on plants and animals in the coastal ecosystem. I'm in charge of the photography."

"That's fantastic, Lola!"

"You are a good interviewer, Jorge."

"Can you help me get the food on the table?"

"I'd be delighted."

Jorge showed Lola into the kitchen he had painted yellow and had refurbished with vintage light fixtures and appliances—sink, stove, oven, and refrigerator—which he had discovered in a retro store in Dahlonega.

"What do you think, Lola? "

"I should be wearing a polka-dotted housedress with a white ruffled apron, and I should be baking cookies while listening to the radio."

"If you feel you're living in the nineteen fifties, then I got it right."

"Seriously, Jorge. I love what you've done with this farmhouse."

At dinner Jorge brought up the conversation Lola had initiated on her previous visit.

"Lola, you asked me, 'If you repopulate the forests with wolves, are the forests still natural?' I say Yes. We reestablishing the original balance of nature. We are trying to bring back the wilderness."

"For aesthetic reasons?"

"Partly, but mainly for ethical reasons. We humans have brought about climate change and destabilized ecosystems across the planet. Because of us, many species have gone extinct, such as the Red wolf. Jaime and I want to return to the mountains a few of the predatory animals that kept the wilderness in balance for ten thousand years."

"I'm on your side there, Jorge. I also know you like wolves and minks. I happen to like skunks and Wood rats, who are also cute."

"Okay. I'll ask Jaime if he would repopulate the woods with skunks and rats if they were on the verge of extinction."

"Delicious stew, Jorge. Thanks so much." Lola finished her wine. "I must be going."

"Let me answer my phone first, Lola. Nick's calling me on FaceTime."

"Hey, Nick. What's up?"

"Shaggy is about to give birth. See?" Nick showed the bison struggling to expel the calf. "Do you want to come watch? Right now?"

"I'll be there in five minutes." Jorge ended the call.

"Do you have time to witness a bison birth before you leave, Lola? It's only six thirty, and it's still light."

"Yes, yes!"

Jorge grabbed his medical bag and a spring scale, Lola grabbed her camera, and they and took off for the pasture in Jorge's jeep.

By the time they arrived, Shaggy's calf was on the ground.

"It's a girl!" Nick said. "Just like Jaime said when he got Shaggy pregnant."

"Jaime got her pregnant?" Lola smiled.

"Jaime and Marco implanted her with an embryo clone of a female Wood bison," Jorge said. "Nick, this is my friend Lola Montoya. Lola, this is my assistant Nick Crane."

"Pleased to meet you, Nick."

"I live here at the zoo," Nick said. "My parents work for Jorge."

"Where's Marco, Nick? Did you call him?"

"He didn't pick up," Nick said. "Jorge, we need a name for the baby bison. How about Zoey, like Zoey Billings in my class?"

"Good name. Is Zoey Billings your girlfriend, Nick?"

"Maybe soon," Nick said.

Jorge weighed the calf.

"Zoey, you weigh fifty-five pounds," Jorge said. "You are a healthy Wood bison calf, and just a bit heavier than an American bison newborn."

Jorge gently laid Zoey on the grass.

Zoey struggled to get on her feet. Within minutes she was standing under Shaggy and searching for a teat.

"I've got good pictures of you, Zoey," Lola said, "and of your mother."

"You've photographed nearly all the zoo's residents, Lola. You know a lot about us."

"But I haven't met Marco."

"You haven't met my parents either," Nick said.

"You'll meet them soon," Jorge said.

"And Marco? What does he do, Jorge?"

"Marco does lots of things. The best thing, in my view, is that he plays the flute—not a fancy silver flute, but a wooden *quena* flute, and also a Peruvian *pan* flute. Marco is from Perú."

"Marco is teaching me to play," Nick said.

"What does Marco do for the zoo?"

"Marco works with Jaime in embryo transfers. He has an undergraduate degree from the University of Lima in biology and a master's degree from Georgia Tech in genetic engineering."

"And Zookeeper Zell feeds the animals?" Lola asked.

"Zell Larson feeds and cares for the animals. He has a degree in animal husbandry. He commutes from Witherston."

"Seven days a week?"

"Five days a week. I feed the animals on weekends. Sometimes Nick helps me."

"Do you ever get time off?"

"Saturday night is time off for all of us," Jorge said. "I often go to my brother's house in Dahlonega for dinner. Eddie and Emma and Nick go to Tallulah Falls to visit family. Marco usually goes away for the whole weekend, except when he's needed here."

"Let's go see the wolves again," Lola said. "I'd like to take more pictures for Benito."

"First, let's stop and smell the honeysuckle, Lola."

CHAPTER FOUR

Monday, April 22, 2030

A s Faye lay sedated on the operating table, Marco Ramos prepared the two-year-old wolf for the embryo transfer. He wiped her belly with alcohol and then inserted a camera needle on the right side.

Nick was holding Faye's head. "Be a good wolf, Faye," he said. "We're making you pregnant." Nick had asked to watch.

Jaime Arroyo looked up from the microscope.

"Are the embryos okay?" Marco asked. "They should be thawed and rehydrated by now."

"Good to go," Jaime said. "You and Nick hold Faye while I inject her. Nick, we're implanting four cloned embryos of a female Red wolf."

The procedure was apparently painless. Faye did not protest.

"Now let's have Luna. Luna gets four female Red wolf embryo clones too, but from a different wolf."

"And Fern gets four female Red Wolf embryos from a third Red wolf," Marco said.

"Three times four makes twelve female pups we'll get," Nick said.

Jaime and Marco followed the same embryo transfer procedure with Luna and Fern. Luna and Fern likewise fared well.

"Why all female embryos, Jaime?" Nick asked.

"We want more female Red wolves for breeding, Nick. We'll implant male embryos in Fran tomorrow."

"I can stay with Luna and Faye and Fern till they wake up."

"Thanks, Nick. They'll probably be ready to return to the woods this afternoon."

"I'll take them back," Marco said. "Say, around three?"

"I'll go with you," Nick said.

"Take food for the pack," Jaime said.

From his rocking chair Jorge watched the sun disappear over Black Rock Mountain. The slopes were covered with the pink and white blossoms of dogwoods and azaleas. The air carried the fragrance of pines.

Jorge called Lola with an invitation.

"Eddie and I will be in Savannah the week of May fifth for the Southeastern Zoo and Menagerie Association annual meeting. We'll be staying at the Marriott Riverfront Hotel. Would you like to meet me there for dinner on Sunday night?"

"Yes! I would love to meet you for dinner if I may bring Benito."

"Of course!"

"Benito turned thirteen today," Lola said.

"Tell Benito *feliz cumpleaños* for me. I'll bring him a birthday present when we have dinner.

"Let's make it early, because Benito and I have to drive back to Charleston afterwards. Sunday is a school night, you know."

"Suits me. I'll meet you and Benito at five thirty in the Marriott Hotel lobby."

"I look forward to getting together."
"*Hasta pronto*, Lola."
"*Hasta pronto*, Jorge."

From: Estela Navarro (EstelaNavarro@zmail.com)
To: Lola Montoya (LolaMontoya@zmail.com)
10:01 pm, Monday, April 22, 2030
HAPPY BIRTHDAY TO BENITO
    Querida Lola,
    How is Benito on his thirteenth birthday?
    I remember so well my adorable grandson's first birthday party.
    I miss you all, but I believe you made the right decision to move to the U.S.
    Come again soon for a visit.
    Con mucho cariño,
    Tu Mami

From: Lola Montoya (LolaMontoya@zmail.com)
To: Estela Navarro (EstelaNavarro@zmail.com)
10:17 pm, Monday, April 22, 2030
Re: HAPPY BIRTHDAY TO BENITO
    Querida Mami,
    Benito and I miss you too.
    Benito was four when we left Juárez. I was twenty-four and already divorced.
    I felt bad leaving you to bring Benito to Charleston nine years ago.
    But it was the right decision. Benito is doing well and making all A's.

I feel happy that you have your position at the university.

Benito will write you a thank-you note for the guitar you sent him, which he loves.

I gave him a tiny "spy" camera. Tío Juan gave him a shaving kit.

As usual, Benito's father did not contact him—no card, no gift.

Stay well, Mamacita.

Muchos besos,

Lola

CHAPTER FIVE

Sunday, April 28, 2030

Jorge took his usual spot in front of the studio microphone. His guest sat beside him with her own mic and headphones. His producer signaled the start time.

"Hello, north Georgia listeners! Welcome to 'People for the Planet' on WITH-FM, broadcasting from Witherston, Georgia. I am Jorge Arroyo, and I am devoting the next few programs to the subject of animal rights. My guest today is Samantha Wheeling, presently from Chattanooga, Tennessee, and formerly from Witherston. Samantha is founder and president of Green Earth International and the author of the new book *Must We Name Animals To Confer Rights?* Hello, Samantha."

"Hi, Jorge. It's good to be with you."

"Tell us about your book."

"Okay. Let me ask you. Have you named the animals you keep at Zoo Arroyo?"

"Yes, every one of them."

"Why have you named them?"

"They all have distinct personalities. They know me and the Zoo Arroyo team. They have thoughts and feelings. They are feathery and furry persons. I consider them friends, like my crow Poe."

"What are some of the names you've given them?"

"Shaggy and Brown-Eyes, who are bison. Sol and Luna, who are wolves. Romeo and Juliet and Jackie, who are bears. Hoot, who is a Barred owl."

"Have you named any of the deer who wander into Zoo Arroyo?"

"No."

"Don't you think that those deer know you and the Zoo Arroyo team?"

"I hadn't thought of it. I suppose they do."

"What about the squirrels who steal seed from your birdfeeder? Do they know you?"

"They must. They peer into my kitchen from outside the window."

"If you named all those deer and all those squirrels, would you want to grant them each the right to a happy life?"

"I would."

"That's the thesis of my book, Jorge. Everybody has thoughts and feelings, just like the individual animals we name. I propose that we grant all animals the right to pursue happiness, the same right that we grant all humans."

"Even skunks and Wood rats?"

"Even skunks and rats and bats and porcupines."

"Are you advocating that we humans become vegetarians?"

"No. I don't mean we can't eat animals. I mean that we grant all creatures the right to happiness. A mouse in the meadow is happy until a fox eats him. The fox is happy until an eagle eats him."

"How are we infringing on the animals' right to pursue happiness, Samantha? Can you give us an example?"

"I can give you a hundred examples, all in the category of 'cage.' Think of chickens packed into tiny cages on a chicken truck bound for the poultry plant. Think of calves confined in small crates until they are slaughtered for veal. Think of the wild animals locked up in zoos and menageries. If we recognized these animals as individuals with consciousness, we'd feel obligated to grant them rights."

"Samantha, I have long wondered why we humans feel superior to other animals."

"That assumption has religious origins, Jorge, that I don't want to get into. But the practical reason is obvious. If we want to cage other animals we don't want to consider them conscious individuals. If we want to eat a chicken, we don't want to know her name. Our conscience would bother us."

"Good point."

"Imagine going to Kroger and picking up a package of chicken labeled 'These thighs came from the late Duchess Eggnog, Princess Lay, and Lady Cluck.'"

"I'd become a vegetarian then and there, Samantha."

"Imagine asking the butcher to cut you a roast from Patty Sue's ribs."

"I'd rather eat alfalfa."

"Me too."

"We've come to the end of our program, Samantha. Is there anything else you'd like to tell our listeners?

"Yes. If you are mistreating any animal in your care, Green Earth will find you and expose you. If you are breeding animals without consideration for their happiness, Green Earth will find you and expose you."

"Thank you, Samantha Wheeling, for being my guest today on 'People for the Planet.'"

"One last comment, Jorge?"

"Go ahead, Samantha."

"Please read my friend Garrison Tucker's new book *Does Every Species Belong to Us?* as well as my book."

"I will read both, Samantha. Thank you, mountain listeners, for tuning in. Come back on May twenty-sixth, for an interview with another fascinating guest. This is Jorge Arroyo, and we've just listened to Samantha Wheeling on 'People for the Planet.'"

CHAPTER SIX

Sunday, May 5, 2030

Jorge was on his phone when Lola and Benito entered the elegant lobby of the Marriott Savannah Riverfront Hotel.

"I'll call you later, Jaime," Jorge said. "Marco just texted me that Juliet is doing fine. But in case there's a problem Eddie and I will return to the zoo tomorrow."

Jorge disconnected.

"Hey there, Lola!" Jorge gave her a hug. "And this must be your son Benito."

Jorge was struck by the good-looking boy's resemblance to his mother. Benito was tall, dark-skinned, with black hair and smiling black eyes. He had the faint shadow of a mustache.

"Yes, sir, Dr. Arroyo. Pleased to meet you." Benito gave Jorge an elbow bump.

"Call me Jorge. I have a twin brother who is Dr. Arroyo too. He's Jaime."

"Pleased to meet you, Jorge."

"I've made reservations for us in the dining room. This way."

They all ordered shrimp scampi.

Jorge told Lola and Benito what was on his mind.

"A half hour ago Eddie got a call from his son Nick. Nick is nine years old, Benito, but he's already learning to be a vet. Anyway, Nick reported that Juliet—one of our bears—seemed dopey this afternoon. I texted Marco, and Marco said that he'd tranquilized Juliet to examine her because she had passed a little blood. He didn't find anything wrong with her."

"Are you worried about Juliet?" Lola asked.

"Not really worried. But I do want to check on her. Eddie and I are driving back to the zoo tomorrow."

"May I change the subject, Mom?"

"Sure, Benito."

"Mom told me that your brother transferred clone embryos into your female wolves. I have two questions. First, do female wolves go into heat like dogs?"

"The answer to that question is yes, Benito. So do bears. So do wolverines. So do lions. So do raccoons."

"Do rats?"

"Rats come into heat every four or five days. Sounds like your mother has talked with you about animals mating."

"Yes, sir. She's told me everything."

Lola gave Jorge a wink.

"My second question is: Does Sol mate with any of the wolves?"

"Sol, the alpha male, has been sterilized, Benito. He still mates with Luna, but he is not the father of her pups, who are all Red wolf clones," Jorge said.

"Does he think he's the father?"

"Yes! And he's quite proud of his pack."

"We should be getting on the road, Jorge," Lola said.

"Wait, you all. I haven't given Benito his belated birthday present. Actually, one present and one commission."

Jorge produced from his backpack a large manilla envelope, which Benito opened.

"Wow! A cartoon of a crow eating off a fork. Look, Mom. It's framed."

"Is that Poe, Jorge? Do you feed Poe at the table?"

"I confess I do, Lola. And when Poe gets to know you he'll want you to feed him at the table too."

"Cool," Benito said. "Thanks so much, Jorge. I really like it. I'll hang it in my room."

"You are an excellent cartoonist, Jorge," Lola said. "Really excellent!"

"Now here's another envelope for you to open, Benito."

Benito extracted a document from the smaller envelope.

ZOO ARROYO
Animals (Mammal and Avian)
RESIDENTS OF BREEDING/RESCUE ZOO

American Bison: Brown-Eyes, Shaggy, and Zoey

Black Bears: Romeo, Juliet, and Jackie

Red Foxes: Foxy Ann, Foxy Belle

Red-shouldered hawk: Quill

American Minks: Mickie, Minkie

North American River Otters: Slippy, Slidey

Raccoon: Bandit

Barred Owl: Hoot

Mexican Puma: Kitty Rather

Gray wolves: Sol and Luna

Red wolves: Faye, Fern, Fran, Gabby, Gert, and Grace

RESIDENTS OF PETTING ZOO

Chickens: Henny, Penny, Buttercup, Beauty, Feathers, and Doctor Doodle Doo

Donkey: Sancho

Horse (miniature): Herman

Goats: Nanny, Patty

Peacock: Narcissus

Sheep: Wooly, Bully

Skunk: Blossom

VISITORS

Deer, cats, rabbits, raccoons, opossums, squirrels, chipmunks, skunks, and armadillos.

"Is this a list of the zoo animals, Jorge?" Benito asked.

"It is, Benito. I invite you to Zoo Arroyo to take a close-up photo of every one of these animals. We'll make a gallery on the wall of a guest room for the portraits."

"Thank you, Jorge. Thank you! *Muchas gracias*. I accept the commission. I specialize in close-ups. I can add to my portfolio."

"I will pay you three dollars per portrait. You can just email them to me and I'll print out the images."

At seven thirty Jorge bade goodbye to Lola and Benito.

NOT READY TO RETURN TO HIS ROOM, JORGE HAD GONE to the bar for a beer when he got a text from Nick.

Hey, Jorge.

Juliet is doing fine. I just checked on her.

Mom said that maybe Romeo had made love to Juliet.

Romeo, Juliet, and Jackie are all asleep in a big black furry pile.

I whittled a bear for Mom for Mother's Day. Marco helped.

Tell Dad I miss him.

Your assistant,

Nick

Jorge responded.

Thanks, Nick.

Your father and I will see you tomorrow.

Sleep tight.

Jorge

Monday, May 6, 2030

From: Lola Montoya (LolaMontoya@zmail.com)
To: Estela Navarro (EstelaNavarro@zmail.com)
9:17 pm, Monday, May 6, 2030
TU VIDA
> *Querida Mami,*
> *I've never asked you this question, but now I'm curious.*
> *How soon after you met Papi did you think you were in love?*
> *And how long after that did you and Papi get married?*
> *Con mucho cariño,*
> *Tu hija*

From: Estela Navarro (EstelaNavarro@zmail.com)
To: Lola Montoya (LolaMontoya@zmail.com)
9:30 pm, Monday, May 6, 2030
Re: TU VIDA
> *Querida Lola,*
> *I met your father in Guadalajara at my my fifteenth birthday party.*

He was nineteen years old and a student at the University of Guadalajara.

I fell in love with him when we first danced.

We didn't get married till September 18, 1995, on my eighteenth birthday.

A mariachi band dressed in white played at our wedding.

Then we moved to Juárez. And you were born on November 20, 1996.

We loved each other till the day he died, in 2010.

Have you met somebody you could love as much as I loved your father?

Un fuerte abrazo,

Tu Mami

From: Lola Montoya (LolaMontoya@zmail.com)
To: Estela Navarro (EstelaNavarro@zmail.com)
9:47 pm, Monday, May 6, 2030
Re: TU VIDA

Querida Mami,

I have met somebody.

A lot depends on Benito.

Besos,

Lola

CHAPTER SEVEN

Sunday, May 19, 2030

Jorge had invited Jaime, Annie, the twins Heather and Holly, and Amigo up to the zoo for their midday Sunday dinner.

At the last minute Jorge persuaded Marco to join them. Marco had followed Jaime through the zoo's entrance gate. Ordinarily on Sundays Marco did not return to the zoo until late afternoon or evening.

"Hi, Mr. Marco," Heather said. "I'm Heather."

"Hi, Mr. Marco," Holly said. "I'm Holly. We dressed alike, so you may have a hard time telling us apart."

"Let me close my eyes for fifteen seconds while you all run around the porch and sit in different chairs. Then I'll guess who is who," Marco said.

After fifteen seconds Marco opened his eyes. One of the girls had found Jorge's straw hat and put it on.

"Let's see. I'm not taking any chances, so I'll guess you are Heather," Marco said, pointing to the girl in the hat, "and you are Heather," he said, pointing to the other one. "Did I get it half right?"

"You did!" Holly said.

The girls squealed in delight.

"Mr. Marco, do you have any children we could play with?"

"I do not, Heather. Or are you Holly? But I would certainly like to have children sometime."

"Do you have any dogs?"

"I don't have any dogs either."

"Do you have a wife?"

Marco hesitated. "I live alone, girls."

"Do you have anybody?"

"I have a cat. Her name is Bonita."

"Oh."

"Oh."

"Marco has a flute, girls," Jorge said. "I bet he'll play some music from Perú for us after lunch. Your father brought his guitar, and your mother brought her voice."

The girls giggled. "Uncle Jorge! Mom always brings her voice."

"And you girls brought your dancing feet," Jorge said.

After their big meal of roasted duck the group moved out to the porch. Marco went back to the A-frame to retrieve a *bombo*, that is, a large wooden drum, for Jorge, and a *pan* flute for himself.

Marco introduced Jaime's family to Incan music, to which the girls danced.

Before long Nick joined them. He had his *quena* flute in hand.

"I heard you all playing, so I came to join you. Marco taught me," Nick explained to Heather and Holly.

"And, Nick, you play the flute like a native Peruvian," Marco said.

"Thanks, Marco. How's your girlfriend?"

"She's fine, Nick."

"She's very pretty, Marco," Nick added.

"I'll tell her you said so, Nick. Now let's make music together."

"We can form a band and call ourselves the 'The Blue Ridge Mountain Incans.'"

"Now that's a good band name, Nick!" Jaime said.

"I've been thinking about it," Nick said.

Heather asked "Could you play some American songs, Nick, like 'Puff the Magic Dragon'?"

"I can't, girls, but your parents can."

The hootenanny lasted till late afternoon.

That evening Jorge took his wine outside to watch the sun disappear over the mountain peaks. Sitting in the swing under the porch lamp he thumbed through the copy of *Wild Beasts Magazine* Lola had sent him. He was pleased with the cover photo of the wolves as well as the story about Zoo Arroyo.

Then he spotted an ad:

We buy and sell wild animals and hybrid predators.
We also buy and sell sperm.
Leave voice mail at 800-340-4838.

Jorge called the number. Nobody picked up. He did not leave a message.

He called Jaime and read the ad to him over the phone.

"Why the secrecy?" Jorge said. "If this market for sperm and wild animals were legitimate, the ad would have named an institution or an organization."

"Right, bro. Sounds like black market communication. Commerce in wild animals is illegal."

At nine o'clock Jorge FaceTimed Lola. Nine o'clock had become their usual time to talk.

"You look *bellísima*, Lola, even this late in the evening."

"And you look *muy guapo* yourself, Jorge."

"I have another invitation for you and Benito," Jorge said. "Would you and Benito like to spend the weekend of July twelfth through fourteenth at Zoo Arroyo? Jaime and Marco are transferring Swift fox embryos into Foxy Ann and Foxy Belle this week, so the foxes could deliver their kits that weekend."

"We would love to come to the zoo then, Jorge. Benito would want to photograph the kits."

"We can't be sure of the due dates, because the Swift fox gestation period is fifty-three days, and the Red fox gestation period ranges between forty-nine and fifty-eight. But I'd love for you all to spend that weekend with me anyway."

"Benito will be thrilled. He'll bring his cameras."

"The farmhouse has two guestrooms, so you and Benito will each have your own room and bath."

"Perfect, Jorge. Thank you."

"One other thing. Thanks for the advanced copy of *Wild Beasts*.

"Did you see the ad for buying and selling wild animals and sperm?" Lola asked.

"I did. What did you think of it?"

"I wondered whether Mr. Tavis placed it himself. Or if not Mr. Tavis, one of his friends."

CHAPTER EIGHT

Wednesday, May 22, 2030

"What are your plans for the future, Marco?" Jaime asked.

Jaime and Marco were implanting the Swift fox clones in Foxy Ann and Foxy Belle in Jorge's operating room. "Do you still want to leave the zoo at the end of June?"

"Until last Sunday I was prepared to leave on June twenty-eighth," Marco said. "But when we were all making music together, with Heather and Holly dancing, I wanted to stay. May I let you know in a month?"

"Certainly. We'd like to extend your contract. You are part of our team, Marco."

"Thank you. I'm truly grateful."

"I'll tell Jorge you're considering it, Marco. He'll try to persuade you to stay here too," Jaime said.

"You asked about my plans for the future. The truth is that I am unsure. I had hoped to enter a PhD program in reproductive genetics at Georgia Tech next fall, and I guess I still want to do that. But let me ask you. What is it about your scientific work that gives you most pleasure?"

"Knowing that I'm making a better world for others, Marco."

"Just for human others, or for everybody?"

"In my work I'm helping restore the populations of endangered species to the wild. So I suppose I'm trying to make a better world for everybody—humans, wolves, foxes, the whole biosphere."

"You're fortunate that you have no moral qualms about your scientific project."

"I don't, Marco. I would not embark on a scientific project if it gave me moral qualms."

"You said in your acceptance speech for the Benningham Prize last October that scientists should always ask: 'Who is helped? Who is harmed?' I've been thinking about xenotransplantation, such as the use of chimpanzees' hearts to save humans with degenerative heart disease. It's a good thing for the person with degenerative heart disease, but not for the chimpanzee. From the chimpanzee's viewpoint, isn't heart xenotransplantation basically a violation of his rights?"

"Good god, Marco! Of course it is. It's homicide."

"That's my view too."

"Heart xenotransplantation requires the surgeon to think of the chimp as a commodity, something for humans to use. What got you thinking about this?"

"I read that the Apex Prize for Biological Innovation was awarded this year to two geneticists who transplanted a chimp's heart into a human being. And the reason the operation was a success, from the human standpoint, was that the chimp had been genetically designed for that purpose. Let me read you something."

Marco took a copy of a *New York Times* article out of his wallet.

The 2029 Apex Prize for Biological Innovation will be awarded to two American scientists for genetically editing a chimpanzee's reproductive cells to create offspring whose organs may be successfully transplanted into humans. The human immune system will not reject the organs of the bioengineered chimp's descendants because it will not recognize the organs as foreign. The genetic changes are passed on to succeeding generations of chimps.

"The scientists, Hernando Ibarra and Olivia Wong of the Taxon Institute for Advanced Biological Studies in San Francisco, created a new species just to harvest their organs," Marco said, "the Ibarra-Wong chimpanzee. Jaime, the chimps' purpose in life is to be killed. That's got to be unethical."

"I agree. But cattle ranchers would say that their cows' purpose in life it to be killed. Marco, why do you keep the article in your wallet?"

"I wanted to show it to you. I've already talked with Jorge about it. If xenotransplantation is the future of genetics I don't want to be a geneticist."

"Marco, if you become a geneticist, you choose how you use your scientific education. Nobody makes that decision for you."

"I want to do something important in science that presents no ethical dilemma whatsoever."

"Such as?"

"I don't know yet. I'm torn. Did you ever have any doubts about what you wanted to do in life?"

"No, not really, Marco. I was fortunate. I always wanted to study nature. When I was in high school I wanted to become an ecologist, but after the accident, when Jorge and I decided to tie our work to each other's, I became a wildlife biologist. Jorge became a vet. We bought this land and created a zoo. We never looked back."

Marco looked out the window at the grassy hill.

"I do love my life here at Zoo Arroyo," Marco said. "I'll decide soon if I can stay on."

CHAPTER NINE

Sunday, May 26, 2030

"Hello, north Georgia listeners! Welcome to 'People for the Planet' on WITH-FM, broadcasting from Witherston, Georgia. I am Jorge Arroyo, with my second program devoted to animal rights. My guest today is Professor Garrison Tucker from Augusta, Georgia. Professor Tucker is the author of the recently published book *Does Every Species Belong to Us?* He has both a law degree and a PhD in philosophy from the University of Georgia. Welcome, Professor Tucker."

"Thank you for having me on your show, Jorge. And call me Garrison."

"Your book is groundbreaking. That's why I invited you. Tell our audience about it."

"The subject of the book is our exploitation of other species for our benefit. I am not just talking about the production of food, which should certainly be made into a kinder industry. And I am not talking about the market for pets. I am talking about the cruel and unnecessary exploitation of non-human animals in general. I have a chapter on the exploitation of pigs, sheep, and chimpanzees for their organs."

"Explain."

"Until recently, we raised or hunted animals for food, clothing, transportation, and companionship. Now we are designing animals whose organs our immune systems won't reject. That's the height of animal exploitation."

"Is it a common practice, Garrison?"

"It's becoming a common medical practice. This year's Apex Prize went to two genetic engineers who created a species of chimpanzee whose organs we humans can use.

"Who were the scientists? I may have heard of them."

"Hernando Ibarra and Olivia Wong. They named the new species after themselves: the Ibarra-Wong chimpanzee. That's a gross violation of animal rights."

"How would you rectify this situation, Garrison?"

"I would give legal standing to the Ibarra-Wong chimps. I would give legal standing to all animals. I would give mistreated animals the right to sue their abusers."

"Elaborate, please."

"I would give standing to all abused animals, to female dogs in puppy mills who have been forced to produce litter after litter until they die of exhaustion, to caged rats, rabbits, and chimps in scientific laboratories who have been deliberately infected with diseases, to unnatural hybrids such as ligers who have been bred simply to satisfy the breeder's curiosity, and to primates abused and exploited by us humans."

"In your hypothetical legal world, would these unfortunate animals sue for money?"

"Yes. For money and a better life. The only way to deter cruel exploitation is to hurt the exploiters financially."

"You would have ligers and other exotic, unnatural hybrids sue their breeders?"

"Yes, because those animals will not be able to lead normal lives. They will not be happy."

"Who will represent them?"

"Lawyers like me. Lawyers who believe that all conscious beings have an inalienable right to happiness. You understand, Jorge, the animal rights that I advocate won't result in legislation in my lifetime. I am simply participating in a conversation that the philosopher Peter Singer started a half-century ago."

"Who is Peter Singer?"

"Peter Singer is the author of the groundbreaking book *Animal Liberation,* which he published in 1975. I have memorized its thesis statement: 'If possessing a higher degree of intelligence does not entitle one human to use another for his or her own ends, how can it entitle humans to exploit non-humans?'"

"That's hard to refute. Tell me, to whom would the financial settlement go?"

"To organizations that employ lawyers to defend animals."

"So the answer to your question 'Does every species belong to us?' is No?"

"Correct, Jorge. Our power to control other species does not translate into our right to control other species. Our ability to design nature does not translate into our right to design nature."

"I have a friend who says that by restoring the wolf population my brother Jaime and I are creating designer forests. What's your position on breeding wolves?"

"I read in *Wild Beasts Magazine* that you and Jaime are reviving the Red wolf population in the Blue Ridge mountains. I think that's great."

"What is your current project, Garrison?"

"I'm suing unethical breeders and traffickers of wild

animals on behalf of the animals. I plan to ruin the breeders and traffickers financially."

"We have been talking for almost fifteen minutes, Garrison Tucker. Is there anything else you'd like to say to our listeners?"

"I'd ask anybody with information on illegal or unorthodox animal trafficking to contact me, Garrison Tucker, at this email address: Garrison Tucker at zmail.com."

"Thank you, Professor Tucker, for being my guest today on 'People for the Planet.' And thank you, mountain listeners, for tuning in. I am Jorge Arroyo inviting you back on June twenty-third for another exciting interview."

From: Jaime Arroyo (Jaime Arroyo@zmail.com)
To: Jorge Arroyo (JorgeArroyo@zmail.com)
12:45 pm, Sunday, May 26, 2030
Re: ANIMAL LIBERATION
 Hey, bro.
 Garrison Tucker just put a target on his own back.
 Jaime

From: Jorge Arroyo (JorgeArroyo@zmail.com)
To: Lola Montoya (LolaMontoya@zmail.com)
1:44 pm, Sunday, May 26, 2030
"PEOPLE FOR THE PLANET"
 Hi, Lola.
 Could I interview you on "People for the Planet" on Sunday, June 23?
 We could talk about your work for Green Earth Charleston.

I would call you on your cell phone at 11:50 am.

You can listen to my interview with Garrison Tucker on my website.

Un abrazo,

Jorge

From: Lola Montoya (LolaMontoya@zmail.com)
To: Jorge Arroyo (JorgeArroyo@zmail.com)
1:52 pm, Sunday, May 26, 2030
Re: "PEOPLE FOR THE PLANET"

Hi, Jorge.

I would be delighted to accept your flattering invitation. Thank you.

I have already listened to the interview. It was excellent.

Un abrazo muy fuerte,

Lola

From: Jorge Arroyo (JorgeArroyo@zmail.com)
To: Lola Montoya (LolaMontoya@zmail.com)
2:00 pm, Sunday, May 26, 2030
Re: "PEOPLE FOR THE PLANET"

Hi, Lola.

It's a deal. Thanks!

We'll talk tonight.

Buenas noches,

Jorge

LOLA CALLED JORGE AT NINE.

"Jorge, would you ever sell any sperm or embryos?"

"No, Lola! Never. Why do you ask?

"My uncle Juan asked me. I think Mr. Tavis asked him."

"Tell, your uncle that under no circumstances would we sell sperm or embryos."

"Don't get upset, Jorge. I just wanted to make sure."

"Why, Lola?"

"I may send a tip to Garrison Tucker. Would you like me to read you my email to him?"

"Go ahead."

Lola read Jorge the draft of her message.

Dear Professor Tucker:

Please consider this email confidential.

I heard your "People for the Planet" interview on May 26.

Someone I know in Charleston may be illegally trafficking in wild animals.

This ad in Wild Beasts Magazine may be his.

**"We buy and sell wild animals
and hybrid predators.
We also buy and sell sperm.
Leave voice mail at 800-340-4838."**

Yours sincerely,
Anonymous

"I called that number when I saw the ad, Lola. I got voice mail. Do you believe that Willard is involved in the illegal trade of wild animals?"

"Yes, I do. And he's particularly interested in your wolves. He asked me all about them."

"When will you send Garrison the tip?"

"Soon. Very soon."

CHAPTER TEN

Thursday, June 13, 2030

D *ing.* Jorge opened his email.

From: Garrison Tucker (GarrisonTucker@zmail.com)
To: Jorge Arroyo (JorgeArroyo@zmail.com)
9:01 am, Thursday, June 13, 2030
ALERT

Dear Jorge.

I enjoyed our interview. Thanks so much for featuring me and my new book.

I write you because you are breeding rare Red wolves.

I recently got a tip about an illegal animal trafficker who resides in the Southeast.

This ad appeared in Wild Beasts Magazine:

We buy and sell wild animals
and hybrid predators.
We also buy and sell sperm.
Leave voice mail at 800-340-4838.

I called the number and left voice mail.

When I identify the trafficker I will sue him and
ruin him financially.
Ring me at noon on Saturday: 706-891-2343.
Sincerely yours,
Garrison

Jorge forwarded Garrison's email to his Zoo Arroyo staff and then replied to Garrison, copying Jaime.

From: Jorge Arroyo (JorgeArroyo@zmail.com)
To: Garrison Tucker (GarrisonTucker@zmail.com)
C: Jaime Arroyo (Jaime Arroyo@zmail.com)
9:09 am, Thursday, June 13, 2030
Re: ALERT
  Dear Garrison:
  Thank you for the alert.
  I enjoyed our conversation too.
  Come visit Zoo Arroyo some time. Bring Mrs. Tucker.
  I will call you at noon on Saturday.
  Jorge

JORGE FIXED LUNCH FOR MARCO AND ZELL.

"We should lock the entrance gate behind us when we leave, now that we have a padlock for it," Jorge said. "I myself get careless and leave it open sometimes."

"Who could have given Garrison Tucker the tip?" Marco asked.

"Somebody with a conscience," Zell said. "Somebody who dislikes the animal trafficking business."

"Have you told Jaime?"

"I copied him on my reply, Marco," Jorge said.

"Could we listen to your 'People for the Planet' conversation with Mr. Tucker?" Zell asked. "I missed it."

"Sure. It's on the zoo's website." Jorge played the recording.

"I want to read Garrison Tucker's book," Marco said.

CHAPTER ELEVEN

Saturday, June 15, 2030

A t noon Jorge called Garrison Tucker. Garrison's wife
Tallie answered Garrison's cell phone.

"Oh, Dr. Arroyo! Garrison's been shot. He's in the
hospital, Trinity Hospital here in Augusta. I'm with him."

"Oh, no! What happened?"

"Someone rang the doorbell about eleven this morning.
Garrison opened the the door. Nobody was there. So he
went outside to look around. Somebody shot him in the
chest and drove away."

"Will he be okay?"

"I don't know. The surgeon, Dr. Howard Worthy, will
operate on him. I'm so frightened."

"Mrs. Tucker, please stay strong. And please keep me
informed."

"I will keep you informed. I am staying at the hospital."

"What are the police doing?"

"Two officers are on the case. They're looking for the
shooter's vehicle. They're calling the crime 'attempted
homicide.'"

"Did you see the vehicle?"

"Yes. It was a black Dodge Ram, just like the red one
Garrison drove twenty years or so ago."

"That's very helpful, Mrs. Tucker."

"Jorge, what could Garrison have done to deserve this?"

"Garrison did not deserve this. But he might have gotten information that somebody didn't want him to share."

LATE IN THE EVENING JORGE GOT A TEXT FROM JAIME.

9:59 pm
Hey, Jorge.
Garrison Tucker was shot and killed today. He was on your show.
Look at Beverly's article in OnlineWitherston.

Hey, Jaime.
Oh no! I knew he'd been shot.
Could there be a connection with my show?
I'll read the article.

BEVERLY EVERETT'S ARTICLE IN ONLINEWITHERSTON was informative.

GEORGIA ENVIRONMENTALIST WRITER MURDERED
BY BEVERLY EVERETT

9:00 pm, June 15, 2030. Distinguished scholar Garrison A. Tucker, age 74, was shot at 11:00 this morning by an unidentified assailant outside his home in Augusta, Georgia. He died at 5:15 this evening at Trinity Hospital.

Tallie Tucker, Dr. Tucker's wife of fifty-two years, said that the shooting might be related to his investigation into illegal animal trafficking.

Dr. Tucker is renowned for his investigative research. His 2026 article about the black market for kidneys resulted in the arrest and conviction of two Atlanta physicians.

Dr. Tucker was Professor Emeritus of Philosophy at the University of North Carolina and is the author of the new book "Does Every Species Belong to Us?"

He was born in Atlanta in 1956. He earned his BA, MA, PhD, and JD from the University of Georgia.

Augusta police officials are seeking information about a twenty-year-old black Dodge Ram cruising Augusta's Hickory Heights neighborhood around 11:00 this morning.

Jorge forwarded the article to his Zoo Arroyo team.

CHAPTER TWELVE

Friday, June 21, 2030

"Want any groceries? I'm going to Atlanta this evening, and I can pick up anything you like on my way back. I'll bring them by on Sunday afternoon." Marco often stopped by the farmhouse for a shopping list.

"The usual coffee beans, grits, rice, and milk," Jorge said. "Thanks. Come in."

Marco sat down.

"Jorge, As you know, I'm trying to get back into graduate school. I'll need to write about what I've been doing these past two years. Do you have a list of the animals in our reproduction program?"

"Yes. Let me print you a copy."

"Could you email it to me?"

"Sure."

"Thanks."

"Would you like a recommendation from either Jaime or me? Or one from both of us?"

"Thank you. Yes, I would. Thank you very much. How about one letter from the two of you together? I'll get you an address."

JORGE DRAFTED THE LETTER OF RECOMMENDATION and emailed it to Jaime.

To whom it may concern:

Mr. Marco Ramos-Martínez has worked at Zoo Arroyo since July, 2028. During these two years we have gotten to know him well. You have his academic record, so we will address his work skills, his character, and his potential for intellectual growth.

Zoo Arroyo is engaged in the restoration of endangered species by artificial insemination and embryo transfer, as well as the rehabilitation of injured individuals. Marco was hired to assist in both undertakings. He has made himself indispensable. Whether in the laboratory, in the clinic, or in the field, Marco has exhibited an aptitude for microscopic procedures. He is intellectually curious, and he learns quickly. He is already an excellent scientist.

Marco has been the ideal employee. He has eagerly helped out wherever he could be of use, whether the job be feeding the animals, cleaning out the enclosures, repairing structures, tending to the garden, or implanting embryos. And he has brought joy and fun to the zoo with his Incan music.

He is also an excellent chess player.

In short, Marco is intelligent, conscientious, reliable, and, most importantly, honest. He will use science to make life better for humanity.

Sincerely,

Jaime Arroyo, PhD

Jorge Arroyo, DVM

Jaime responded: "Good letter, bro. It would warm Marco's heart if you showed it to him."

Jorge wrote back, "I will."

CHAPTER THIRTEEN

Sunday, June 23, 2030

"Hello, north Georgia listeners. Welcome to my radio program 'People for the Planet' on WITH-FM, broadcasting from Witherston, Georgia. I am Jorge Arroyo, and my guest today is Ms. Lola Montoya from Charleston, South Carolina. Lola Montoya is an immigrant from México who is now a naturalized citizen of the United States. She has became a first-class animal photographer and an environmental activist. She is the newly elected president of Green Earth Charleston. I met Lola Montoya in March when she came to Zoo Arroyo to photograph our wolves for *Wild Beasts Magazine*. Hello, Lola Montoya."

"Hello, Jorge. Thank you for having me on your show."

"Tell us, Lola, about your early life in Juárez."

"I grew up in Juárez with loving parents in a blue adobe house with a patio. We had a very talkative Amazon parrot named Conchita, a small dog named Diego, and canaries and parakeets whose names I've forgotten. My father, who died when I was fourteen, was a pharmacist, and my mother was a secretary at a university in Juárez. I got a scholarship to the University of Texas at El Paso. In El Paso I met a handsome doctor named Carlos Benito Montoya, married him, gave birth to our son Benito, and two years later divorced him. I wanted to raise Benito in the United States. My uncle Juan Navarro had gotten a job as a cook in a Mexican restaurant in Charleston, so in 2021 Benito and I went to Charleston. Benito and I are both naturalized Americans now. I am a photographer, and so is he. The end."

"That's not the end, Lola!"

"That's the end of my autobiography, Jorge. Do you want more?"

"Of course. What animals do you photograph??"

"I photograph animals that evolved naturally and animals that were created by humans. You are breeding wolves and foxes, which evolved naturally in the Appalachian mountains, and other men are breeding jackal-dogs and pumapards, which did not evolve at all. Pumapards are a puma-leopard hybrid. You release the wolves and foxes back into the wild, and the other breeders sell the one-of-a-kind creatures to collectors who keep them in cages."

"Who wants jackal-dogs and pumapards?"

"Collectors of man-made beasts. Jackal-dogs and pumapards are rich men's toys. Their sole purpose in life is to alleviate the boredom of their unscrupulous creators and collectors. Let me add that the breeders calls these anomalous animals 'wild beasts.' They should be called 'caged beasts.' My son would call them 'caged souls.'"

"Who are these unscrupulous creators and collectors, Lola?"

"I'm not free to give you their names, but I expect you will meet one or two of them tomorrow at the reception for the *Wild Beasts Magazine* conference."

"Let me ask you. In your view, could any of these breeders or collectors be breaking the law?"

"Possibly, Jorge. For certain they are violating ethical norms."

"Explain, please. What ethical norms?"

"The first one that comes to mind is Biblical: 'Do unto others as you would have others do unto you.' Jesus probably meant other humans, but now that we know that humans aren't the only species with consciousness, we must expand our ethical community to include mammals and birds. The breeders and collectors I have met do not."

"Do not do what?"

"Do not include the jackal-dogs, pumapards, and lions, tigers, and bears in our ethical community."

"Would you name any of the breeders or collectors?"

"No."

"Would you tell our listeners how you've met these breeders and collectors, Lola?"

"I photograph predatory animals in captivity for *Wild Beasts Magazine*."

"Who is the editor of *Wild Beasts Magazine*?"

"Willard Tavis."

"Let's turn our attention to your environmental work. When were you elected president of Green Earth Charleston?"

"I was elected president on March 1, 2030."

"What is the current project of Green Earth Charleston?"

"Green Earth Charleston is concerned with the rise in sea levels caused by global warming. Our coastal areas are sinking, and the marshland ecosystems are rapidly changing. So Green Earth Charleston will document the changes by creating a book of photographs and data called 'Coastal South Carolina 2030.' I view it as a census of the area's flora and fauna to be repeated once every ten years. I am the editor. My son and I photograph the mammals, reptiles, and amphibians."

"That's an important project. I hope that Green Earth chapters in other states do something similar."

"We are communicating with each other."

"I see that our time is up. So I thank you, Lola Montoya, for being my guest today on 'People for the Planet.' I thank you, mountain listeners, for tuning in. This is Jorge Arroyo reminding you to return on July twenty-eighth for an interview with another person who is making the planet a healthier place for humans and its other residents."

After going off the air, Jorge called Lola.

"Thanks, Lola. You were terrific."

"I probably revealed too much. I should not have criticized the breeders."

"Is your work for Green Earth Charleston compatible with your work for *Wild Beasts Magazine*?"

"No, it is not. I personally oppose the breeding of bizarre hybrids. But as a professional photographer for *Wild Beasts Magazine* I glorify it. Maybe I should do as my son does, and photograph the suffering in the animals' eyes."

"Would you tell me privately the names of the breeders?"

"I mustn't, Jorge. I promised Mr. Tavis to keep their names confidential."

"I'm glad Charleston can't pick up WITH-FM."

"Me too. Mr. Tavis might take revenge."

"Do you want to keep working for Willard Tavis?"

"No. And I won't for long. However, he did get us together."

"I owe him a thank-you note," Jorge said.

"I'll see you at the reception, Jorge."

CHAPTER FOURTEEN

Monday, June 24, 2030

L ola had not told Jorge he was to be honored at the *Wild Beasts* reception. Lola had not told him that "Zoo Arroyo Resurrects the Red Wolf" had been voted favorite story by *Wild Beasts* subscribers. She had told him only that he was invited to a reception for preservationists.

When he entered the Witherston Inn ballroom at seven o'clock on Monday night, Jorge saw a thirty-by-forty inch framed, dry-mounted photograph of Sol and Luna on an easel. It was the magazine's cover photo.

At that moment Lola appeared. Lola had dressed up in a white cotton pantsuit with a red silk scarf. She turned toward Jorge.

"Will you have a glass of champagne, Jorge? Did you come alone?" Lola carried two flutes of champagne.

"Good evening, Lola. You look stunning tonight. Yes, I'll have a glass, thank you. And yes, I came alone. But I see Zell and Eve and Abbie are joining us."

Eight-year-old Abbie Larson raced over to hug Jorge.

"This is Abbie Larson, Lola."

"So nice to meet you, Abbie," Lola said.

"Nice to meet you."

Lola turned towards Jorge. "Jorge, did you know that *Wild Beasts Magazine* will honor you tonight as its Preservationist of the Year?"

"Really, Lola? No kidding? I am totally surprised."

"I wanted you to be surprised, Jorge."

A tall, well-dressed man in his early forties approached them.

"Good evening, Lola. Whom do we have here?"

"Hello, Mr. Tavis. Let me introduce Jorge Arroyo, director of Zoo Arroyo, and his friends Zell and Eve Larson and their daughter Abbie. Zell is the zookeeper."

"How do you do," Jorge said.

"Mr. Tavis founded *Wild Beasts* last year. He owns a deer preserve near Charleston called Tavis Ranch," Lola said.

"Pleased to meet you all," Willard Tavis said. "Congratulations, Dr. Arroyo. I first read about Zoo Arroyo in the University of Georgia alumni magazine."

"I am surprised and honored to receive the award, Mr. Tavis."

"By the way, I listened to you and Lola on last Sunday's 'People for the Planet.'"

"How did you pick it up, Mr. Tavis? Does WITH-FM reach Charleston?" Lola asked him.

"I was alerted. I have connections."

Willard Tavis moved away.

Rhonda Rather entered the hall, followed by Marco Ramos, and Eddie, Emma, and Nick Crane.

"Hello, hello!" Rhonda said. "We're here!"

Rhonda held a glass of champagne in one hand and the leash of Blanche, her white standard poodle, in the other. In her red linen pantsuit, Rhonda did not look sixty-eight years old.

Jorge had never seen his friends so dressed up. Marco wore a blue *guayabera* shirt. He had shaved off his beard. Emma wore a blue sundress and white strappy sandals. Eddie had put on a white shirt and tie. Even Nick had on a tie, a red Atlanta Falcons bow tie.

"I made you a present," Marco said. He handed Jorge a Rosewood and Mahogany chessboard. "Congratulations."

"Wow, Marco. This is exquisite."

"It's a chessboard—to thank you for all the chess games."

Jorge introduced Lola and Marco.

"I've already met Marco," Lola said.

"Jorge taught me to play chess," Marco said.

"Marco learned chess quickly, and now he beats me," Jorge said to Lola.

"Sometimes," Marco said.

"You must teach me, Jorge."

"I'd gladly teach you, Lola."

"I heard your interview on 'People for the Planet,' Lola," Marco said. "I found it very thought-provoking."

"I'm glad you did. Willard Tavis, who hired me to do the photos for the Zoo Arroyo story, obviously did not."

"Willard Tavis heard it?" Marco asked.

"Willard Tavis said his connections informed him of it."

"Oh."

"Hey, Marco! Come here!" Nick called from across the room. "There's food."

Marco joined his biggest fan.

"Now back to business," Lola said. "Jorge, after you receive your award, will you make a short acceptance speech? Say, five minutes?"

"Of course, Lola."

Jorge looked around at the guests, most of them men,

most of them sporting *Wild Beasts* baseball caps.

"There must be fifty people here," Jorge said. "Who are they? Is this a convention?"

"It is," Lola said. It's the first annual convention of the Wild Beasts Association, the subscribers to the magazine. According to Mr. Tavis, the purpose is to introduce subscribers to each other. Some of them are hunters. Some are breeders. And a few may be collectors of exotic animals. I've told you about them."

A man in a blue denim shirt and jeans took off his cap and climbed the steps to the stage.

"Hey there, Wild Beasts. I'm your president, Lester Wexton, here from the Georgia coast. If you haven't already guessed, I'm a hunter. I hunt boars and alligators, and that's not easy these days after the Tipping Point."

Jorge was well aware of the consequences of global warming. The climate change Tipping Point, triggered by the melting of the polar ice sheets in 2024, had raised sea level by five inches, leaving the marshlands and the low-lying areas of Charleston under water. Many of the wild animals inhabiting those areas had moved inland, changing the dynamics of other ecosystems and endangering the populations of other species. The mosquito population had increased exponentially. Fires had devastated the forests. In five years the average coastal temperature had risen three degrees. The Tipping Point was a lesson in interconnectivity.

Lester Wexton spoke for five minutes about the Tipping Point's effects on the boars, alligators, bobcats, deer, and other coastal wildlife.

Lola whispered in Jorge's ear. "That's what Benito and I are photographing. By the way, you may not see me after your speech. I have to return home to Benito tonight."

"We'll talk, Lola."

Jorge kissed her cheek.

"Now let me announce the recipient of our first Preservationist of the Year award," Lester said. "He is Dr. Jorge Arroyo, co-founder and executive director of Zoo Arroyo. Please join me on stage, Dr. Arroyo."

With the help of his cane Jorge ascended the steep stairs to the rostrum.

"Dr. Arroyo is a graduate of Witherston High School and the University of Georgia. He received his doctorate in veterinary medicine from UGA in 2026, after which he and his twin brother Dr. Jaime Arroyo founded Zoo Arroyo. Dr. Arroyo is not only a vet. He is also a writer and an artist, and he hosts the WITH-FM interview program 'People for the Planet.' Dr. Arroyo, the Wild Beasts have selected you as Preservationist of the Year."

Lester handed Jorge a weighty crystal vase with his name engraved under the words Wild Beasts Preservationist of the Year 2030.

"Thank you very much, Mr. Wexton. I share this award with my brother Jaime, and I accept it on behalf of our whole Zoo Arroyo team. I wish Jaime were here."

"I am here, Jorge!" Jaime ran up the steps to Jorge's side. "I wouldn't miss this."

The twins embraced, and the audience cheered. The two men, both dressed in khaki suits, were practically indistinguishable from each other.

"Dr. Arroyo—I mean, Dr. Jorge Arroyo—please say a few words about your passion for rescuing hurt creatures and reviving endangered species," Lester said.

Jorge handed the vase to Jaime and went to the lectern.

"As you all can see, this is my twin brother Jaime. Jaime and I founded Zoo Arroyo to rescue individual animals who could not survive in the wild and to reestablish threatened and endangered species. We are working with environmentalists, such as my sister-in-law Annie Arroyo, to resist the encroachment of humans on old-growth forests."

"Hey, Jorge!" Annie waved her arm. "I'm here!"

"Hey, Annie." Jorge continued. "I once wrote in my column, 'In an apocalyptic vision I imagine a planet with no wilderness, where cities stretch from shore to shore on every continent, and where all the once wild animals are enclosed in parks and zoos.'"

Jorge spoke about the effects of COVID-19 on minks and COVID-27 on canines.

"As you know, COVID-27 not only killed a half-million Americans but also reduced the populations of wolves, foxes, and coyotes in the wild. The disappearance of these predatory mammals has destabilized forest ecosystems. So Zoo Arroyo aims to restore the wolf population to Appalachia."

Applause.

"Let me put in a personal plea. If any of you knows who stole two American minks from Zoo Arroyo last March, please let me know."

"Thanks for mentioning it, Jorge," Jaime said.

"In conclusion, let me say that Zoo Arroyo could not survive without the financial support of our generous friend and benefactor, Rhonda Rather. Rhonda enabled us to launch our operation to restore the Red wolf to the Appalachian mountains. Our petting zoo carries her name. Thank you, Rhonda."

Rhonda blew a kiss to Jorge.

"Thank you again for this honor, Wild Beasts," Jorge said.

From the back of the ballroom, Lola waved him good-bye.

"Good-bye, Lola," Jorge said from the podium. "And thank you."

Willard Tavis raised his hand. "I have a question. Would you ever sell a Red wolf?"

"No, never," Jorge said. "We are not breeding wolves for sale."

"I'll speak to that," Jaime said. "No animal in our zoo is for sale. Our zoo is not a pet store. It is not a menagerie. It is a project, to restore the Appalachian mountains to what they were when the Cherokees lived here."

"It's a dream," Jorge said.

Jorge and Jaime left the stage and joined Annie.

"Now let's have dinner," Jaime said. "Zell, Eve, and Abbie will join us."

On their way out of the Witherston Inn ballroom Jorge was stopped by an impeccably groomed, clean-shaven man with thick white hair, wearing a seersucker suit and alligator cowboy boots.

"I am Dr. Louis Bordeau," he said. "I would love to visit Zoo Arroyo. Since I'm in the area for this convention may I come by later this week?"

"Pleased to meet you, Dr. Bordeau. I'd be happy to show you around on Wednesday. Can you be there at ten?"

"Yes. Here is my card. Please tell me your address."

"Twelve hundred Bison Highway. It's a half hour's drive from here."

"Thanks. I'd especially like to see the wolves."

Louis Bordeau turned back to Rhonda.

"And you are the phenomenal Rhonda Rather, former mayor of Witherston?"

"Good evening, Dr. Bordeau. I am Rhonda Rather."

"Let me bring you another glass of champagne, Ms. Rather," Louis Bordeau said. He disappeared into the crowd.

Jorge looked at Dr. Bordeau's card.

Dr. Louis T. Bordeau, Large Animal Veterinarian
Columbia Zoo, Columbia, South Carolina
LouisBordeau.ColumbiaZoo@zmail.com
https://www.ColumbiaZoo.org

He showed the card to Jaime.

"So Dr. Bordeau is a zoo vet," Jorge said. "That's why he's interested in Zoo Arroyo."

"I wonder if he knows about our cloning projects."

"If he doesn't already, let's keep that secret," Jorge said. "At least the *Wild Beasts* article doesn't mention cloning."

———

THE VAULTED GLASS CEILING OF THE WITHERSTON INN dining room allowed the sun to illuminate the space on a clear day and the moon and the stars to shine through on a clear night. This evening it brought the sound of rain.

Jorge thought about Lola driving through the storm to Charleston.

Jorge, Jaime, and Annie were seated with Zell, Eve, and Abbie Larson at a long table by the window. Eddie, Emma and Nick were seated nearby.

"I invited Marco to join us," Jaime said, "but he had to get back to the zoo."

"And Lola had to get back to Charleston," Jorge said.

"I heard your interview with Ms. Montoya yesterday," Zell said. "I really liked it."

"Thanks, Zell," Jorge said. "It turns out that Willard Tavis also heard it. He disliked it, of course."

"How could he have heard it down in Charleston?"

"He said he had connections who alerted him."

"He used that word, 'alerted'? That's weird," Zell said.

"He did. Definitely weird."

"How can we tell who's who?" Abbie asked Jorge and Jaime.

"Jorge parts his hair on the left side," Jaime said. "And I part my hair on the right."

"But your hair is so curly, it's hard to tell," Abbie said.

"Okay. So here are more differences. Jaime is right-handed, and I am left handed," Jorge said.

"Jorge makes animals healthy, and I make them pregnant," Jaime said.

"Jaime plays the guitar, and I write stories."

"And Jorge draws and paints and collects art," Jaime said. "Jorge is right-brained, and I am left-brained."

"Yea, I'm sensitive, and Jaime is practical."

"You are both cute," Eve said.

"Thank you," Jorge and Jaime said in unison.

Over chianti and lasagna, Jaime spoke about his research.

"Word of our cloning projects is spreading, Jorge, whether we like it or not. Yesterday I got a request for Kitty Rather to be a surrogate mother for an Eastern cougar embryo. The Eastern cougar was caught in North Carolina. My colleague will send me the cloned embryo."

"Male or female?" Zell asked.

"Female."

"I thought the Eastern cougar was extinct," Jorge said.

"The Eastern cougar was declared extinct in 2011, but apparently a few survived. The wildlife biologist who wrote me knew we had Kitty, who can't run but can be a good surrogate mother."

"Why Kitty?"

"Kitty is a Mexican puma, Annie. Very closely related to the Eastern cougar, so she would be a good carrier for the clone," Jaime said. "A puma is basically a cougar, as is a mountain lion. The cougar goes by many names."

"Kitty was born with a deformed front foot. We got her as a kitten. She's sweet and cute, so we named her Kitty Rather." Jorge turned to his brother. "You plan to impregnate Kitty with the Eastern cougar's embryo, bro?"

"If you agree, Jorge."

"I agree."

"Where does Kitty live?" Abbie asked.

"Kitty lives in the back of Sol's Woods where Foxy Ann and Foxy Belle hang out, honey," Zell said to his daughter. "I'm taking you to the zoo tomorrow to play with Nick. Maybe you'll see them."

"Who are Foxy Ann and Foxy Belle?" Eve asked.

"Foxy Ann and Foxy Belle are the three-year old female Red foxes we got in January," Jorge said. "They were implanted with Swift fox clones a few weeks ago. The Swift fox is a threatened species."

"How about coffee?" Jaime asked as they finished dinner. "I'm not through celebrating Jorge's award."

"Good idea, Jaime. I'll have mine with strawberry ice cream pie."

Eddie came over with his phone. "Hey, Jorge. I'm looking at OnlineWitherston. Beverly has already posted an article about your award, Jorge. I'll read it aloud."

JORGE ARROYO ACCEPTS PRESERVATIONIST AWARD
By Beverly Everett

8:00 pm, June 24, 2030. Dr. Jorge Arroyo, who owns and operates Zoo Arroyo with his brother Dr. Jaime Arroyo, accepted the Wild Beasts Magazine "Preservationist of the Year 2030" award tonight at a ceremony in the ballroom of the Witherston Inn. Dr. Jorge Arroyo was featured in an article titled "Zoo Arroyo Resurrects the Red Wolf" published in the summer issue.

Dr. Arroyo, who has a doctorate in wildlife veterinary medicine, is the zoo's executive director.

According to Willard Tavis, founder and editor of Wild Beasts Magazine, "Zoo Arroyo deserves recognition for its use of cloning techniques to restore the populations of wolves to the Appalachian forests."

Zoo Arroyo is located in the Saloli Valley at 1200 Bison Highway. The working zoo is closed to the public, but the petting zoo—the Rhonda Rather Petting Zoo—welcomes visitors by appointment on Saturdays from 10:00 am to 2:00 pm.

"Oh, no!" Jaime said. "Why did Beverly mention cloning the wolves?"

"She was quoting Willard Tavis. How did Willard Tavis know that Jaime was using cloning techniques?" Eddie said.

"He listened to Lola Montoya's recording of our interview," Jorge said. "Lola asked him not to mention our use of cloning, but he did anyway."

"Tavis sent Lola to Zoo Arroyo to get pictures and information," Jaime said.

"Beverly posted Jaime's picture instead of yours, Jorge," Annie said.

"That's okay, Annie," Jorge said. "We use the same picture."

ENJOYING HER NIGHTCAP—A HONEY-BOURBON TODDY— Rhonda emailed her daughter.

From: Rhonda Rather (RhondaRather@zmail.com)
To: Sandra Rather Anders (SandraRather@zmail.com)
10:49 pm, Monday, June 24, 2030
HAPPY ANNIVERSARY!

My darling Sandra,

Happy anniversary! I loved seeing you and Phil and Maisie this weekend. Thanks so much for coming up from Atlanta to visit me. I can't believe that my darling granddaughter is old enough to date.

This evening I went to a reception where Jorge was named Preservationist of the Year 2030 by Wild Beasts Magazine. Such an honor for Jorge and for Zoo Arroyo! Jaime and Annie were there too.

FASTEN YOUR SEATBELT! At the reception I met a tall, attractive, debonair, well-spoken, charming, charismatic and somewhat mysterious widower whom I actually liked. He's a veterinarian named Louis Bordeau from Columbia, South Carolina.

Anyway, after the reception Louis took Blanche and me to Dot's Trout House, where we wined and dined and talked till ten. Louis loves animals as much as I do, and he asked me all about my involvement in Zoo Arroyo. Get it? He asked me about ME! He asked if I had family. I told him about you and asked him if he had children. He said he didn't.

I haven't cared seriously for anyone since your father died. I've preferred the attention my dogs and cats have given me to the attention my dates have given themselves.

I invited Louis to dinner at my house on Wednesday. Good night, sweet Sandra.

Love you, Mom

As always, her daughter replied right away.

From: Sandra Rather Anders (SandraRather@ zmail.com)
To: Rhonda Rather (RhondaRather@zmail.com)
11:04 pm, Monday, June 24, 2030
Re: HAPPY ANNIVERSARY!
Hi, Mom.
So glad you had a good evening. I'm happy when you're happy.
For our anniversary Phil is taking Maisie and me to Myrtle Beach for the weekend.
Love you,
Sandra

CHAPTER FIFTEEN

Tuesday, June 25, 2030

"You say a man is dead in Sol's Woods?"

Jorge and Marco were installing a microwave oven when Zookeeper Zell, Abbie, and Nick descended from Zell's pickup. The rain had soaked the three of them.

"Yes, Jorge. Nick and Abbie found his body," Zell said. "The man was sprawled across a rotting log. The wolves had mauled him."

Zell had brought Abbie to the zoo to collect Chanterelle mushrooms with Nick. When Nick and Abbie ran across the body, Abbie called him.

"He was murdered," Nick said. "He was shot in the head. But Abbie thinks he was attacked by the wolves."

"The wolves ate him," Abbie said. "Daddy saved us, or the wolves might have eaten us too."

"No, they wouldn't," Nick said. "The wolves were just defending themselves."

"Was the body recognizable?" Marco asked.

"No. He was all torn apart," Abbie said. "I saw his bones."

"He was not recognizable," Zell said. "His face was pretty bloody. So was his body. The man must have offended the wolves."

"He was fat," Nick said. "And he had red hair."

"I'm calling Detective Dunning," Jorge said.

Detective Mira Dunning and Jorge's old friend Officer Sequoyah Waters arrived first.

"Hey, Mira," Jorge hailed her. "Good to see you again. Well, I mean, sorry to see you again."

"We follow dead bodies wherever they lead us, Jorge," Mira said.

"You doing okay, Seq? It's good to see you too."

"I'm fine, Jorge. Thanks. Turns out I like police work."

A minute later Dr. Dev Reddy, the medical examiner, parked in front of the farmhouse. So did Beverly Everett.

"A dead body draws a crowd," Beverly said, climbing out of her ten-year-old Camry.

"Hello, Mrs. Everett," Abbie said. "Nick and I just discovered a dead man. Do you want to interview us? You could mention us in your article."

"I'll have to," Beverly said. "We wouldn't know about the dead man if it weren't for you all."

"Let's go to the scene," Mira said, "before the rain destroys the evidence. Beverly can ride with Seq and me. I've got umbrellas in the back seat."

"I'll take my van," Dev Reddy said.

"I'll take my truck." Zell said. "Abbie can ride with me."

"I'll take my Outback," Marco said. "Jorge and Nick can ride with me."

"I'll stay here," Jorge said.

"Does anybody have a stun gun? Just in case a wolf gets aggressive."

"I do," Zell said.

Within a minute the storm began, and the rain turned the road into mud.

Shielding themselves with umbrellas, the party hurried after Abbie and Nick through Sol's Woods to the drenched corpse.

"Don't touch anything," Mira advised, "Seq will take pictures, and Dr. Reddy will do a preliminary examination."

"I'll take pictures, too," Beverly said.

"So will I," Zell said.

Dr. Reddy examined the body of a heavy man wearing camouflage, already stiff with rigor mortis.

"The rain makes ascertaining the time of death difficult, but I think the man died between eight and ten last night."

"While everybody was at the reception," Marco said.

"So this guy drove into the zoo, past the farmhouse, past the enclosures, past Eddie's cabin, and up to Sol's Woods without anybody here to notice him," Zell said.

"Them," Seq corrected. "There had to be at least two of them. One shot the other. And the shooter drove their vehicle away."

"What were they doing here, I wonder," Mira said.

"Stealing the wolves, probably," Seq said. "They weren't just taking their picture."

"Maybe one of them was Marco's shooter," Zell said. "Too much of a coincidence. The mink thief shoots Marco. The wolf thief shoots this guy."

"I'll see if the bullets match," Mira said. "Dr. Reddy, can you tell whether this fellow was killed before the wolves got him?"

"No, Detective, I'll have to look at the cadaver in the morgue."

"Who knew the premises would be vacated," Mira asked, "besides Marco, Eddie, and Zell?"

"Lola Montoya knew," Zell said. "She invited all of us to the reception. And she was at the reception for a while, but she left early."

"How did the intruders get in?" Seq asked. "The entrance gate has a padlock."

"Can you all help me turn the body over, Seq?" Dev said.

"This stiff weighs a lot," Seq complained.

"Looks like he was shot in the head," Dev said. "In the back of the head."

"So he was murdered," Zell said.

"That depends on whether he was alive when he was shot."

"No wallet. No driver's license," Mira said, emptying his pockets. "No phone either. No identification whatsoever."

"Fellows, help me get this body into a body bag."

Marco and Zell slid the corpse into the body bag and lifted it onto the gurney.

"By tomorrow morning, if not tonight, I'll have an autopsy report for you," Dev said to Mira. "I'll do the autopsy this afternoon."

"Detective Dunning, do you think the perps left prints on the gate?" Marco asked Mira as they got into their vehicles.

"Probably not in last night's rain, but possibly. Seq, would you please come back here tomorrow morning to check for prints. The rain will have cleared out by then. Dust the zoo entrance gate as well as this one," Mira said. "We need to figure out how the perps got into the zoo."

"I'll write up the story now," Beverly said. "Abbie, would you like a ride back to Witherston?"

"Yes, please."

"Seq and I will leave you all," Mira said. "There's nothing more we can do here in this rain."

Mira and Seq departed.

"Let's check the wolves," Zell said. "In the truck I have some beef, which we can put near the entrance. It's their mealtime anyway."

Once they were outside the fence Zell whistled for the wolves. Within ten minutes Sol and Luna emerged from the brush with six other wolves.

"Look at Luna, Daddy," Abbie said. "She's awfully fat. So is Faye."

"They're about to whelp their pups, Abbie. Maybe today, maybe tomorrow."

"Sol's injured," Nick shouted. "He's been shot."

Sol was limping. His left shoulder was caked with blood.

"But he's still hungry."

"Maybe he's okay."

"Sol needs to be examined," Zell said. "Let's take him back to Jorge."

Zell went into the enclosure and tranquilized Sol. After a minute he picked up the seventy-five-pound wolf and brought him out.

"I'll be happy to keep an eye on the other wolves this afternoon," Marco said. "I'll let you know if anyone whelps."

Zell drove back to the farmhouse with Sol lying in the bed of the truck and Nick sitting in the cab.

With Nick's help Zell moved Sol onto a gurney and brought him in. Jorge gave the wolf a pain killer.

"The bullet's still here. I can get it out."

Jorge removed a nine millimeter bullet from Sol's shoulder. "Same kind of bullet that was lodged in Marco's shoulder."

Jorge and Zell carefully lifted the sedated wolf into a large kennel.

"This bullet came from a handgun," Jorge said to Nick. "Do you want to wash it off?"

"Sure." Nick carefully washed off the bullet and placed it on a towel. "Do you think the person who shot Marco also shot Sol and the fat man?"

"And possibly Garrison Tucker," Zell said.

"We'll find out soon when Detective Dunning compares the bullets.

"When can Sol go back to his pack?"

"Zell can take Sol back to his pack tomorrow morning."

"I want to be a vet like you, Jorge," Nick said.

Ping. Jorge got a text from Jaime.

12:49 pm
> *What's happening, Jorge?*
> *I just read Beverly's story.*
> *I can be at the zoo by six.*
> *May I spend the night?*
> *Heather and Holly are hosting a sleepover for their preschool class.*

Jorge replied.

> *Yes, spend the night! I'll fix paella.*
> *Rhonda will be coming too.*
> *Hasta pronto.*

Jorge went to OnlineWitherston on his tablet and found Beverly's story. He read it aloud to Zell.

MAN KILLED AT ZOO ARROYO
By Beverly Everett
12:39 pm, June 25, 2030. A man's mauled body was discovered about 9:00 this morning in a heavily forested

part of Zoo Arroyo called Sol's Woods. Abbie Larson, age eight, and Nick Crane, age nine, were hunting mushrooms when they came across the corpse.

"The body got chewed by wolves," Abbie said. "There was almost nothing left."

Detective Mira Dunning of the Witherston Police Department would not say whether the individual was attacked and killed by the wolves or killed by a human and then attacked by the wolves. She said that the medical examiner, Dr. Dev Reddy, would determine the cause of death in the next day or so.

Dr. Reddy estimated the time of death to be between 8:00 and 10:00 last night.

Sol's Woods is the home of eight wolves. Drs. Jorge and Jaime Arroyo are attempting to reestablish the endangered Red wolf species.

Because of a reception in Witherston in honor of Jorge Arroyo, all zoo personnel were off the premises between 6:30 and 10:00 pm.

No vehicle was found on the access road. Detective Dunning surmised that the victim entered the woods last night with a partner who left him for dead and drove away before anybody returned.

Detective Dunning is investigating a possible connection between this death and the shooting of Marco Ramos in March. In the earlier case, two American minks were stolen.

Zoo Arroyo, on Bison Highway, was established by Jorge and Jaime Arroyo in 2026. It is a non-profit dedicated to rehabilitating injured wildlife and restoring endangered species.

"How did the intruders know we'd be gone?" Zell asked.

"Maybe they didn't," Nick said.

"Maybe they did," Jorge said.

Only Zell joined Jorge for lunch. Nick ate his pimento sandwich in the operating room with Sol.

"Have you ever been contacted by anybody wanting sperm from our animals, Zell?"

"No. I'd tell you if I had been."

Jorge showed him the ad in *Wild Beasts Magazine*.

We buy and sell wild animals and hybrid predators.
We also buy and sell sperm.
Leave voice mail at 800-340-4838.

"Sounds like a black market to me."

"To me too."

———

Jaime and Rhonda both arrived at six, each with a dog and a bottle of wine. Jorge sent Amigo and Blanche out to play, and poured the Rioja.

Jaime offered the toast. "*¡Salud, amor, y dinero, y tiempo para gastarlo!*"

"Health, love, and money, and time to spend it!" Jorge repeated. "What I need is love."

"You'll find it, bro."

"Jorge, you've become a gourmet cook!" Rhonda said.

After recounting the day's events, Jorge brought to the table a seafood *paella* with squid, shrimp, scallops, and mussels.

Poe flew from Jorge's shoulder onto Jaime's shoulder, where he picked pieces of shrimp off Jaime's fork.

"I wonder if Poe can tell us apart," Jaime said. "Crows remember faces, you know. But we have the same face."

"How would we know if he could tell us apart?" Jorge said. "Maybe he just likes us equally."

"Poe, wanna come here?" Rhonda extended her arm. Poe flew onto Rhonda's shoulder.   "He likes me, too."

Jorge gave Jaime and Rhonda a print-out of Garrison's email, as well as the list of Zoo Arroyo's caged animals.

"How's my namesake doing?" Rhonda asked, looking at the list.

"Kitty Rather is still her lovable self, Rhonda," Jaime said. "She has been chosen to carry a cloned embryo of a female Eastern cougar. So she'll soon be pregnant."

"Well, I declare! I'll be having another granddaughter."

"We have to figure out what happened last night," Jaime said.

Taking a long sip of wine, Rhonda said, "Here's a possible scenario for what happened. The perps—let's call them Thief and Accomplice—know that Zoo Arroyo has wolves because they read *Wild Beasts Magazine*. They decide they want a wolf for a pet. Nincompoops feel *muy macho* when they have fierce animals under their control. They drive up to the Sol's Woods gate in a truck with a couple of large cages in the back. They go inside the enclosure with a smelly dead rabbit and a net. Sure enough. The whole pack comes out of the trees to investigate. Sol and Luna attack Thief. So Accomplice shoots Thief to avoid taking him to a hospital and shoots at the other wolves to scare them away. He gets Sol in the shoulder. Then he escapes."

"Your scenario is credible, Rhonda," Jorge said. "But I think Thief and Accomplice may have been already familiar with the zoo. They may be the ones who shot Marco and stole Minkie and Mickie in March."

"Here's another scenario," Jaime said. "Thief and Accomplice are working for the breeder Garrison mentioned. We can call him Breeder. Breeder knows that we'll be away from the zoo Monday night, so he sends Thief and Accomplice to bring back a wolf. Thief goes after Sol. Sol kills Thief. So Accomplice shoots at the wolves to scare them away and gets Sol in the shoulder."

"Here's a third scenario," Jorge said. "Thief and Accomplice want to capture Sol, take his sperm, and return him to the pack. If they had been successful we would never have known."

"In that case, Thief and Accomplice are unaware that Sol has been sterilized," Jaime said.

"You all, we're overlooking something," Rhonda said. "How did Thief, Accomplice, and Breeder know that everybody would be in Witherston last night? They must have been tipped off by someone. And they must have gotten keys."

"The same key that unlocks the Zoo Arroyo padlock unlocks the padlock to Sol's woods."

"So who would have given the thieves a key, and who would have told them that the zoo would be vacated?"

"It wouldn't be Marco," Jaime said. "Marco helped me implant the Red wolf clones. He wouldn't want anyone to take a wolf."

"It wouldn't have been Eddie. He's been a devoted friend for ten years. It wouldn't have been Zell either. We've known him since we were sixteen."

"Maybe the thieves are associated with Lola Montoya, who knew that Jorge would be at the reception and that the others were coming too."

"No, Rhonda. Not Lola. Lola is an honest person," Jorge said, "a good person. I know her pretty well. And she doesn't have a key."

"I'm thinking," Rhonda said. "Marco was shot in March. Garrison Tucker was shot right after you interviewed him. And now this man was shot last night. Do you all suppose the deaths are connected?"

"I'll contact Mira. She will find out whether the bullets match."

"You know what all the shootings have in common, Jorge? A connection with you." Jaime laughed.

After dinner the three of them rocked on the front porch till dark, drinking coffee and listening to Marco's flute across the pond. The wolves howled. The owls hooted. The tree frogs chirped.

Jaime mimicked the wolves. Rhonda mimicked the owl.

"Who would guess that a man was killed here last night?" Jorge said.

"It's nine o'clock, folks." Rhonda stood. "But before I leave, I want to tell you that I had a date last night. A real date. One where the man paid for the meal."

Ten years before, Rhonda had lost her husband Rich Rather to a massive heart attack, shortly after she succeeded him as Witherston's mayor. Although she had had many opportunities, she had not dated since his death.

"After the Wild Beasts ceremony?" Jaime asked.

"With whom, Rhonda?" Jorge asked.

"With Dr. Louis Bordeau. Remember him from last night? After the reception he took Blanche and me to Dot's Trout House, where we had a very pleasurable dinner on the veranda."

"Did you like him?"

"Oh, yes. We talked about hybrid animals. He is very familiar with breeding techniques. He asked about your work, Jaime. You and he would have much to talk about."

"What did you tell him?"

"Only that I don't understand your work. Anyway, Louis likes me. Tomorrow he is coming to my house for dinner."

"That's after he visits our zoo," Jorge said. "You can debrief us on Thursday."

"We'll let you know whether Dr. Bordeau has our approval, Rhonda," Jaime said.

"I will report back," Rhonda said. "I do appreciate you all looking out for me. Now I must go home."

Rhonda blew her police whistle for Blanche.

After a couple of minutes Blanche returned with Amigo. The poodle carried a gold and black baseball cap in her mouth.

"That's not ours," Jorge said.

"No way," Jaime said. "It has Georgia Tech's colors."

"It's a clue," Jorge said.

At nine Jorge FaceTimed Lola.

"Hi, Lola. I enjoyed seeing you last night. I wish you could have joined us for dinner after the ceremony."

"I should have brought Benito with me. Then I wouldn't have had to return to Charleston. And in the rain. The rain followed me home."

"Lola, all hell has broken loose here at the zoo. Last night a man was killed in Sol's Woods, either by the wolves or by a human. He had a bullet in his head. You can read about it in OnlineWitherston."

"What? You're kidding! When?"

"Between seven and nine last night, when all of us were at the reception."

"What do you think happened?"

"Two or more individuals opened the zoo's gate with a key. They drove up the lane, entered Sol's Woods, and did something to rile up the wolves. The wolves attacked the man, either before or after he was shot."

"What did the man look like?"

"I don't know. I didn't see him. But I was told he was a fat red-head wearing camouflage."

"What did the police say?"

"The medical examiner will give us an autopsy report soon."

"That's scary, Jorge. Do you have a gun?"

"No, I don't. And I don't want one. I have a stun gun that I take with me when I'm feeding the animals."

"Maybe a stun gun would work on people if you should be in danger."

"On a different topic, would you and Benito like to come to the zoo for lunch on Sunday?"

"We would, Jorge. Thank you! Benito will be thrilled."

"I will be too, Lola."

From: Estela Navarro (EstelaNavarro@zmail.com)
To: Lola Montoya (LolaMontoya@zmail.com)
10:19 pm, Tuesday, June 25, 2030
PROMOTION!

Querida Lolita,

I have been promoted to office manager for the president. And the promotion comes with a big raise!

My friend Elena took me out to dinner to celebrate.

How is my grandson?

How are you?

Muchos besos,

Mami

From: Lola Montoya (LolaMontoya@zmail.com)
To: Estela Navarro (EstelaNavarro@zmail.com)
10:24 pm, Tuesday, June 25, 2030
Re: PROMOTION!

Querida Mamacita,

I am proud of you for getting the prestigious position. Congratulations!

I am proud of your grandson too. Benito won second place in the Charleston Amateur Photographers contest with a photograph of two turtles mating.

Last night Benito and I attended a reception in Witherston, Georgia, to honor a a wildlife veterinarian named Dr. Jorge Arroyo. Jorge and I have begun dating—that is, Jorge and Benito and I have begun seeing each other. Jorge and his identical twin brother, Dr. Jaime Arroyo, operate a zoo, which is actually a rescue operation for injured wild animals and endangered species.

In August I will get my online master's degree in photography from the University of Charleston. Benito wants me to go through the graduation ceremony. Would you be able to come? It's on Saturday, August 24. You could meet Jorge.

This morning my parrot said, "Cha Cha wanna go in a car. Ahora!" Cha Cha speaks Spanglish.

Un fuerte abrazo,

Lola

From: Rhonda Rather (RhondaRather@zmail.com)
To: Sandra Rather Anders (SandraRather@zmail.com)
10:50 pm, Tuesday, June 25, 2030
SWEET DREAMS

Dearest Sandra,

A man was killed at Zoo Arroyo last night! Just awful. And Sol, the leader of the wolf pack, was shot in the shoulder. Check Beverly's article in OnlineWitherston.

This evening I went up to Zoo Arroyo for dinner with Jorge and Jaime. When I got home I saw a dozen red roses awaiting me on the front porch! They were from Louis. The card read, "Louis thinks you are lovely."

Need I say more?

I fixed myself a double Irish coffee to celebrate. Sleep well, my precious daughter.

Love you,

Mom

From: Sandra Rather Anders (SandraRather@zmail.com)
To: Rhonda Rather (RhondaRather@zmail.com)
10:59 pm, Tuesday, June 25, 2030
Re: SWEET DREAMS

Hi, Mom.

The red roses seem to have achieved their purpose. You sound positively giddy.

Maybe Dr. Bordeau will invite you down to Columbia to visit him.

Maisie plans to join her high school's environmental club. I'm proud of her. She is very progressive, like you.

I read Beverly's account of the murder. Appalling!
Love,
Sandra

CHAPTER SIXTEEN

Wednesday, June 26, 2030

J orge's day started with a text from Lola.

> *7:29 am*
> *Hi, Jorge.*
> *I got an email from Mr. Tavis saying he would not be needing me any more.*
> *Call me when you can.*
> *Abrazos,*
> *Lola*

Jorge called her immediately.

"I am so sorry Mr. Tavis sent you that email, Lola! I should not have asked you questions about your work. Do you have enough other clients?"

"No problem! I have plenty of clients whom I actually like. I was about to quit working for Mr. Tavis anyway. But I have other news for you."

"Tell me."

"Yesterday Mr. Tavis fired Tío Juan, and evicted him."

"Why?"

"He gave no reason. But I suspect it has something to do with you and me, with our friendship. Juan may have mentioned that you and I were seeing each other. Mr. Tavis has secrets he doesn't want disclosed."

"What will Juan do, Lola?"

"Juan is talking to the manager of La Cocina Mexicana about a job as a cook. I've invited him to live with Benito and me."

"His life has taken a turn for the better."

JORGE OPENED THE GATE FOR SEQ AT EIGHT IN THE morning.

"Hello, Jorge. Thanks for getting your staff together," Seq said, as he dismounted from his Harley-Davidson.

"Would you like breakfast? Or at least a cup of coffee?"

"Both, thanks."

Seq joined Jorge, Jaime, Marco, Eddie, and Nick at the table, where he helped himself to peaches, fried eggs, bacon, and biscuits. Jorge poured coffee.

Poe perched on Nick's shoulder, stealing pieces of biscuit. Amigo lay under the table.

"Can you account for all of your keys?" Seq asked the group.

"Is anybody missing a key?" Jorge asked. "Eddie, Marco, Zell?"

"No," Eddie said.

"No," Marco said, "not so far as I know."

"No," Zell said. "I have only one, and it's on my key chain with my car key."

"I'm thinking that the same guys who took the minks went after the wolves," Seq said.

"But Sol defended his pack. Good for Sol!" Zell said.

"Maybe they wanted a pregnant wolf," Nick said, "to start their own pack."

"Could be. Four of our wolves are pregnant, Olli," Zell said. "Fern, Faye, Fran, and Luna."

"Keep thinking, folks, while I look around the zoo for clues," Seq said.

"Spend as much time as you like. The only clue we have is this bullet I retrieved from Sol's shoulder." Jorge gave Seq the bullet. "Oh, and a Georgia Tech baseball cap. Here it is. It could have dna on the rim."

"I'll report back," Seq said.

The others lingered over coffee. Jorge scrolled through articles on his tablet. He stopped.

"Let me read you all something," Jorge said. "It's on the *USA Today* website."

SCIENTIST CREATES WOLF-BEAR CHIMERA
BY ROY EMERSON

7:00 am, June 26, 2030. Dr. Patricia B. Maloney, until recently an assistant professor of genetics at the Callaghan Research Institute in Atlanta, has created an embryo of a 50/50 wolf-bear chimera and transplanted it into the uterus of a Black bear.

Dr. Maloney reports the achievement in an article titled "On the End of Species" in the July issue of Reproductive Frontiers.

Dr. Maloney is the daughter of Danyon Patrick Maloney, winner of the 2026 Nobel Prize for Chemistry.

Dr. Maloney stated that the surrogate mother is due to give birth to the wolf-bear cub in late November or early December. She said that the surrogate mother belonged to a private zoo.

Chimeras are produced when cells from one species are introduced into the developing embryo or fetus of another. In a chimera, each cell contains the genetic material of either one parent species or the other, unlike a hybrid, in which each cell contains genetic material from both.

Dr. Maloney's work was supported by the Embryonic Science Foundation.

Dr. Maloney resigned from the Callaghan Research Institute on May 31. She left no forwarding address.

"Have you ever heard of Patricia Maloney, Jaime? Have you, Marco?"

"I haven't," Marco said.

"I haven't either," Jaime said. "But my colleagues and I are not doing chimera research. Most of us would view the attempt to create freaks of nature as unconscionable."

"Dr. Maloney must be alluding to Darwin's *On the Origin of Species*," Marco said.

"Dr. Maloney is playing god," Jorge said. "She's manipulating dna to make whatever being she imagines."

"Would chimeras have souls?" Nick asked. "I think animals have souls. Bernie has a soul. So does Poe."

"Yes, Nick," Jaime said. "But I would use the word 'consciousness' instead of 'soul.' Chimeras would have consciousness, just like birds and other mammals."

"And also octopuses," Jorge added. "Octopuses have consciousness."

"Jaime, what's the difference between hybrids and chimeras?" Eddie asked. "Why is creating hybrids okay and creating chimeras not?"

"Hybrids are produced by selective breeding. Take the mule, which has a horse mother and a donkey father. In the mule, each cell is mulish. The mule results from sexual reproduction, even if done by artificial insemination. A horse-donkey chimera is not a mule, and it's not a product of sexual reproduction. A horse-donkey chimera is artificially created by injecting donkey cells into a horse embryo and transplanting the embryo into a mare. The mare's offspring would have some horse cells and other donkey cells. It might have a horse-ish head and a donkey-ish body. It would be a freak."

"What if you made a human-donkey chimera?" Nick asked. "That would be gross."

"Gross, unethical, and illegal," Jorge said.

"Illegal?"

"You favor sexual reproduction over the laboratory creation of chimera, Jaime. But cloning is not sexual reproduction," Eddie said. "Therefore a clone is not natural."

"A clone is natural, Eddie. It just comes into the world in an unnatural way," Jaime said.

"So, Jaime, you approve of clones because they are natural. You don't approve of chimera because they are unnatural, or artificial."

"I don't approve of the creation of chimera. A chimera has consciousness, like all mammals. A chimera can still feel happiness and sadness. A chimera can still suffer. A chimera has no place in an ecosystem."

"I found a statute prohibiting human chimeras, Nick," Jorge said. "Here it is."

> *It shall be unlawful for any person to knowingly, in or otherwise affecting interstate commerce, create or attempt to create a human chimera; transfer or attempt to transfer a human embryo into a non-human womb; transfer or attempt to transfer a non-human embryo*

into a human womb; or transport or receive for any purpose a human chimera.

"Good god, Jorge," Jaime said. "The very prohibition implies that someone has tried it."

"That's horrifying," Eddie said. "What's the penalty, Jorge?"

"It says, 'imprisonment for not more than ten years.' I would give the perpetrator of this vicious act life plus ninety-nine years."

"I would sentence the perpetrator to death," Marco said.

"Let's figure this out later, you all. It's almost ten. I'll go let Dr. Bordeau in. Come, Amigo." Jaime poured the rest of his coffee down the sink and walked out the door. Amigo followed him.

"Nick and I are cleaning out the barn, so we'll be going too," Eddie said. "Thanks for breakfast, Jorge."

"I'll take Sol back to his pack," Marco said.

———

"Hello, there," Louis Bordeau said, as he walked into the farmhouse with Jaime and saw Jorge. "Now who is the real Dr. Arroyo?"

"We both are," Jaime said.

"I am Jorge. I met you Monday night."

"I am Jaime. I didn't."

"Thanks for letting me see your operation here," Dr. Bordeau said. "You have a unique home, Jorge."

"I enjoy it," Jorge said. "I have my veterinary clinic in the back."

"And you?" Dr. Bordeau turned to Jaime.

"I live in Witherston with my family. I teach genetics at the University of North Georgia."

"So you're a veterinarian, Dr. Bordeau," Jorge said.

"Yes. I have a private practice but I work primarily for the Columbia Zoo."

"What would you like to see, Dr. Bordeau?" Jaime asked him.

"All of it, if I may. The article about your wolves in *Wild Beasts* intrigued me. So I'd like to see the wolves. And I'd like to hear about your latest breeding techniques."

"I'll give you a tour," Jaime said. "But we won't see the wolves. They are shy. I'll tell you about our zoo while we walk."

Jaime and Louis set off through the petting zoo and up the lane toward the enclosures. Amigo followed.

They encountered Seq near the bears. Seq got off his motorcycle.

"Hey there, Jaime," Seq said. "I found something."

"Hey there, Seq. This is Dr. Louis Bordeau, a veterinarian. Dr. Bordeau, this is Officer Seq Waters, from the Witherston Police Department."

"Pleased to meet you," Seq said. "I'm here investigating a possible homicide, of a human."

"Who was murdered?" Dr. Bordeau asked.

"We don't know his name, sir. And we don't know whether he was killed by a human or a wolf."

"Thanks, Seq. We won't keep you. Jorge's waiting for you," Jaime said.

"Somebody left a shoe print right behind the body. I'll tell Jorge," Seq said. "Size nine or so, narrow. I got a picture of it."

LOUIS BORDEAU WAS GONE BY ELEVEN.

"For the life of me I can't see why Louis came out here," Jaime said. "He seemed bored with my talk of our dual mission."

"He came to see the wolves," Jorge said.

"He asked about our reproductive techniques. I answered, 'Sex. Would you like to watch our rabbits?' He didn't."

"You didn't say anything about cloning, did you?"

"No, Jorge. And he didn't ask."

"Do you think he'd be a good suitor for Rhonda?"

"No, he's too slick."

"He has the air of money."

"He does," Jaime said.

"He's having dinner with Rhonda tonight."

"He's fast as well as slick."

Jorge's phone rang. "It's Marco," he said to Jaime.

"What's up, Marco?"

"Luna has whelped. She's doing fine. Three pups. You don't need to come."

"Jaime is here with me. We're on our way, Marco, both of us. Where is Luna?"

"At the creek, about a quarter mile into Sol's Woods. Take your jeep up here. The lane is muddy."

When Jorge and Jaime got to Luna she was already nursing four pups.

"Woohoo! She's got four pups," Jorge said.

Then he spotted Faye about fifty feet away.

"There's Faye," Jorge said. "She's whelping right now. Didn't you see her, Marco?"

"I didn't."

Faye whelped a single pup.

"Only one pup?" Jaime asked. "That's a surprise."

"In one day we've got five more wolves," Marco said. "What shall we name them?"

"Let's give flower names to Luna's pups," Jaime said. "How about 'Pansy,' 'Petunia,' 'Azalea,' and 'Orchid'?"

"Good names, bro. I'll bring collars for them next time I come out here. And for Faye's pup?"

"How about Sasha? Faye's pup is a clone of a wolf named Alexandra."

"Something's wrong with Faye," Jorge said. "She's rejecting Sasha."

Faye was pushing Sasha away from her belly.

"Faye is not doing well," Jaime said.

After examining Faye, Jorge said, "Faye's heartbeat is too fast. And she's not lactating. No wonder she's pushing Sasha away. Let's take Faye and Sasha back to the farmhouse. We'll clean up Sasha and give her some formula. Marco, would you please monitor Luna and her pups for an hour or so."

"Glad to."

"I'll drive, Jorge," Jaime said. We'll put Faye on the back seat and you in the front with Sasha in your lap."

By the time Jaime and Jorge got Faye onto the operating table, Faye was bleeding heavily and her blood pressure was dropping. Jorge intubated her, gave her fluids, and moved her onto a heating pad. She died within a minute.

Jaime teared up.

"She's gone, Jaime. I'm so sorry. I know she was your favorite wolf. But we have to save Sasha now. I'll warm up some formula."

Jorge cleaned up Sasha and weighed her. "Sasha weighs fifteen ounces. She'll be okay."

Jorge wrapped her in a blanket and gave her to Jaime to feed.

"Funny that both Luna and Faye whelped on the same day."

Marco and I implanted them on the same day, April twenty-second."

Sasha pulled at the nipple of the baby bottle.

"Sasha seems healthy, but she doesn't look well-formed, Jorge. Her back is humped."

"I will x-ray her later today."

"How about giving me the rest of the umbilical cord. And a blood sample. I'll send her DNA to a colleague at Zoo Atlanta. Her dna should match the Red wolf we cloned."

Jorge gave his brother a blood sample and the cord.

"I have to get back now, Jorge. I have a seminar at four thirty."

"That's fine. I'll ask Nick to feed Sasha today. I'll feed her tonight."

Nick was delighted with the responsibility.

"I'll take good care of her," he said. "I'll be there in ten minutes."

From: Rhonda Rather (RhondaRather@zmail.com)
To: Sandra Rather Anders (SandraRather@zmail.com)
10:28 pm, Wednesday, June 26, 2030
MY SECOND DATE WITH LOUIS

My dear Sandra,

I have just said good-bye to Louis. We had a marvelous evening. He greeted me with flowers and wine and gentlemanly kisses on both cheeks.

He praised my gazpacho.

I invited him for pork roast on Friday, before he goes home Saturday morning.

Although I dated lots of men before I married your father, I never met one as attentive to me as Louis is. He said I was "pretty as a peach" and "fascinating." Gracious! At the age of sixty-eight I've become fascinating. Who would have thought it!

I must say that I did get all gussied up. I wore my black silk harem pants and my pink lace blouse with puffy sleeves.

Louis seemed to know that Zoo Arroyo was dear to my heart, and he liked my tales of the animals there. I told him that Jorge and Jaime had named their puma after me—Kitty Rather—and that Kitty Rather was going to get pregnant.

Kitty Rather really is going to get pregnant—with a cloned embryo of a female Eastern cougar.

Please forgive my chattering on about myself. I know it's bad manners. But I want to share my happiness with you.

Give my love to Phil and Maisie.

Hugs and kisses,

Mom

From: Sandra Rather Anders (SandraRather@ zmail.com)

To: Rhonda Rather (RhondaRather@zmail.com)

10:56 pm, Wednesday, June 26, 2030

Re: MY SECOND DATE WITH LOUIS

Hi, Mom.

Everyone who knows you thinks you're pretty as a peach and fascinating.

Phil and Maisie and I will pass through Columbia on Friday on our way to Myrtle Beach. I'll see what I can find out about Dr. Bordeau.

'Night, Mom.

Love,

Sandra

CHAPTER SEVENTEEN

Thursday, June 27, 2030

From: Detective Mira Dunning (MiraDunning@wpd.gov)
To: Jaime Arroyo (Jaime Arroyo@zmail.com), Jorge
Arroyo (JorgeArroyo@zmail.com)
C: Officer Seqyoyah Waters (SeqWaters@wpd.gov)
9:05 am, Thursday, June 27, 2030
MEETING - DEATH AT ZOO ARROYO
    Dear Jaime and Jorge:
    Are you all available to meet tomorrow for an
update on the case?
    4:00 pm in my office at the Witherston Police
Station.
    Mira

From: Jaime Arroyo (Jaime Arroyo@zmail.com)
To: Detective Mira Dunning (MiraDunning@wpd.gov)
C: Jorge Arroyo (JorgeArroyo@zmail.com),
Officer Sequoyah Waters (SeqWaters@wpd.gov)
9:11 am, Thursday, June 27, 2030
Re: MEETING – DEATH AT ZOO ARROYO
    Dear Mira:
    Jorge and I will be happy to meet with you
tomorrow at 4:00 pm.

Thank you for keeping us informed.
Jaime

JORGE TEXTED HIS BROTHER.

9:21 am
Jaime,
I read your reply to Mira. I'll meet you at the police station at 3:55.
Bad news. Sasha's X-ray shows deformation.
Her back is rounded, almost like a badger or a raccoon.
Nick has taken charge of feeding her. She is on his lap now.
Sasha in still in the incubator.
I'll take over nursing duties—every four hours or so—when Nick's not here.
Jorge

Jorge,
Could I have implanted the wrong embryo?
I'll see you at 3:55.
How about dinner at my house after we meet with Mira?
On Saturday morning I'll drive up to the zoo in time for breakfast.
I'd advise not telling anybody about Sasha. OK?

Jaime,
I accept dinner invitation for tomorrow.
I'll ask Marco to look after Sasha.
Eddie, Emma, and Nick will be away.
Thanks.

CHAPTER EIGHTEEN

Friday, June 28, 2030

"Big news," Mira said to Jorge and Jaime as soon as they were seated at her conference table with Officer Seq Waters. "Dr. Reddy stated that the cause of death was homicide. He found a bullet in the deceased man's head. The man was shot from behind at close range. Jorge, the bullet matched the ones removed from Sol and Marco."

"So the most likely scenario is that two men entered Sol's Woods and attempted to steal a wolf," Jaime said. "One of them was mauled. The other man shot at the wolves and hit Sol, and then shot and killed his buddy."

"And fled," Seq said. "The shooting was intentional. If the shooting had been an accident, the shooter would have called nine-one-one."

"Furthermore," Mira said, "this bullet matched the bullet that killed Garrison Tucker. The same gun was used in both murders."

"Which means that the same shooter killed Tucker and this man," Jorge said.

"It means that the same gun was used to shoot Tucker and this man," Seq said. "And Marco."

"Since the victim's wallet and phone were not on his body, the shooter must have taken them," Mira said. "But the shooter left a credit card receipt in the victim's pocket. Apparently, the victim's name is Simon Pate. We tracked him down. He's from Charleston, South Carolina. Forty years old."

"Vehicle?"

"According to the South Carolina Department of Motor Vehicles, he owns a 2009 black Dodge Ram."

"Anything else?"

"Mr. Pate is a felon. He was arrested in 2027 for selling heroin. He served two years in prison."

"Now we have to find his partner," Jorge said.

"Seq is working on that. We'll let you know. We're also getting a warrant to see his bank account."

"One mystery is how they got into the zoo," Seq said.

"They must have had a key. Or else somebody left the gate unlocked," Mira said.

"I think they had a key. Otherwise they couldn't have gotten into Sol's Woods," Jorge said. "All the padlocks have the same key."

"Maybe you have a traitor on the zoo staff who gave them a key," Seq said.

"I don't think so," Jorge said. "We all like each other too much."

"Has anything else out of the ordinary occurred at Zoo Arroyo?" Mira asked. "I'd like to get the big picture."

"We had an unusual whelping," Jorge said, "but I don't see how it could be related to the murder."

"I want to know anyway," Mira said.

Jorge told the police officers about the pups born to Luna and Fern, and about Sasha's birth and Faye's death.

"SASHA IS NOT A WOLF, AT LEAST NOT A PURE WOLF," Jaime said, looking at the X-ray Jorge showed him.

"She looks like a weasel," Annie said.

Jorge, Jaime, and Annie sipped margaritas on Jaime's deck while the steaks cooked. Heather and Holly played in the backyard sandbox.

"Well, whatever she is, Sasha is ravenous, wanting her bottle constantly. And she's bonded to Nick, who's with her from eight in the morning till dinnertime."

"Her DNA will tell us what she is. Yesterday I emailed Sasha's DNA to Dr. Kavita Bakshi at Zoo Atlanta to see whether she could determine Sasha's identity. She said she'd get me an answer right away."

"If Sasha is not a Red wolf clone, then your colleagues in North Carolina shipped you the wrong embryo. And that would be a colossal mistake."

"My colleagues are not that incompetent."

"Then somebody substituted Sasha's embryo for the one that was in the embryo freezer. And that person knew to take precautions. The freezer temperature is minus three hundred twenty-one degrees Fahrenheit. Who would know about an embryo freezer?"

"Marco would know. So would Eddie. Just to be cautious, Jorge, let's put a lock on the freezer."

"I've already bought a lock for the freezer. Here's the combination." He handed Jaime a card with the set of numbers.

"Who else will have the combination?"

"Nobody. Just the two of us—unless you want me to give it to Marco."

"No, I think not," Jaime said. "He texted me that he's leaving soon."

"Could Marco have made the substitution, Jaime? Do you trust him completely?"

"I do."

"Marco is the only person here other than you who knows how to implant embryos."

After dinner Jaime played the guitar, Annie played the mandolin, and everybody sang. Heather and Holly knew some of the songs well, especially "Old McDonald Had a Farm."

"With a moo moo here," sang Heather.

"And a moo moo there," sang Holly.

"Here a moo, there a moo, everywhere a moo moo." Annie finished the verse. "Old McDonald had a farm, ee I ee I o."

"Dad, does Marco know 'Old McDonald'?" Heather asked.

"I don't think so, Heather. He knows mostly Spanish songs."

"Could Marco come to our house sometime?"

"We need Marco here," Holly said. "He could play his flute."

"I'll call him," Jorge said. "I'm wondering how he's doing with Sasha anyway."

He rang Marco. The call went to voice mail. He tried again a half hour later. Again it went to voice mail. He sent him a text.

> 8:29 pm
> Hello, Marco.
> I assume that all is well at the zoo.
> Jaime and I wanted to know about Sasha.
> Was she hungry? Did she drink her formula?
> I won't be home till ten thirty.
> So please feed her again about ten. Thanks.
> And please call me.

Jaime says Hello.
Heather and Holly miss you.
Jorge

"This is strange," Jorge said. "Why is Marco out of touch?"

"He could have forgotten to charge his phone," Jaime said. "Anyway, we'll see him tomorrow. I'll be there for breakfast, Jorge."

From: Rhonda Rather (RhondaRather@zmail.com)
To: Sandra Rather Anders (SandraRather@zmail.com)
10:49 pm, Friday, June 28, 2030
LOUIS NO LONGER
  Dear Sandra,
  I had invited Louis to my house for dinner tonight.
  At six o'clock, when the wine was poured, the salad was on the table, the pork was in the oven, and the candles were lit, he called to say that he couldn't come, that he was returning to Columbia tonight.
  I asked him what was up. He said, "Business." That was all.
  I said, "Call me when you're on the road."
  He didn't.
  I called his cell phone. He didn't answer.
  So a half hour ago I called his land line in Columbia.
  A woman picked up! I disconnected.
  The cheater had told me he was a widower. The creep.
  I shared the pork with Blanche. I didn't share the wine.

Don't worry about me. I just fell out of love.
Have fun at Myrtle Beach.
Love,
Mom

From: Sandra Rather Anders (SandraRather@zmail.com)
To: Rhonda Rather (RhondaRather@zmail.com)
10:59 pm, Friday, June 28, 2030
Re: LOUIS NO LONGER
Hi, Mom.
I am so sorry! Well, actually I'm not.
From my perspective Louis was moving awfully fast.
Good thing you found out he was a creep. What did he want with you?
On our way to Myrtle Beach we saw a jackal on the Columbia courthouse steps!
It must have escaped from the Columbia Zoo.
Sleep well, dear mother.
Love,
Sandra

From: Rhonda Rather (RhondaRather@zmail.com)
To: Sandra Rather Anders (SandraRather@zmail.com)
9:40 pm, Friday, June 28, 2030
Re: LOUIS NO LONGER
Dear Sandra,
I hope the jackal eats Louis.
Love,
Mom

From: Rhonda Rather (RhondaRather@zmail.com)
To: Jorge Arroyo (JorgeArroyo@zmail.com)
9:56 pm, Friday, June 28, 2030
LOUIS BORDEAU THE CREEP

Hey, Jorge.

Forget all the nice things I said about "Dr. Louis Bordeau." He's a creep.

He dumped me and returned to Columbia "on business" after he had accepted my invitation for dinner tonight.

I've been thinking. All he wanted from me was information about Zoo Arroyo. He told me nothing about himself.

Sandra told me they saw a jackal loose in downtown Columbia today. Could there be any connection between that event and the creep's sudden need to go back to Columbia?

Don't feel sorry for me. I'm enjoying the wine that I no longer have to share with him.

Kisses,

Rhonda

From: Jorge Arroyo (JorgeArroyo@zmail.com)
To: Rhonda Rather (RhondaRather@zmail.com)
10:48 pm, Friday, June 28, 2030
Re: LOUIS BORDEAU THE CREEP

Oh, Rhonda.

I'm sorry that Bordeau used you for information about our zoo. There might be a connection between the jackal's escape and Bordeau's decision to make the 4-hour drive tonight.

You're always welcome to join me for dinner here at the farmhouse. But we'll share the wine!

Affectionately,

Jorge

CHAPTER TWENTY

Saturday, June 29, 2030

Jaime arrived at Zoo Arroyo in time for a breakfast of freshly-laid eggs, home-grown watermelon, grits, biscuits, and coffee.

As Jorge put the dirty dishes into the dishwasher, Jaime got an email.

"It's from Dr. Bakshi. I'll read it," Jaime said. "Oh, no, Jorge! Sasha is a chimera! She's a wolverine-wolf!"

"Holy smoke!"

"No wonder Faye died."

"A chimera! Who would create such a chimera? And who would transfer it into Faye?"

"Only someone experimenting with chimera, and with interspecific pregnancies. Faye had an interspecific pregnancy, which means she carried a fetus not of her own species."

"What's the gestation period for a wolverine, Jaime?"

Jaime looked it up on his phone. "Sixty days, same as a Red wolf."

"I just had an awful thought. Maybe someone got into the embryo freezer and exchanged the wolverine-wolf embryo for the Red wolf clone embryo because he or she wanted the Red wolf embryo."

"I have a more awful thought. Someone got into the freezer and exchanged the wolverine-wolf embryo for the Red wolf embryo because he or she wanted a wolverine-wolf pup."

"Or kit. A wolverine offspring is a kit," Jorge said.

"Let's x-ray her again, to see how she's developing."

Jorge and Jaime found Nick back in the operating room feeding Sasha.

"Sasha is growing!" Nick said.

Jorge x-rayed the pup. The three of them stared at the screen.

"Now she looks more like a wolf pup," Jorge said. "Is this the same pup I x-rayed on Wednesday?"

"Sasha is getting healthy," Nick said. "She's hungry. And she's getting darker."

Jorge brought up Sasha's older x-ray for comparison."

"This is not the same pup. Sasha's back is straight in today's x-ray, not like a wolverine's."

"I think I'd better do another dna test, Jorge. Could I have samples of her blood and saliva?"

Jorge produced them.

"If they don't match," he said, "somebody has switched the pups."

"Let's take this Sasha to Luna, who might nurse her with her other pups," Jorge said. "You want to come along, Nick?"

"Yes, but will Luna have enough nipples?"

"Teats, Nick. Female wolves have teats, eight teats, in fact. The question is whether Luna will welcome a strange pup."

Jaime and Jorge rode in the front seat of the jeep and Nick rode in the back with Sasha and a sack of wolf chow.

They found Luna near the creek where she had whelped her four pups. Luna was nursing them, and she hardly noticed Sasha when Sasha attached herself to a free teat. Sasha was darker than the others.

"I wanna see the foxes," Nick shouted, running further into the woods.

Jaime took pictures of Luna's offspring close up while Jorge distributed the dried food.

In five minutes Nick returned.

"Follow me, you all! I found Fern! She's got puppies too!"

Nick led them to Fern, who was nursing three female pups who appeared the same age as Luna's but darker.

"These pups look like Sasha," Nick exclaimed.

Jaime took their picture.

"Maybe we should bring Sasha back here to Fern, since she has only three pups," Nick said. "May I go get her, Jorge?"

"Sure," Jorge said. "Fern was supposed to have four pups anyway."

After placing Sasha on one of Fern's teats, Nick said, "These pups need names. Could we give them S names to go with Sasha? I thought of Sylvia, Sonya, and Sassy."

"Great names, Nick. Next trip out you can give them their collars. You're an excellent assistant."

"I'm going to call this Sasha 'Sasha Two,'" Nick said, "and the original Sasha 'Sasha One.'"

"I just had an awful thought, Jorge," Jaime said. "Somebody substituted one of Fern's pups for Sasha One, the wolverine-wolf. That somebody had to know Fern was about to whelp. Only Marco would have had that information."

"That's what I'm thinking, bro."

"If that's what Marco did, then he has Sasha One. Call Marco. Ask him to meet us here. We'll watch his reaction to Fern."

Jorge called Marco. No answer.

"Let's drive over to his house," Jaime said.

Marco's Subaru Outback was not in the driveway.

"He's gone somewhere. He goes away on weekends," Jorge said.

"I'll ring his doorbell." Nick jumped out of the jeep and ran to the front door. He rang the doorbell and then turned the doorknob.

"Marco left the house unlocked!" he yelled.

Nick opened the door and looked in. "Marco has moved out."

"I'll text him," Jorge said.

"I'll check the mailbox," Jaime said.

Jaime came back with a handwritten note.

Hello, Jorge and Jaime.
    I decided to leave late last night.
    I'm sorry I didn't have a chance to say good-bye.
    Here are the keys to the house and Jaime's lab.
    Thanks for everything.
                      Marco Ramos

"He didn't give us a forwarding address."

"What did you know about him, Jaime?" Jorge asked.

"Basically what you know about him. He was skilled in reproductive techniques. He was a good musician. He loved children. He was a gentle soul."

"You taught him about cloning."

"He learned quickly. And you taught him to play chess."

Nick came back holding a loudly meowing long-haired white cat. "I found Bonita in the bushes. Why would Marco leave Bonita behind?"

"Why indeed," Jaime wondered.

"She's hungry. May I keep her?"

"Sure," Jorge said. "Bonita needs a keeper."

They returned to the farmhouse with Nick cuddling Bonita.

Jaime looked at his phone again. "He didn't respond to my text. I'll email him."

From: Jaime Arroyo (Jaime Arroyo@zmail.com)
To: Marco Ramos (MarcoRamos2004@zmail.com)
11:34 am, Saturday, June 29, 2030
WHERE ARE YOU?
> *Hello, Marco.*
> *I was surprised you left without contacting either Jorge or me. Is there a problem?*
>> *Please reply this message.*
>> *Jaime*

"I think he's with his girlfriend," Nick said.

"What do you know about his girlfriend, Nick?"

"She's pretty. She was with Nick when he tended to Juliet. That was the Sunday you and my father were at the convention, Jorge."

"May fifth. What's her name, Nick?"

"Marco just introduced her to me as his girlfriend. Then she left."

"I have a hunch." Jaime googled Patricia B. Maloney and found her image. "Nick, look carefully at this picture. Is this woman Marco's girlfriend?"

"Yes!"

"Nick's girlfriend is Dr. Patricia B. Maloney," Jaime said to Jorge.

"Now that's really really interesting. I wonder how they met?"

"Maybe Dr. Maloney contacted Marco."

"Because Marco was working for you, Jaime."

"May I take Bonita home now?" Nick asked.

"Sure, Nick. You're parents will be surprised," Jorge said. "I'll call them."

JORGE AND JAIME FOUND EDDIE WAITING FOR THEM ON the farmhouse steps.

"Nick told me that Marco had left. And with Sasha. Unbelievable. I wouldn't have expected Marco to disappear like that. He must have carried around some secrets."

"We didn't know him as well as we thought we did," Jorge said.

"Do you want me to clean out his A-frame?" Eddie asked.

"Yes, please. And bring me anything unusual you find."

"Will do. I'll take my truck."

"I just realized something," Jaime said to Jorge after Eddie had gone. "It was most likely Marco who put the chimera embryo in our embryo freezer. And then Marco watched me implant it in Faye. So could Marco have left other embryos in our freezer? I'm going to check."

Jaime returned a minute later. "Nothing."

"Maybe the Red foxes are carrying chimeras."

"I guess we won't know till the kits are born."

EDDIE WAS BACK AT THE FARMHOUSE BY NOON.

"Here's what I found at Marco's place," Eddie said, setting a cardboard box on the floor and a shoebox on the kitchen table.

"What's in the big box?" Jaime asked.

"The big box is for you, Jaime," Eddie said. "It's labeled 'For Jaime.' Open it."

Jaime did.

"Wow. A *pan* flute, a couple of *quena* bamboo flutes, a *charango*, and a *bombo*. Jorge, I'm giving you the *bombo* right now."

"He also left a wrapped present that said 'To Nick, on his birthday, from Marco,'" Eddie said.

"When is Nick's birthday?" Jorge asked.

"The Fourth of July."

"Marco left his wood carving knives to Nick and his larger tools to me. I didn't bring them. But I did bring a coffee table that he marked 'For Jorge.' It's in my truck. I'll go get it."

Eddie brought in a Rosewood coffee table inlaid with mahogany. "Marco left you a Rosewood floor lamp too."

"Marco has to be a good man to create such art," Jorge said. "Artists speak with the angels."

"I think we don't know what was going on in Marco's head," Jaime said.

"What's in here?" Jorge asked, opening the shoebox.

"What Detective Dunning would call evidence. A credit card receipt from a gas station in Charleston that I found in his wet garbage and a barely legible bank receipt for three thousand dollars which was in the pocket of a shirt in the dryer."

"Which bank?"

"Wells Fargo in Witherston."

"You're a good sleuth, Eddie. That's a trove of clues."

"The bank receipt is dated Monday, June twenty-fourth, at eight fifty pm. It's for a cash deposit of three thousand dollars. Can you imagine? Feeding the ATM machine thirty hundred-dollar bills?"

"Apparently, the person who paid Marco in cash didn't want it traced," Jaime said.

"I just realized something," Jorge said. Marco must have made the deposit right after the Wild Beasts reception. So he probably got the cash at the reception."

"What's the date of the credit card receipt, Eddie?" Jorge asked.

"March eleventh."

"So Marco was in Charleston on March eleventh. I wonder if he knows Willard Tavis. Willard Tavis lives in Charleston."

"I think Marco intended to leave the country," Jaime said. "That's why he left the musical instruments. If he went to Perú he could buy new instruments. We should tell Mira."

"I will email Mira," Jorge said, "and I'll ask her to check Marco's Wells Fargo bank account.

"Tell her about Lola. Willard Tavis sent her to photograph our animals. She may be the key to solving the mystery."

"I'll tell Mira everything I know."

CHAPTER TWENTY-ONE

Sunday, June 30, 2030

L ola and Benito arrived at eleven forty-five. Jorge unlocked the zoo's entrance gate for them and locked it after they drove through.

"*Bienvenidos, amigos míos*," Jorge said. "Welcome to Zoo Arroyo, Benito. So great to have you here again, Lola."

Jorge gave Lola a hug and Benito an elbow bump.

"I brought three cameras, Jorge," Benito said. "One is this super Nikon, which is a hand-me-down from Mom. It has a built-in telephoto lens. This one is a miniature spy camera. The third is my phone."

"How do you use your spy cam, Benito?"

"I mount it to record what happens in our back yard overnight. I've photographed deer, foxes, raccoons, opossums, and a skunk eating the deer corn we put out for them. And I got a really good picture of two skunks mating."

Lola winked. "Benito likes to capture young love."

Poe flew onto Lola's shoulder.

Benito took several close-up photos of Poe.

Over lunch Jorge told Lola and Benito of Garrison Tucker's warning.

"And two days after the warning he was shot to death," Jorge said. "On June fifteenth."

"When did you interview him, Jorge?"

"May twenty-sixth."

"I was interviewed on June twenty-third, and on June twenty-fifth Willard Tavis fired Juan and me."

"That raises a question," Jorge said. "What do you and Garrison Tucker have in common?"

"We both abhor animal trafficking."

"What does 'trafficking' mean?" Benito asked.

"'Trafficking' means buying and selling something illegal, like drugs," Lola said.

"Is Mr. Tavis involved in animal trafficking?" Benito asked.

"I think so, Benito, or he wouldn't be keeping his work secret," Lola said.

"May I please be excused, Dr. Arroyo? The soup was delicious. But I'd like to take more close-ups of the animals' faces for our project."

"Of course, Benito. You can start with close-ups of the animals in the petting zoo."

Jorge poured coffee for Lola and himself.

"Now I want to find out about you, Lola. What do you do for work? What do you do for fun? What do you think about when you're alone?"

"Oh, my. Do you have a minute?"

"I have all afternoon."

"For work, I take photographs of people getting married, of high school seniors, and of corporate executives. I used to take photographs of animals in cages. For fun, I go on road trips with Benito, play the guitar with Benito, cook, and read."

"Did you bring your guitar?"

"No, I didn't."

"Another time, bring your guitar. I'll invite Jaime and Annie. Jaime plays the guitar and Annie sings."

"I'd love it."

"So what do you think about when you're alone?"

"Lately? Well, when I traveled on photo shoots for Mr. Tavis I thought about caged animals. I wondered what reasons different people have for caging them. You, Jorge, have good reasons. You cage wounded animals to get them well. And you keep a few healthy individuals in enclosures, huge enclosures, to save their species."

"We want our animals to be happy."

"But the other men I visited for Mr. Tavis are not like you. They want to control 'wild beasts' for their personal pleasure.'"

"How long had you worked for Willard Tavis?"

"Since last July. Mr. Tavis hired my uncle, Juan Navarro, when Juan got arrested for drunk driving a year ago. Mr. Tavis bailed him out of jail for some unknown reason and gave him a job on his ranch. He never paid Juan much, but he allowed Juan to live in a house on his land. With another hired man named Gordo. Juan felt trapped."

"What did Juan do before he got arrested?"

"He worked in Charleston at La Fiesta as a cook. I owe him a lot. He brought Benito and me to Charleston right after the covid-19 pandemic and got me work at his restaurant. His wife Gloria had just died from the virus."

"But you left the restaurant?"

"I got a graduate fellowship in photography at the University of Charleston and started taking pictures for companies. The companies paid well. I'll get my degree in August."

"How did Tavis come to hire you?"

"Juan must have told him that I was a photographer, and a year ago he hired me to take pictures for *Wild Beasts*. He paid me by the shoot, which is about once a month. But he didn't always publish my pictures. He didn't publish my picture of a badger-wolverine."

"What did Juan do for Tavis?"

"He prepared food for the animals Mr. Tavis keeps on the ranch. I've never seen them. But once when I visited Tío Juan I heard howling. So maybe he keeps wolves."

"Why did Tavis found *Wild Beasts Magazine*?"

"He says he wanted to learn about wild animals. But I think he is networking. He writes all the stories. He wrote the story about Zoo Arroyo. And he finds the advertisers."

"Who are the advertisers?"

"Gun shops, bow shops, outdoor apparel stores, feed stores. Benito finds it contradictory that the magazine features zoo animals and advertises guns."

"Benito is perceptive."

"Sometimes I take Benito with me on weekend photo shoots. That's how Benito started shooting close-ups of animals. Benito saw sadness in their eyes. He believes his close-ups revealed their souls."

"Lola, I have to tell you that Zoo Arroyo has been violated. Our young wolf Faye, whom Jaime had implanted with a Red wolf clone, or so he thought, whelped a wolverine-wolf chimera this past Wednesday."

"Oh, my god."

"You know what a chimera is?"

"Yes."

"And Friday night, somebody got into Jaime's lab and substituted a newborn Red wolf pup for the wolverine-wolf chimera pup. We think that person was Marco. He left the zoo without giving us a forwarding address."

"Could this event be related to the murder?"

"Could be. But I hate to think that Marco is involved in a murder. He seems too nice a guy."

Lola put down her coffee cup. "Let's show Benito around your zoo, Jorge. You can ask him about his portfolio."

"Good idea. We'll take the jeep. Poe, stay here."

Poe flew onto the top of his cage.

"I have to ask you something, Lola. Do you know Dr. Louis Bordeau?"

"Not really. I encountered him at the Wild Beasts convention."

"Good. Don't make the effort."

Jorge went into his operating room and took a large package out of the refrigerator.

"We'll take some chow for the wolves."

Jorge and Lola found Benito outside the bears' enclosure.

"I got a great close-up of the bear cub, Jorge," Benito said.

"That would be Jackie, Benito."

"She wanted to touch me."

Benito was eager to talk.

"I have this theory, Jorge, that eyes reveal suffering, in animals and in humans. And I think that the main cause of suffering for animals, besides physical pain, is being caged. So I plan to take pictures of as many caged animals as I can and then make a book titled "Caged Spirits.""

"Wow, Benito. Do you think your theory applies to humans too?"

"Yes, of course. Tío Juan is a caged spirit. I look into his eyes and see the same suffering I see in caged lions. I took some pictures of him too."

The scent of the meat brought the pack to the fence. As Sol watched warily, Benito photographed the wolves with his telephoto lens. Then Jorge fed them.

"Do you see suffering in their eyes, Benito?" Jorge asked.

"No, I don't. I guess they're happy here. But you haven't really caged them, so they are still free spirits."

They returned to the farmhouse.

"I agree with Benito, Jorge," Lola said. "And I agree with Samantha Wheeling, who talked about cages on your radio show. We humans have caged life on Earth. We have converted Earth's wilderness to land we control for our own use. We have enclosed America's wild animals in national or state parks where we can manage them, or we have caged them in zoos where we can view them."

"And we are now breeding chimpanzees, pigs, and other animals for their organs."

"What's the difference between breeding pigs for their organs and breeding pigs for bacon?" Benito asked.

"I sense an ethical difference, Benito, but I can't articulate it," Jorge said. "We humans think we have the right to control every living thing on earth. To me that's wrong."

"I didn't see suffering in the eyes of your animals, Jorge. I took close-ups of the chickens, and of Blossom, Herman, and Sancho. I took close-ups of Nanny and Patty too, and I didn't see suffering in their goaty eyes either. You know what I saw?"

"What?"

"Slits!" Benito laughed uproariously. So did Jorge and Lola.

"Now it's my turn," Jorge said. He used his cell phone to take their pictures.

Lola and Benito departed at three thirty, with promises to return.

JORGE SET UP HIS EASEL ON THE FRONT PORCH, OPENED a box of sixty-four chalk pastels, and worked for an hour on a portrait of Lola. The temperature hovered at seventy-five degrees, and the air was fragrant with the scent of mown grass.

Late in the afternoon Nick and Bernie appeared. Nick carried a two-foot-tall balsa-wood bear.

"Hey, Jorge. I brought you a bear I carved. It has arms!'

"And it has a smile. You've carved a great bear, Nick! Thank you."

Nick sat down behind Jorge to watch him finish the drawing. Bernie settled himself at the top of the steps.

"Is she your girlfriend, Jorge? She's beautiful. What's her name?"

"She is my girlfriend. She is beautiful. And her name is Lola."

Jorge enjoyed Nick's companionship.

After a while Nick asked, "Why don't you put some of those pink flowers in your drawing? They would look good with your girlfriend's blue blouse."

"The hydrangeas? Good idea, Nick."

Jorge quickly chalked in multiple pale pink hydrangea blossoms behind Lola's head. "How's that, Nick?"

"That's good, Jorge. The flowers float like clouds. Your girlfriend will like it."

"I hope so. She'll see it on my living room wall."

Ping. "Wow, Jorge. It's a text from Marco! He's in Perú."

"Is he okay?"

"I guess so. He's gonna send me a *pinkillo* flute. Do you want to read his text?"

Nick showed Jorge an exchange of text messages. Nick had initiated the correspondence with a thank-you note for the wood carving knives.

"Good idea to write Marco. I hope that you all stay in touch, Nick."

"We will, Jorge."

Jorge sprayed fixative on the artwork. "Now time for you to go home."

Shortly thereafter Jorge got a call from Detective Dunning. "Hey, Mira."

"May I pay you a visit to Zoo Arroyo tomorrow, Jorge? Say, at one o'clock? I have some information to share with you."

"Certainly."

"*Hola, Lola! Are you home now?*"

"Hi, Jorge. Thanks for calling. Benito and I just got home. We had wonderful day. Thanks so much for everything, especially for the attention you paid Benito."

"Benito won me over, Lola."

"Benito talked about you and the zoo the whole ride home. He got a great picture of Poe that he wants to enter into a competition. He said he'd like to work for you next summer."

"You can tell him that I'll give him a job with room and board."

"Jorge, you asked me what I thought about when I was alone, and I said 'caged souls.' Now I ask you. What do you think about when you're alone?"

"What do I think about when I am alone? These days my thoughts fall into two categories: the mystery of the dead man; and you."

"I think about you too, Jorge."

"Are you and Benito free on the Fourth of July? If so, can we meet at noon in Augusta at the Alligator's Smile, on Lock and Dam Road? It's near the Phinizy Swamp Nature Park. We can eat lunch and walk through the park."

"Sure! Benito will bring his camera."

"I have a question. You said you had photographed a badger-wolverine? Can you tell me where?"

"If I could tell you where I photographed the badger-wolverine I would, but Mr. Tavis made me sign a non-disclosure agreement promising not to give out any information about my photo shoots."

"Even after he's fired you."

"If I should be subpoenaed, I would talk."

"I'll think about that, Lola."

From: Lola Montoya (LolaMontoya@zmail.com)
To: Estela Navarro (EstelaNavarro@zmail.com)
11:30 pm, Sunday, June 30, 2030
JORGE ARROYO

Querida Mamá,

I hope you can come to my graduation on August 24. I want to introduce you to my friend Jorge Arroyo. Benito and I spent the day with him, and now Benito wants me to marry Jorge. Benito thinks I will do what he wants in this matter, since I do whatever he wants in other matters.

I do care for Jorge, very much.

I attach a picture that Benito took of Jorge and me. Jorge is a wildlife veterinarian. His identical twin brother Jaime is a wildlife biologist. Together they own and operate Zoo Arroyo, in north Georgia. I will send you a copy of Wild Beasts Magazine, which has an article about the zoo with photos that I took.

So that's the good news.

The bad news is that Mr. Tavis, the editor of Wild Beasts Magazine, fired Tío Juan and me this week.

Actually, that's not such bad news. I invited Tío Juan to move into my house with Benito and me. And he has found work at La Cocina Mexicana.

I hope you're well. I can't wait to see you!
Con cariño,
Lola

From: Estela Navarro (EstelaNavarro@zmail.com)
From: Lola Montoya (LolaMontoya@zmail.com)
11:40 pm, Sunday, June 30, 2030
Re: JORGE ARROYO
Querida hija mía,

I am happy that you have a nice companion now. I have worried that you would never find anybody to love.

I will see you on August 24.
Con mucho cariño,
Tu mamacita

CHAPTER TWENTY-TWO

Monday, July 1, 2030

Every Monday morning at nine o'clock Jorge held a staff meeting over breakfast. The staff normally included Zookeeper Zell, Eddie, and Marco, but today Nick occupied Marco's chair. Poe perched on Nick's shoulder.

"So glad you came, Nick. As my assistant, you are on the Zoo Arroyo staff now."

"I've been thinking, Jorge," Zell said. "I suspect the thieves wanted Faye. She was pregnant with a wolverine-wolf fetus, which Marco had gotten Jaime to implant. And if that's the case, then Marco is an accomplice."

"Marco knew that Faye, who was carrying the chimera, was close to her delivery date," Jorge said. "If Marco wanted to take Faye away from the zoo before she whelped, he might have hired the thieves to steal her. He could have told the thieves that Faye was the wolf with the yellow collar."

"And if the wolf thieves had taken Faye, we would never have found out about Sasha. I mean Sasha One," Nick said.

"Do you all think that Marco is really in Atlanta preparing to go to graduate school? If that's where he went he would have told us his address," Zell said.

"I'll ask Mira to try to locate him," Jorge said. "Now is there any other business for us today?"

"The Fourth of July is coming up," Nick said. "And that's my birthday. You all are invited to my party. And you can bring me presents if you like. Come at six thirty."

"I may be a little late, but I'll be there, Nick. I guess you'll turn ten, right?"

"No, I'll turn fifteen." Nick laughed and laughed.

"Anything else before we adjourn? Nick?"

"Bonita is pregnant."

WHILE DOING THE BREAKFAST DISHES, JORGE THOUGHT about Lola. How much more he would enjoy preparing meals with her. Having a devoted identical twin brother, he hadn't really felt the need for another human being in his life until he'd met Lola, but now he thought constantly about her. Paradoxically, she made him feel lonely.

Jorge's reverie was interrupted by a phone call from Rhonda.

"Hey, Jorge. I've got information for you. I checked the OnlineColumbia website and found an article published last night about a loose jackal."

"Read it to me."

COLUMBIA ZOO JACKAL ARRESTED DOWNTOWN
BY ELLIE PARSONS

8:00 pm, June 30, 2030. The jackal that threatened pedestrians in downtown Columbia on Friday was recaptured late Friday night.

A Golden jackal named Sameera escaped from a veterinary clinic in Columbia where she had been

*artificially inseminated. After chasing her along the
Columbia Canal to the courthouse steps, police officials shot her with tranquilizer darts and returned
her to the Columbia Zoo.*

*The jackal was a gift from the government of
South Africa.*

Local police are investigating the incident.

"Since Dr. Louis Bordeau, veterinarian, was more eager
to return to Columbia than to share a dinner with me, I
conclude that he is Sameera's vet."

"You may be right, Rhonda."

"I'm telling you, Jorge, the creep has secrets."

⸻

Jorge googled "Columbia Zoo," and found Bordeau's resumé.

*Louis T. Bordeau, Doctor of Veterinary Medicine,
specializes in large animal medicine. He has served
on the staff of the Columbia Zoo in Columbia, South
Carolina, since 2008.*

*Dr. Bordeau earned his BS degree in biology from
the University of South Carolina and his DVM at the
University of California at Davis School of Veterinary
Medicine. He did his residency at the San Diego Zoo's
Program in Zoological Medicine associated with the
UC Davis School of Veterinary Medicine. He has
ACZM (American College of Zoological Medicine)
board certification.*

Jorge stopped browsing when Mira and Seq arrived.

"I've got big news," Mira said. "We've located Simon Pate's 2009 black Dodge Ram. It was abandoned in the Witherston High School parking lot."

"Then the thieves were in the vehicle of Simon Pate's accomplice," Jorge said.

"Seq searched the Ram. He found four packets of cocaine taped to the axel."

"So Simon Pate returned to dealing drugs after prison," Jorge said. "But what could drugs have to do with the two murders?"

"Simon Pate was subject to blackmail," Seq answered.

"Do you all know anything about Willard Tavis?" Jorge showed Mira and Seq the ad he had seen in *Wild Beasts Magazine*. "The person who placed this ad may have something to do with Garrison Tucker's murder, which has something to do with Simon Pate's murder. I have reason to believe that person is Willard Tavis and that the telephone number 800-340-4838 is his."

"Tell us what you know about Tavis, Jorge."

"Willard Tavis owns a ranch in the Charleston area. He founded *Wild Beasts Magazine*. And, according to Garrison Tucker's tipster, he has developed an interest in Zoo Arroyo's wolves. So here are my questions: Did Simon Pate work for Willard Tavis? Does Willard Tavis traffic in wild animals? Does Willard Tavis traffic in drugs?"

Mira jotted down the questions in her notebook. "Got it," she said.

"That's one mystery," Jorge said. "Another mystery is Marco Ramos. Did you find out anything about him?"

"I got a search warrant to check Marco's Wells Fargo bank account in Witherston," Mira said. "Automatic deposits of his Zoo Arroyo salary. And then two unusual transactions.

A deposit of three thousand dollars in cash on Monday, June twenty-fourth, at eight-fifty pm."

"Probably for something he did regarding the wolves," Jorge said.

"And a withdrawal of more than eight thousand dollars in cash on Friday, June twenty-eighth, at three fifty-five pm leaving only three hundred and five dollars in his checking account."

"Eight thousand dollars would buy Marco an airline ticket to Perú," Jorge said, "and plenty more."

"I checked Simon Pate's account in the Bank of South Carolina and found irregular cash deposits ranging from three thousand dollars to ten thousand dollars."

"Always cash?"

"Yes, always cash, which is typical of a drug dealer. Simon Pate had plenty of income. His savings account and his checking account combined totaled approximately forty thousand dollars."

"What was the most recent deposit?"

"There were two recent deposits, three thousand dollars on Monday, June seventeenth, at eight-thirty am, and two thousand dollars on Monday, June twenty-fourth, at eight fifty-five am."

"The first was the Monday someone shot Garrison Tucker, and the second was the day Simon Pate entered Sol's Woods and met the wolves," Jorge said. "So Simon Pate may have shot Garrison Tucker."

"Could be that Marco Ramos and Simon Pate were being paid by the same person," Seq said. "Maybe Willard Tavis."

"So let's start solving the mystery of Simon Pate's death," Mira said. "We'll make a timeline of associated events. We can add to it as we get more evidence."

"You might include the visits of Lola and Dr. Bordeau to Zoo Arroyo. Lola gathered a lot of information back in March that she or somebody could have used," Seq said. "And Dr. Bordeau had no obvious reason to tour the zoo."

"Lola is not a suspect," Jorge said.

"She is not. But she was reporting to Willard Tavis, wasn't she?"

"Yes. And I'd consider Willard Tavis a possible suspect."

"I would too. Willard Tavis has a police record. He was convicted of drug dealing in 2015, when he was twenty-five years old, but his conviction was overturned. He served only three months in prison."

"Sounds like Willard Tavis and Simon Pate are bad characters," Seq said.

"And in some way they are connected," Mira said. "I will interview Willard Tavis. Let's see what we know." Mira opened up her laptop computer and started typing.

MONDAY, MARCH 4—Lola Montoya visited Zoo Arroyo, took pictures, and recorded her interview with Jorge for Willard Tavis, of Charleston, who used the information to write the Wild Beasts article.

Friday, March 8—Marco Ramos was shot after midnight by an intruder who, apparently, stole the zoo's two minks.

- *Questions: Is there any connection between Lola's visit and the shooting of Marco Ramos? Did Marco Ramos interrupt the robbery of the minks? Who knew about the minks?*

- *Speculation: Willard Tavis learned of the minks through Lola Montoya's recording of her interview with Jorge.*

Monday, April 22—Jaime and Marco implanted female Red wolf embryos into Faye, Fern, and Luna. However, it turns out that they implanted a wolverine-wolf chimera embryo in Faye.

- *Speculation: Marco substituted a wolverine-wolf chimera for a wolf embryo Jaime thought he was transferring into Faye.*

Sunday, May 5—Nick ran into Marco and his girlfriend Dr. Patricia Maloney at the bears' enclosure.

- *Question: How did Marco meet Dr. Patricia Maloney?*

Wednesday, May 22—Jaime and Marco implanted embryos in Foxy Ann and Foxy Belle.

- *Question: Could they be carrying chimeras?*

Sunday, May 26—Jorge interviewed Garrison Tucker on "People for the Planet."

Friday, May 31—Wild Beasts summer issue, with Sol and Luna on the cover, came out.

Thursday, June 13—Garrison Tucker warned that the zoo's wolves were targets for theft. He also threatened to bring financial ruin to a particular animal trafficker. Jorge shared his email with the staff. Did Marco share it with Willard Tavis?

Saturday, June 15—Garrison Tucker was murdered. Mrs. Tucker saw an old black Dodge Ram in Tucker's neighborhood. Simon Pate drove a 2009 black Dodge Ram.

- *Question: Who shot Garrison Tucker?*

- *Speculation: Simon Pate shot Garrison Tucker in Augusta. Willard Tavis ordered him to do so.*

- *Question: Why?*

- *Speculation: To stop Tucker's investigation into animal trafficking. According to Lola, Willard Tavis traffics in wild animals.*

Monday, June 17—Simon Pate deposited $3,000 in cash into his bank account at 8:30 am.

- *Question: Who paid him and for what?*
- *Speculation: Willard Tavis paid him for killing Garrison Tucker.*

Sunday, June 23—Lola Montoya was interviewed on "People for the Planet." Willard Tavis heard it, somehow.

Monday, June 24—Simon Pate deposited $2,000 in cash into his bank account at 8:55 am.

- *Question: Who paid him and for what?*
- *Speculation: He was paid by somebody to steal a wolf that night.*

Monday, June 24— Eddie, Emma, Nick, Marco, and Jorge went to the Wild Beasts reception, leaving the zoo locked but unattended.

MONDAY, JUNE 24—Dr. Louis Bordeau, a veterinarian from Columbia, South Carolina, who works at the Columbia Zoo, Willard Tavis, the founder and editor of Wild Beasts Magazine, and Lola all attended the reception. Lola departed early. Dr. Bordeau asked to visit Zoo Arroyo.

Monday, June 24—Simon Pate and an accomplice entered the zoo at night, and went into Sol's Woods. Wolves attacked Simon Pate, and Pate's accomplice shot and killed him, and escaped. The gun used to shoot Simon Pate had previously been used to shoot Marco Ramos, Sol, and Garrison Tucker.

- Question: Who killed Simon Pate and why?
- Speculation: Accomplice killed Pate either to save him from being mauled to death by the wolves or to silence him.
- Question: How did Simon Pate and his accomplice get into the zoo?
- Speculation: Marco gave Simon Pate and his accomplice a key.
- Question: Why were the thieves interested in the wolves?
- Speculation: Simon Pate and his accomplice intended to steal Faye because she was carrying the wolverine-wolf. Marco told them or the person who hired them that Faye with the yellow collar was the wolf carrying the chimera.
- Question: Who directed Marco?

Monday, June 24—Marco deposited $3,000 into his bank account at 8:50 pm.

- Question: Who paid him and for what?
- Speculation: He was paid by somebody for transplanting the chimera embryo into Faye and for helping the thieves steal Faye before she whelped.

Tuesday, June 25—Rhonda revealed that Dr. Bordeau, whom she had met at the reception, was interested in her and in her stories about the zoo's animals.

- Question: Why was Dr. Bordeau interested in Rhonda? Why was he interested in the zoo?

Wednesday, June 26—Willard Tavis fired both Lola and her uncle Juan Navarro.

- *Speculation: Both knew too much about Tavis's business. And Lola was dating Jorge.*

Wednesday, June 26—Dr. Bordeau visited the zoo, briefly.

- *Question: Why? What did he want to learn?*

Wednesday, June 26—USA Today published an article about Dr. Patricia Maloney's creation of a wolf-bear chimera. Dr. Maloney is Marco's girlfriend.

- *Speculation: Dr. Maloney produced the wolverine-wolf chimera embryo. She is working with Marco.*

Wednesday, June 26—Faye whelped Sasha One, the wolverine-wolf. Faye died.

Friday, June 28—A jackal named Sameera escaped from a veterinary clinic in Columbia, South Carolina.

- *Question: Was the veterinarian Dr. Louis Bordeau?*

Friday, June 28—Somebody substituted a female newborn wolf for Sasha One late Friday night.

- *Question: Did Marco make the substitution?*

Friday, June 28—Dr. Bordeau departed suddenly for Columbia.

- *Speculation: As a vet for the Columbia Zoo, Dr. Bordeau wanted to get back to Columbia for Sameera.*

- *Question: Did Dr. Bordeau use Rhonda to get information about the zoo's animals? If so, why?*

Saturday, June 29—Marco disappeared.

- *Speculation: Marco took Sasha One with him.*

- *Question: Where is Marco?*

- *Speculation: Marco is either with Dr. Maloney somewhere or in Perú. But if he went to Perú what did he do with Sasha?*

"How's that for a timeline?" Mira asked.

"I have a speculation on the jackal," Jorge said. "If Dr. Bordeau gave regular physical examinations to the Columbia Zoo's animals, he had the opportunity to take cells from them, as well as sperm and embryos."

"To make chimera embryos? But would he have the skills? I doubt it."

"Who would have the skills?" Seq asked.

"Dr. Patricia B. Maloney. Marco knows how to clone animals, but as far as I know he does not know how to create chimeras."

"What does the 'B' stand for in Dr. Maloney's name?" Mira asked.

"Let me google her." Jorge went on the web and found a short bio from her post-doctoral experience at Georgia Tech. "Holy moly! Her full name is Patricia Bordeau Maloney! She must be related to Dr. Louis Bordeau."

"I have a conjecture," Mira said. "Everything follows from Lola's visit to Zoo Arroyo on March fifth, starting with the theft of Minkie and Mickie on the night of March seventh."

"That's what I'm thinking," Seq said.

"Wait, Lola is innocent."

"Jorge, I'm not implicating Lola," Mira said. "I'm guessing that the publication of 'Zoo Arroyo Resurrects the Red Wolf' in *Wild Beasts Magazine* was the source of somebody's information about the wolves."

Seq interrupted. "Here's my theory. Mr. Tavis sent Lola here to take pictures and interview Jorge. He wanted information about the wolves because he was looking for a female wolf to carry a chimera embryo. Lola came here and got you to tell her everything about the zoo. Then she told Mr. Tavis."

"No, Seq. You've got Lola all wrong."

"Here's a more likely theory, Jorge," Mira said. "Mr. Tavis used Lola's recorded interview to write the article. That's how he got his information. Mr. Tavis had time to have a wolverine-wolf chimera embryo sent frozen to Marco. Jaime and Marco implanted the chimera embryo on April twenty-second."

"If you all are right, then Willard Tavis is the ringleader," Jorge said. "At the reception he could have given Marco the three thousand dollars in cash that night for switching the embryos before April twenty-second."

"Or for giving Simon Pate a key to the zoo," Seq said.

"And he could have given Simon Pate the two thousand dollars that morning to capture a wolf. Both Pate and Tavis live in Charleston. Pate must work for Tavis."

"But who sent the embryo to Marco?" Seq asked.

"It could have been Dr. Bordeau, or it could have been Willard Tavis," Mira said. "Willard Tavis could have ordered Bordeau to send it."

"At minus three hundred twenty-one degrees Fahrenheit?"

"It could have been Dr. Maloney," Jorge said. "Dr. Maloney is the one with the skill to create a chimera. She could have handed it off to Marco."

"Lola's uncle, Juan Navarro, worked for Tavis. You could talk to Juan Navarro, Detective Dunning," Seq said.

"Lola told me that Tavis bailed Juan out of jail when Juan was arrested for drunk driving. Juan is not an American citizen. Now why would Tavis offer him a job? Surely not out of the goodness of his heart."

"That's an easy one, Jorge. Tavis could control Juan, whom he could turn in to the police if Juan were insubordinate," Seq said.

"Simon Pate was a convicted felon," Mira said. "Convicted felons have difficulty finding work. Maybe Willard Tavis employed him to do odd jobs, such as stealing wolves. I have to talk with Tavis."

"I'll talk with Lola about Willard Tavis, Mira. I'm meeting Lola and Benito on the Fourth of July at Phinizy Swamp Nature Park. May I show them this timeline?"

"It can't do any harm."

CHAPTER TWENTY-THREE

Wednesday, July 3, 2030

Jorge opened the brown envelope that came through the U.S. Postal Service and found a set of car keys and two notes written on notebook paper, plus a vehicle certificate of title.

> *Dear Jorge.*
>
> *Here is the key fob to my Subaru.*
>
> *The car is yours (and it's paid for).*
>
> *I left it at the Atlanta airport in the south long-term parking garage.*
>
> *Look for it under the sign "Level 2, Section K8."*
>
> *By the time you get this message I will be in Perú.*
>
> *I don't think I've broken any laws, but I've betrayed your trust. That's worse.*
>
> *I will write later.*
>
> *Marco*

> *To Whom It May Concern:*
>
> *I, Marco Ramos-Martínez, give this Subaru to Dr. Jorge Arroyo.*
>
> *Marco Ramos-Martínez*

Will I ever see Marco again? Jorge wondered. I will miss hearing the sounds of his flute. I will miss playing chess with him. I thought I knew him but I didn't. He had secrets. Does Lola have secrets? Time will tell.

Jorge called Rhonda.

"Hey, Rhonda. Would you take me to the Atlanta airport this evening to pick up a Subaru Outback that Marco left for me, and then follow me back to your house? Eddie and I will pick it up tomorrow."

"I'd enjoy it, Jorge. Did Marco flee the country?"

"Yes. I'll explain. Can we go in your car? Zell will drop me off at your house at three o'clock. And to show my gratitude I'll fix you dinner on Saturday."

"Louis phoned me last night," Rhonda said to Jorge when Jorge got into her car. "He apologized for his abrupt departure."

"Does he want to see you again?"

"Yes. He told me he has resigned his position as a Columbia Zoo vet and has put his property on the market."

"How did he explain his behavior?"

"Louis said that he had been informed on Friday afternoon that a pregnant jackal from the Columbia Zoo he'd brought to his clinic had escaped. His niece was caring for Sameera—the jackal—in his absence because she was performing some routine surgery on her. He said he drove at top speed back to Columbia to retrieve Sameera. The police captured Sameera before he got there and returned her to the zoo. Louis said he felt so bad that he resigned from the zoo's veterinary staff."

"A niece? Did he mention her name?"

"No. That was the first time I heard of a niece. He asked me about you, Jorge. He asked whether you had ever mentioned a Dr. Patricia Maloney. I told him you had never spoken of her to me. Maybe Dr. Patricia Maloney is his niece."

Jorge spent the rest of the trip bringing Rhonda up to date on what they knew.

They entered the south long-term parking deck, ascended to level two, and promptly found Marco's car in section eight.

WHEN HE GOT HOME JORGE OPENED A COLD BEER, WENT out onto the porch, and texted Marco.

> *9:55 pm*
> *Hey, Marco.*
> *Thank you very much for your Subaru Outback.*
> *The zoo can use an extra all-wheel drive vehicle.*
> *And thank you very much for the beautiful Rosewood table and lamp.*
> *As I've said, "Artists speak with the angels."*
> *Tell me what's going on with you, Marco.*
> *Jorge*

Marco replied.

> *Artists who speak with the angels may still be seduced by the devil.*
> *Who will get the better of me?*
> *I despair.*

CHAPTER TWENTY-FOUR

Thursday, July 4, 2030

J orge found Lola and Benito on the front porch of the Alligator's Smile Café taking selfies of themselves beside a twelve-foot-long alligator. The taxidermist had given the reptile a big smile.

"*Hola*, Jorge!" Benito shouted. "May I take your picture with Grin? That's his name."

Jorge spotted a sign. MEET GRIN, THE ALLIGATOR WITH A SMILE.

"Sure, Benito."

Just as Benito aimed his camera Jorge pulled up his pant leg.

"Did I ever tell you that an alligator took my leg?"

Benito turned pale.

"An alligator did that?"

"He's kidding you, Benito," Lola said.

"I lost my leg in an automobile accident, Benito, on an icy road. I hope that when you start driving that you'll remember what an automobile accident can do."

"I will, Jorge. I will remember forever. I'll also be careful when I'm around live alligators."

"Good idea," Lola said.

The three went inside the restaurant and took a table by an open window. Jorge looked around. Alligators everywhere. Baby alligators, juvenile alligators, and one fourteen-foot-long alligator. The Alligator's Smile Café must have had a taxidermist on staff, Jorge figured.

"This is my all-time favorite restaurant," Benito said.

Over batter-fried catfish Jorge informed Lola and Benito of Marco's disappearance with Sasha One. He showed them the timeline of events.

"It looks like the interview started things, Jorge. What did I do?"

"You took pictures of Zoo Arroyo and recorded our interview, as Willard Tavis paid you to do."

"I emailed the recording to Mr. Tavis that Tuesday night, and on Thursday night the minks disappeared."

"Does Willard Tavis employ anybody besides Juan Navarro?"

"Yes. A man named Gordo."

"What do you know about Gordo?" Jorge asked.

"He's fat," Benito said. "He works for Mr. Tavis. And according to my uncle Juan, he spent two years in prison and didn't learn anything. He still sells drugs."

"That's very helpful, Benito."

"Maybe Gordo does Mr. Tavis's dirty work," Benito said. "You know, like stealing minks."

"He might have been Simon Pate's accomplice," Jorge said. "Do you know Gordo's last name?"

"I don't," Lola said.

"Tío Juan doesn't know Gordo's last name either," Benito said.

"Have you all ever heard Tío Juan mention a man by the name of Simon Pate?"

"No."

"No."

"Have I mentioned Dr. Patricia Maloney's name to you?" Jorge asked Lola.

"I don't think so."

"Dr. Patricia Bordeau Maloney, a geneticist, resigned from the Callaghan Research Institute in Atlanta on May thirty-first. She had implanted an embryo of a wolf-bear chimera into a Black bear that, quote, 'belonged to a private zoo.' Benito, do you know what a chimera is?"

"I do," Benito said. "It's an animal that has genetic material from two different species, but it's not a hybrid. A chimera has some cells with genes from one species and some cells with genes from the other species. A hybrid has genes from both species in every cell."

"I'm impressed," Lola said. "Where did you learn all that?"

"In my science class."

"Dr. Bordeau works for the Columbia Zoo," Jorge said. "And he is probably kin to Dr. Patricia Maloney."

"I bet that Dr. Maloney and Dr. Bordeau made the chimera to put into your animals, Jorge."

"You may be right, Benito. And Marco may be involved. Dr. Maloney is Marco's girlfriend. On a different topic, let me ask you, Lola. How long does it take to drive from Charleston to Augusta?"

"Under three hours."

"So Gordo could have driven from Charleston to Augusta on the morning of June fifteenth and murdered Garrison Tucker."

Jorge called Mira.

"Hey, Mira. I'm with Lola and Benito in Columbia. Have you reached Willard Tavis?"

"Yes. We talked for twenty minutes on the phone. He says he doesn't know Gordo's last name. He says

Gordo works for him on an irregular basis. He pays him in cash."

"Does he know where Gordo is now?"

"He says that he hasn't seen Gordo for a couple of weeks."

"Does he know Simon Pate?"

"He said he'd read about his death but didn't know him."

"Do you believe him?"

"No."

———

Jorge almost missed Nick's birthday party, which had started at seven o'clock. Abbie, Zell, and Eve, and Eddie and Emma were still eating barbecued pork when Jorge arrived at eight. The drive from Augusta had taken four hours.

"Hi, Jorge," Nick shouted. "I've already opened my presents, but I saved Marco's and yours to open when you got here."

"Thank you, Nick!"

"I'll open yours first."

Nick unwrapped a big box.

"Wow! A microscope! Thank you, Jorge!"

"I figure that you'll need a microscope if you're going to be a vet, Nick."

"Open Marco's present, Nick," Eddie said.

Nick tore the wrapping off another box. Inside he found a *pan* flute. "Wow! It's just like Marco's!" Then he saddened. "But I may never get to play with him again."

"Marco's gone now, but you can remember him as a your friend. He loved you like a son."

CHAPTER TWENTY-FIVE

Friday, July 5, 2030

"Jorge, you've got to come here!" Zell said to Jorge on the phone. Jorge was still eating breakfast.

"What's up?"

"Juliet is either delivering a cub or aborting it."

Jorge grabbed his surgical kit, a couple of towels, and a stun gun, got into the jeep, and drove up the lane to the bears' enclosure. Nick was inside with Zell.

"Hey, Jorge," Nick said. "Juliet's cub came out. I saw it all."

"Hi, Nick. I'll take a look."

Jorge opened the enclosure door and joined Zell and Nick.

"When I gave them their food I noticed that Juliet was on the ground having a hard time," Nick said. "Then I saw the little cub poking his head out of her. That's when I called you. It's out now. She's licking it."

"Juliet couldn't have been due before fall, Zell. We didn't discover her pregnancy till May."

"She was sick when you and my dad were in Savannah, Jorge," Nick said. "Remember?"

"You're right, Nick. That would have been on Sunday, May fifth," Jorge said.

Zell pulled up the calendar on his phone. "That was

sixty-one days ago. That's enough time to make a dog or a wolf but not enough time to make a bear cub."

Neither Zell nor Jorge wanted to approach Juliet, who was now protecting her offspring.

"I'm going to knock her out so we can get close," Jorge said.

"Better knock out Romeo," Zell said. "And Jackie too."

Jorge did.

Zell gently took the premature cub from the mother bear, wrapped him in a towel, and handed him to Jorge. "It's a male," he said, "but very premature. I've never seen a bear cub this premature."

"Nick, do you want to come with me?" Jorge asked. "Zell should stay to make sure the bears revive okay."

"Sure," Nick said. "May I hold him?"

"That's why I want you to come with me, Nick, to hold him. You're my assistant."

In the operating room Jorge cleaned up the cub, weighed, and measured him.

"Sixteen ounces, that's heavy for a premature bear cub. Nine inches long, which is about right."

"Should we x-ray him too? To make sure he's a bear?"

"Good idea, Nick."

Jorge x-rayed newborn.

"What in the world?"

"What, Jorge?"

"I can't believe it, Nick. This little creature is not a bear."

"What is it?"

"I don't know. I have an awful suspicion that he is another chimera."

"May I give him wolf formula?"

"Yes, of course. And keep him warm."

Jorge settled Nick in the chair with a heating pad, a towel, and a baby bottle of warm formula. He set the cub on Nick's lap.

"What shall we call the little guy, Nick?"

Nick thought for a moment. "Can we call him Nicky Bear?"

"Sure, Nick. You watched his birth, and now you're taking care of him."

"I can stay all day."

"Can you take care of Nicky Bear tomorrow?"

"Sure."

Jorge texted Jaime.

> *9:02 am*
> *Hey, Jaime.*
> *This morning Juliet produced a male creature that is NOT a bear cub.*
> *I'm wondering if it's another chimera implanted by Marco.*
> *I'm emailing you the x-ray.*
> *Should I send DNA samples to your colleague Dr. Bakshi?*
> *I think Marco used Faye and Juliet as incubators for chimera embryos.*
> *Nick named the "cub" Nicky Bear.*

> *Hey, Jorge.*
> *Good god!*
> *Could Eddie or Zell take a dna sample to Dr. Bakshi at Zoo Atlanta today?*
> *She can give us an answer within hours.*
> *I will alert her.*

Send me a picture of Nicky Bear.

I wonder which other females at our zoo could be incubating a chimera embryo?

If you have time, could you google Patricia B. Maloney?

Eddie said he would take the sample to Dr. Bakshi, and he would take Nick with him to see Zoo Atlanta while they awaited the results.

ON THE CALLAGHAN INSTITUTE WEBSITE JORGE FOUND an abbreviated curriculum vitae for Patricia Maloney, PhD.

Patricia B. Maloney, PhD

EDUCATION

BS, Biology, 2016-2020 (Summa Cum Laude, Phi Beta Kappa), University of California, Berkeley; MS, Biomedical Engineering, 2020-2022, Stanford University; PhD, Reproductive Technology, 2022-2026, Virginia Polytechnic Institute and State University

EMPLOYMENT

Post-doctoral Fellow, 2026-2028, Department of Genetic Engineering, Georgia Institute of Technology;

Assistant Professor, 2028-present, Department of Genetics, Callaghan Research Institute

RESEARCH INTERESTS

Biological engineering; Reproductive technology; Chimera

PAPERS

P.B. Maloney, "Our Chimeric Future," *Stem Cell Frontiers* (May 12, 2030). Pages 12-25.

P.B. Maloney and E. Belmonte-Cardozo, "Reproductive Viability in Genome Altered Organisms," *Germline Genome Quarterly* (February 6, 2030). Pages 49-54.

P.B. Maloney, "Interspecies Embryo Transplantation," *Journal of Xenotransplantation* (November 5, 2029). Pages 23-32.

P.B. Maloney, "Embryo Transfer in Non-Human Mammals," *Embryology Today* (December 8, 2028). Pages 40-49.

P.B. Maloney and A.R. Zhang, "Uterine Receptivity to Foreign Embryos," *Embryology Today* (September 12, 2027). Pages 39-49.

P.B. Maloney and J.D. Hoffer, "Diseases of the Ruminant Placenta," *Journal of Bovine Reproductive Disorders* (April 9, 2027). Pages 28-37.

BOOK PROJECT: *"Nature is Ours"* (in progress)

On a hunch, Jorge searched his files for the CV Marco had submitted in 2028 when he had asked for a job at the zoo. Jorge found it.

Marco Ramos-Martínez

EDUCATION

BS, Biology/English, 2022-2026, *Universidad de Lima*; MS, Genetic Engineering, 2026-2028, *Georgia Institute of Technology*

EMPLOYMENT

Research Assistant, 2026-2028, Department of Genetic Engineering, Georgia Institute of Technology

RESEARCH INTERESTS

Agricultural Reproductive Technology; Cloning

A set of emails was attached.

From: Marco Ramos (MarcoRamos2004@zmail.com)
To: Jaime Arroyo (Jaime Arroyo@zmail.com)
4:09 pm, Friday, April 28, 2028
EMPLOYMENT AT ZOO ARROYO?

Dear Dr. Jaime Arroyo:

Tomorrow I shall receive my Master's degree in genetic engineering from Georgia Tech. I cited your dissertation on "Innovative Techniques for Cloning Canidae" in my thesis. I have become interested in wolves.

Would you consider hiring me at Zoo Arroyo for two years, from July of 2028 until July of 2030, as your assistant/apprentice/intern to learn your cloning techniques before I return to Georgia Tech for my PhD? I would not require much in the way of salary. And I would happily do any work you had for me at the zoo. I really enjoy the company of animals.

I could start in June.

I am originally from Perú, and I speak both Spanish and English.

Muchas gracias.

Marco Ramos

From: Jaime Arroyo (Jaime Arroyo@zmail.com)
To: Marco Ramos (MarcoRamos2004@zmail.com)
C: Jorge Arroyo (JorgeArroyo@zmail.com)
2:30 pm, Tuesday, May 2, 2028
Re: EMPLOYMENT AT ZOO ARROYO?

Dear Mr. Ramos:

My brother Jorge and I would be happy to interview you for such a position at the zoo.

Would you be free to come up this Saturday afternoon, May 6?

We could offer you the minimum wage for a 40-hour week plus free lodging.

We look forward to meeting you.

Sincerely,

Jaime Arroyo, PhD

Zoo Arroyo

1200 Bison Highway

Lumpkin County GA 30533

From: Marco Ramos(MarcoRamos2004@zmail.com)
To: Jaime Arroyo (Jaime Arroyo@zmail.com)
C: Jorge Arroyo (JorgeArroyo@zmail.com)
4:10 pm, Tuesday, May 2, 2028
Re: EMPLOYMENT AT ZOO ARROYO?

Dear Dr. Arroyo:

I will see you all at Zoo Arroyo this Saturday at approximately 1:00 pm.

I would be most grateful for the opportunity to work with you and your brother.

Yours truly,

Marco

From: Jaime Arroyo (Jaime Arroyo@zmail.com)
To: Marco Ramos (MarcoRamos2004@zmail.com)
C: Jorge Arroyo (JorgeArroyo@zmail.com)
8:30 am, Tuesday, May 9, 2028
CONTRACT

Dear Mr. Ramos:

Jorge and I really enjoyed meeting you. Our scientific goals seem aligned.

I have attached a two-year contract for you.

Your employment will begin Monday, July 3, 2028, and end on June 28, 2030. You will have lodging in a newly constructed one-bedroom A-frame at Zoo Arroyo. You will have Saturday and Sunday off. The contract shows your pay schedule.

You will notice that Jorge and I both signed the contract. You will be working primarily for Jorge and assisting me only when I am at the zoo.

I look forward to working with you. Please call me Jaime, and call my brother Jorge.

By the way, I must compliment you on your mastery of the English language.

Sincerely,

Jaime

From: Marco Ramos(MarcoRamos2004@zmail.com)
To: Jaime Arroyo (Jaime Arroyo@zmail.com),
Jorge Arroyo (JorgeArroyo.zmail.com)
9:17 pm, Tuesday, May 9, 2028
Re: EMPLOYMENT AT ZOO ARROYO?

Dear Jaime and Jorge:

I accept. I have signed the contract, scanned it, and attached it to this email.

Thank you. I will see you all at Zoo Arroyo at 8:00 am on July 3.

With regard to my English: My father spoke English to me at home, and my mother spoke Spanish. I was fluent in both languages by the age of six. I write better in English than in Spanish. I like literature. My favorite poets are Walt Whitman and Federico García Lorca.

Yours truly,

Marco

Jorge also found a handwritten note to the file.

NOTE TO THE FILE 5-9-2028:

Marco Ramos appears well-trained and smart.

Very forthright.

Very eager to please.

Likes poetry.

Will be a good employee.

—Jaime

Jorge called his brother.

"Two things, Jaime. One, Eddie has taken the dna sample to Dr. Bakshi, and he'll stay there while she runs the test. And two, we've got an academic connection between Marco and Dr. Patricia Maloney. Dr. Maloney had a post-doc at Georgia Tech in genetic engineering from 2026 to 2028, at the same time that Marco was getting his master's degree in genetic engineering and was employed as a lab technician. I'll bet Marco worked in Maloney's lab."

"I recall Marco's interview. Marco wanted to be my apprentice and to learn how to transfer embryos."

"Marco might have been innocent then, Jaime. Remember how we liked him? In your notes to the file you said he was very forthright and eager to please. He might have really wanted to study your techniques. I'm thinking that Dr. Maloney contacted him later. She might have offered him money to implant the embryos."

"Or she seduced him."

"Right. On May fifth Marco introduced her to Nick as his girlfriend."

"Are you going to tell Mira?"

"As soon as Eddie gives me Nicky Bear's DNA report."

EDDIE REPORTED TO JORGE AT NINE O'CLOCK THAT night. "Nicky Bear is a wolf-bear chimera."

BEFORE GOING TO BED JORGE TOOK NICKY BEAR OUT OF the incubator, sat down with the newborn wolf-bear on his lap, and fed him.

Holding Nicky Bear Jorge wondered whether Juliet would care for her newborn. Would she suckle him? Could the wolf-bear find a place for himself in the wild? Probably not, not without a mate. He was a freak who would be forever dependent on humans.

Jorge's mind wandered. Was there no ethical guide to what humans could do to other animals? Have humans taken charge of all life on the planet? Jorge thought again of Garrison Tucker's book title: "Does Every Species Belong to Us?"

Jorge remembered what Nick had revealed. On May fifth, sixty-one days ago, Nick ran into Marco and his girlfriend, Dr. Patricia B. Maloney, in the bears' enclosure. Marco had sedated Juliet. Could Marco and his girlfriend have transferred the wolf-bear embryo into Juliet that day?

According to the *USA Today* article of June twenty-sixth, Dr. Patricia B. Maloney had announced that she had implanted an embryo of a wolf-bear chimera into the uterus of a Black bear in a private zoo, and that the chimera would be born in late November or early December. That would be seven and a half months from May fifth, the gestation period of a Black bear. Major miscalculation.

Jorge texted Jaime.

> *Hey, Jaime.*
> *Nicky Bear is a wolf-bear chimera.*
> *Maloney and Marco implanted the embryo in Juliet on May 5.*
> *Maloney calculated that the chimera would be born 225 days later.*
> *Nicky Bear was born 61 days later.*
> *Maloney assumed that the chimera would gestate for as long as a bear.*
> *Nicky Bear gestated for as long as a wolf.*

> *Hey, Jorge.*
> *Maloney made a big mistake.*
> *No good scientist would have such a mistake.*

Of course no good scientist would have hijacked Juliet's womb.

Maloney is a no-good scientist.

Let's get the news out. Let's shed sunshine on this chimera business.

I will call Beverly.

Good night, Jaime.

Jorge called Beverly and talked with her for twenty minutes.

"This is big news," she said. "I'll put the story on the Associated Press."

As he fell asleep he wondered: Were the wombs of other mammals destined to be receptacles for whatever embryos bioengineers might create? Are their wombs ours to use? What would Garrison Tucker say?

CHAPTER TWENTY-SIX

Saturday, July 6, 2030

A fter feeding Nicky Bear, who was still in the clinic's incubator, Jorge read *USA Today*.

WOLF-BEAR CHIMERA BORN
AT ZOO ARROYO:
Two Scientists Sought for Questioning
BY BEVERLY EVERETT

8:00 am, July 6, 2030. Zoo Arroyo, in the mountains of north Georgia, is the birthplace of the world's first genetically 50/50 wolf-bear chimera. He has been named Nicky Bear.

A 50/50 genetic chimera is an animal containing a 50/50 mix of genetically different tissues, formed by the fusion of two embryos.

Nicky Bear, born on July 5 to a female Black Bear named Juliet, has 50 percent wolf genes and 50 percent bear genes.

Zoo Arroyo is owned and operated by twin brothers Dr. Jorge Arroyo and Dr. Jaime Arroyo. Its dual mission is to rescue individual wild animals and to restore endangered species to their natural habitat.

This is not the first time Zoo Arroyo has produced a chimera. On June 26, a wolf named Faye gave birth unexpectedly to a 50/50 wolverine-wolf chimera named Sasha. Sasha survived, but Faye did not. Then on Friday night, June 28, Sasha disappeared.

The birth of the two chimeras surprised the Arroyo brothers, who had no inkling that Juliet and Faye had been incubating them.

Dr. Jorge Arroyo asked, "Who has identified Zoo Arroyo's females for gestational surrogacy?"

Detective Mira Dunning of the Witherston Police Department is investigating possible connections between the implantation of the chimera embryos and the murders of Garrison Tucker on June 15 and Simon Pate on June 24.

Detective Dunning is working with the FBI to interrogate Marco Ramos-Martínez, former Zoo Arroyo employee; Dr. Patricia B. Maloney, former assistant professor of genetics at the Callaghan Research Institute of Atlanta; Willard Tavis of Charleston; and an employee of Willard Tavis who goes by the name "Gordo." They are all persons of interest in the case.

Anyone with knowledge of the activities of Ramos, Maloney, Tavis, or "Gordo" should contact the Witherston Police or the FBI immediately.

Zoo Arroyo is now closed to the public until further notice.

"MAY WE TAKE NICKY BEAR TO SEE HIS MOTHER?" NICK asked Jorge as the two of them loaded the jeep with food for the Zoo Arroyo animals. "I'll hold him on my lap."

"Sure, Nick. Better now than later. But I'll take him inside the bears' enclosure. And I'll have my tranquilizer gun handy just in case she objects."

On Saturdays and Sundays Nick accompanied Jorge on his rounds.

To their surprise Juliet showed great interest in Nicky Bear, and with her powerful jaws she gently took her newborn out of Jorge's hand. Jorge and Nick watched her disappear into the bushes with Nicky Bear in her mouth. Nicky Bear was not protesting.

"Nicky Bear will be okay, Jorge, won't he?"

"I think he will, Nick."

"Who made Nicky Bear, Jorge? I mean, who made the chimera fetus?"

"I suspect Marco had something to do with it, Nick. You saw Marco and his girlfriend with Juliet on May fifth. Do you think they could have implanted Nicky Bear in Juliet then?"

"Yes. They could have been doing that."

"Marco said that he had tranquilized Juliet."

"And he made Juliet groggy. Do you think Marco broke a law? Marco didn't steal anything."

"You're right, Nick. Marco did not steal anything. However, he used Juliet's womb without our permission. And Juliet belongs to Zoo Arroyo. That's at least unethical. Maybe it's illegal."

"Would Marco's crime be rape? Marco made Juliet pregnant without her permission."

"That's an interesting idea. If Garrison Tucker were still alive, he would want to sue Marco and his girlfriend Dr. Maloney on behalf of Juliet. But I'm thinking that the greater wrongdoing was the creation of Nicky Bear in the first place."

"Is making a chimera illegal?"

"Probably not. But it should be."

Nick showed up just as Jorge and Rhonda sat down for dinner.

"I took a picture," he said. The picture showed Juliet sitting against a tree trunk licking Nicky Bear.

"Would you like to join us, Nick?"

"No, thanks, Jorge. I just wanted to show you the picture. Juliet loves Nicky Bear."

"Juliet is a good mother, Nick. And you're a good zookeeper."

"I have news," Rhonda announced after Nick left. "Louis Bordeau has gone to the FBI. He emailed me that he has been 'tangentially'—his word—involved illegal activities and that he wants to confess. He said he might have to go to jail but that he'd get a lighter sentence if he initiated the discussion."

"Wow, Rhonda. That is news. Did he read Beverly's article in the *USA Today*?"

"He did. He said the article prompted him to call the authorities."

"Does Mira know?"

"Yes. She and Special Agent Troy Washington are meeting Louis in her office at ten o'clock tomorrow morning."

"On a Sunday?"

"Yes. So I invited Louis for lunch afterwards—that is, if he doesn't get incarcerated on the spot."

"Why did you do that?"

"To find out what he told Detective Dunning and the FBI agent. Why do you think?"

Ding. Jorge looked at his phone.

"I have an email from Samantha Wheeling."

From: Samantha Wheeling (SamanthaWheeling@ zmail.com)
To: Jorge Arroyo (JorgeArroyo@zmail.com)
8:16 pm, Saturday, July 6, 2030
MINKS

Dear Jorge,

I think I tracked down your minks. An animal trafficker named Willard Tavis in Charleston, South Carolina, put this ad online:

"American mink cubs for sale. Leave voice mail at 800-340-4838."

Recognize the number? I called and asked how old the cubs were. A man called me back and said two months. I asked how much? He said $1,500 each. In 2020 lots of minks contracted COVID-19 and died. I guess that's why they are so expensive.

Check out Willard Tavis, 809 Oaks Highway, Charleston.

Samantha

Jorge read the email aloud to Rhonda and forwarded it to Mira.

"Rhonda, did Dr. Bordeau ever mention Willard Tavis?"

"No, Jorge, not that I recall. But if Beverly's article prompted him to squeal to the FBI he might be connected to Willard Tavis."

"You know that my girlfriend, Lola Montoya, worked for Willard Tavis—until he fired her."

"Jorge! You have a girlfriend? Yeah!" Rhonda got up and hugged him.

From: Marco Ramos (MarcoRamos2004@zmail.com)
To: Jorge Arroyo (JorgeArroyo@zmail.com), Jaime
Arroyo (Jaime Arroyo@zmail.com)
10:05 pm, Saturday, July 6, 2030
MY SINCERE REGRETS

Dear Jorge and Jaime,

I write to apologize for whatever harm I may have caused to Zoo Arroyo. I am so very sorry.

Thank you for hiring me, lodging me, and teaching me about embryo transfer. I will miss you all. And I will miss your families.

I will also miss Eddie and Zell and their families. Please give them my best wishes. And please tell Nick that I invite him to visit me in Perú some time.

I have left the United States covered in shame.

In an attachment you will find my the entries in my journal from October 27, 2029 through today, July 6, 2030. I want you both to read my journal and to share it with law enforcement officials. I hope you will understand why I did what I did. The journal is a confession of sorts.

As you will see, today I received an email from Patricia Maloney, who is my wife. I included it so that you all would read it.

If the authorities want me to return for questioning, I will do so without complaint.

Gracias,

Marco

Jorge replied.

From: Jorge Arroyo (JorgeArroyo@zmail.com)
To: Marco Ramos (MarcoRamos2004@zmail.com)
10:39 pm, Saturday, July 6, 2030
Re: MY SINCERE REGRETS

Hola, Marco.

I will read your journal tonight. Thank you for sending it to Jaime and me.

We all miss you. Especially Nick.

I'll write you again soon.

I hope you're okay.

Jorge

Jorge poured himself a glass of wine and opened the attachment.

PART II

Marco

CHAPTER TWENTY-SEVEN

Saturday, July 6, 2030

To Jaime and Jorge, from Marco:
My Journal, October 27, 2029—July 6, 2030

SATURDAY, OCTOBER 27, 2029

Today Jaime, Annie, Jorge, and I returned home from Washington, DC, where Jaime had received the Benningham Prize for Young Scientists at the White House. He won it for a scientific paper he published in the journal *Nature*.

I won't forget two sentences of Jaime's acceptance speech. I wrote them down. "1) A scientist is trusted to pursue the truth and make public his or her findings, to put benefit to society above private gain, and not to let personal emotions and expectations affect his or her judgment. 2) We scientists must always ask ourselves of any of our actions: Who is helped? Who is harmed?"

On the flight to Atlanta, I showed Jaime and Jorge the notes I'd made in my phone.

"Thank you, Jaime," I said. "You've just given me an ethical guide for my life."

"The hardest part is keeping emotions and expectations out of science," Jaime said.

"I'll remember that," I said.

We had fun on the way back from the airport. Jorge drove, I sat in the front seat with him, and Jaime and Annie sat in the back. Annie started singing "This Land is Your Land" and a number of other songs I didn't know. After a while I brought out my *quena* flute, which I keep in my pocket, and played an Incan song. They liked it.

Tonight I thought about Jaime's ethics, which will be my own. Then I thought about my mother, who had instilled similar values of honesty and generosity in me. My mother would like Jaime and Jorge. I hope they meet some day.

I found in my wallet the note Mamá sent me when I graduated from Georgia Tech. She had written, in Spanish: "Querido Marco, I am proud of you. I know you will use your science to benefit others and not yourself. You have always been truthful and kind. May God bless you. With all my affection, your devoted mother."

"God bless you too, Mamá." I folded the note and put it back in my wallet.

I haven't seen Mamá for three years. I'll go see her for Christmas. I'll surprise her.

I hear the owls calling to each other, and the wolves howling. Time to play my flute.

Jaime and Jorge were thoughtful to take me with them to Washington, D.C. They are the best friends I've ever had.

MONDAY, NOVEMBER 5, 2029

This morning I got terrible news. My cousin Cisco called me at 6:15 to tell me that my dear mother, Alicia Martínez-Cisneros, had died of a heart attack. She was only 53. She never remarried after my father passed away and never had another child. I left Perú three years ago when I got the fellowship to Georgia Tech, and I haven't gone back. Mamá must have missed me. She must have thought about me daily, while I went about getting my education.

I will go home to my village tomorrow. Until I get there Cisco will stay with her body. The *vela* will be tomorrow night in Cisco's home. The mass and burial will be on Wednesday. I will clean out my mother's small house and then fly back to Atlanta on Sunday.

If I had known my mother's time on earth was to be so short I would have stayed in Perú. But I could not have stayed in Chasca, where I grew up. I desired education, and Mamá desired education for me, more than she had gotten for herself. She encouraged me to go to Lima to study. I know she was proud of me when I graduated. She kept a picture on her bedside table of me wearing a cap and gown with my arm around her.

Mamá, please forgive me.

I am fortunate to have the job at Zoo Arroyo. Jaime and Jorge have been very kind to me. When I told Jorge that my mother had died, he said that he and Jaime would pay for my round-trip ticket to Lima. I will accept their kind offer.

Life is bitter and sweet, all at once. Tonight I got an email from my Georgia Tech mentor Dr. Patricia Maloney. What a surprise! Dr. Maloney asked about my work at Zoo Arroyo. She had heard that I was learning cloning techniques from Dr. Jaime Arroyo. I replied that my apprenticeship with Jaime had given me the educational equivalent of another degree. I also wrote that I was going to Perú for my mother's funeral. She invited me to dinner in Atlanta on Sunday night after I returned from Perú. She said she had a proposition for me. We will meet at 6:00 at the Peachtree Plaza downtown. I must admit that I am excited about seeing her again.

Monday, November 12, 2029

My week in Perú was full of weeping. I didn't realize how many friends my mother had in a village of only 900 people. All her elementary school pupils were there, present and former, and all the other teachers. The 60-year-olds cried as hard as the 6-year-olds. The food was plentiful, thanks to Cisco, who must have spent a good portion of his mechanic's wages on the event. I will reimburse him. I gave him my mother's car and her rosary.

I took for myself the silver chain Mamá always wore around her neck, which was a wedding present from my father. I took her *charango*. She played the *charango* and other stringed instruments as well as any Andean indigenous musician I ever heard. I also brought back the small *bombo* that I played as a child. I sold her house for cash. I gave Cisco's children her two Persian cats, Chiquita and Flojita.

On my way to the airport I stopped at the art studio of my childhood friend Rosa Elena. Rosa Elena carves flutes, bowls, and cutting boards out of Guadua bamboo, Rosewood, and Black walnut. I bought four Rosewood cutting boards and four Black walnut boxes. For Nick I bought a bamboo *quena* flute. Nick wants me to teach him to play. And for myself I bought a bamboo *pan* flute and several planks of various woods which I had Rosa Elena ship to the zoo.

At the airport I bought six leather friendship bracelets for Christmas presents. I bought some recordings of Andean music for myself.

I had a fantastic time with Patricia Maloney last night. I had not seen her since I graduated from Georgia Tech and she took a job at the Callaghan Research Institute. That was in May of 2028.

Patricia told me to call her Patricia. She is tall and beautiful, with blue eyes and long brown hair. I have feelings for her, even though she is 31 years old and I am 26.

Patricia invited me to collaborate with her on a project. I said Yes almost before she told me about it. She wants to compete for a big prize of $5 million called the "Apex Prize for Biological Innovation." It has been awarded annually since the year 2020 to pioneers in biology and medicine. She showed me an article in the *New York Times* that appeared on October 31 of this year and asked if I had ever heard of the Apex Prize. I said, "Of course." She thinks she can win it by creating "50/50 mammalian chimeras," such as a wolf-bear. She said our work had to remain secret and asked whether I could keep it confidential. I said I could, even though secrecy is not usual in science.

If she wins the prize she will give me $1 million of it, she said.

We talked for a couple of hours over wine and dinner and dessert. She told me about her job, her colleagues, and her research. I told her about my apprenticeship with Jaime.

I asked her what she did for fun. She said she didn't really have any hobbies because she spent all her time on science, but she liked listening to classical music. She once played the cello.

She asked me the same question. I said I played traditional Peruvian instruments, carved wind chimes, and made furniture. I also said that I loved animals, that I had grown up with cats and that I missed them.

At the end of the evening I asked her when we could see each other again. She proposed that we meet for dinner at 6:30 on Saturday, November 24, at the Corfu Greek Café in northeast Atlanta. I said it would be my treat.

I think Patricia must live near there.

I am awed that Patricia chose me to collaborate with her, and not any of the other students in her Georgia Tech lab. Maybe I was the best graduate student in the lab after all. Or maybe she is attracted to me.

Monday, November 19, 2021

At the staff meeting I passed out my gifts from Perú. I gave Jorge the cutting boards I got for him and Jaime, and I gave Zell and Eddie their friendship bracelets. I sent another friendship bracelet home with Eddie for Emma, along with the *quena* flute for Nick.

Jorge announced that the zoo will get two female Red foxes in January, and that we will transfer Swift fox clones into them in May.

Thursday, November 22, 2029— Thanksgiving

Jorge and Jaime invited me to spend Thanksgiving day with them at Jaime's house. I had a really nice time and ate too much. I guess that's the tradition for this holiday. They told me not to bring anything, but I brought two bottles of California Chardonnay for the adults and Black walnut boxes for Heather and Holly.

Jorge invited me to play chess with him after Thanksgiving dinner while the others went for a walk. He won both games, but I didn't do poorly. I asked him how he got so good, and he said his father had taught him and Jaime when they were four years old. He and Jaime had played chess with each other ever since. Jaime was now teaching his daughters. I thanked Jorge for teaching me.

Tonight Patricia wore a tight black low-cut dress. She is really gorgeous. I have never met a scientist as gorgeous as she is.

I enjoyed the evening, all of it. We ate lemon hummus, stuffed grape leaves, moussaka, and baklava at the Corfu Greek Café. Patricia took selfies of us.

Patricia explained her technique for creating large-animal chimera embryos. She showed me the notes she had made. I asked her what my role would be. She said we would work together in a lab in South Carolina to create the chimera embryos. Then I would transfer the embryos into the host animals we selected. She said that my skills in transferring embryos, which I'd gained from working with Jaime, would be essential to the project. That's why I would get $1 million if we won the Apex Prize. She said that two other collaborators would each get $1 million too, but she didn't say who they were.

Patricia doesn't want her Callaghan Institute colleagues to know about this project. Her Callaghan colleagues know only that she and her graduate students study interspecies organ rejection.

She asked me again to keep our project secret. I promised her I would.

She said that on my next trip to Atlanta she would cook for me at her house. I said I hoped that would be soon.

I got home an hour ago. I had to drive through sleet coming up from Atlanta. All I could think of, besides Patricia, was the story Jaime told me about Jorge's losing his leg in an automobile accident on snow and ice.

I hope I can stay overnight with Patricia next time we get together in Atlanta.

Sunday, December 9, 2029

Today Patricia invited me, by email, to have Christmas Eve dinner with her at her house, 612 Thrasher Avenue. I looked up the address. Very nice Atlanta neighborhood.

I accepted right away.

I must take her a Christmas present.

Monday, December 17, 2029

This morning after the staff meeting Jorge asked me to feed the zoo animals on Christmas day if I had no other plans. Jorge wants to spend Christmas at Jaime's house in Dahlonega, and Eddie and his family want to spend Christmas with their relatives in Tocoa. Zell has the holiday off, of course.

I said I'd be happy to spend Christmas with Sol and Luna and Shaggy and Brown-Eyes and Romeo and Juliet and Mickie and Minkie.

I didn't say that I was spending Christmas Eve with Patricia. Actually, I haven't told Jorge—or anybody else— about Patricia. But I can get back in time the next day to feed dinner to Sol and Luna and their pack.

This evening I started work on a Rosewood coffee table. Making furniture transports me to another world where I think about nothing but what I am creating and where I am happy.

Tuesday, December 18, 2029

Tonight Jorge and Jaime celebrated their 29th birthday at the zoo. And what a joyful occasion it was.

I felt honored to be among the guests, who were: Jaime's wife Annie and their 5-year-old daughters Heather and Holly; Eddie, Emma, and Nick Crane; Zell and Eve Larson and their daughter Abbie; and Rhonda Rather (one of the funniest and most delightful women I've ever met). Also included were the dogs: Bernie, Amigo, and Blanche. And Poe the Crow, who perched on Rhonda's shoulder the whole time.

Poe the Crow is named after Edgar Allen Poe, even though Poe's bird was a raven. Poe chose a raven for his poem because ravens can talk.

Jorge and Jaime grilled shrimp-kabobs for the group, and Rhonda brought a case of Spanish red wine—Priorat.

After dinner Jaime played the guitar, and Annie sang a lot of songs I didn't know.

Jorge and Jaime had said "No birthday presents," but they hadn't said "No Christmas presents," so I gave each of them a set of bamboo wind chimes I had carved.

Rhonda brought Jorge a chain-saw bear cub and brought Jaime an antique Appalachian fiddle.

"For Christmas," she said.

TUESDAY, DECEMBER 25, 2029

Christmas Eve was marvelous. I spent the night with Patricia. And I came home with a kitten!

Patricia had hung mistletoe from her dining room ceiling, her living room ceiling, and the doorway to her bedroom. We did a lot of kissing. She told me I looked sexy with my black beard, that I looked like a handsome Pancho Villa.

Patricia made a stew of lamb and bacon and potatoes, which she said was traditional Irish fare. We ate by candlelight and listened to Handel's *Messiah*.

For her Christmas present I gave Patricia the bamboo cutting board I had saved for someone special. Patricia is someone special. I also brought a really good Cabernet for the two of us.

I expected Patricia to use the cutting board, but she said she didn't want to scratch the fine wood. She hammered a nail into her dining room wall, which is blue, and hung the cutting board there. She has painted all the walls blue, even though she rents the house. And she's filled it with white leather furniture. Very nice.

Patricia gave me a very fluffy white Persian kitten, plus cat food, kitty litter, and a litter box.

All I could say was "¡*Mil gracias!*"

"You told me your mother had Persian cats."

"She had Persian cats in her house until the day she died. I will call this kitten 'Bonita.'"

That gift warranted a big kiss and a hug.

She also gave me a book titled *The History of Embryonic Stem Cell Research* and told me to read the last chapter, "The Future of Chimeras."

I asked Patricia about her family. She said she had no immediate family, just an uncle and a cousin in South Carolina. I asked her if she was related to the famous chemist Danyon Patrick Maloney. She said Yes, that he was her father but that she and he were "estranged." She said her mother had died in 2027.

Patricia said she'd rather talk about me. I told her about attending the University of Lima and discovering my aptitude for science. She asked how ambitious I was. I told her I wanted to work on the frontiers of genetic technology. I thanked her for involving me in her project.

At midnight we toasted each other with brandy. Then we went to bed.

Patricia seems lonely. Maybe that will be good for our relationship. Or vice versa.

This morning we got up late, at least late for me. After breakfast Patricia followed me to Zoo Arroyo. I liked seeing her red SUV in my rearview mirror. We talked on the phone for the whole two-hour drive.

At the zoo we fed all the animals. Patricia loves wolves. I impressed her by entering Sol's woods and letting Luna lick my hand. She took my picture.

Patricia takes lots of pictures. She said that she loves "commemorating special moments in her life." She said that life can go by fast "if there is no punctuation." So she takes photographs to punctuate it.

After a late lunch—chicken from my freezer, which I served with a spicy Peruvian chili sauce—Patricia left for Columbia, South Carolina. She said she had a meeting there tomorrow.

I will spend New Year's Eve with her.

I think I'm in love.

SATURDAY, DECEMBER 29, 2030

Nick came over at 8:00 this morning for a flute lesson. He was head-over-heels happy to meet Bonita. I told him that we could share Bonita if he would take care of Bonita on weekends when I was out of town. Nick promised to take good care of Bonita.

"I'm going to be a vet," he said, "so I need experience caring for all kinds of animals."

I told him he was going to be a musician too.

Nick is a quick learner. I can't teach him to read music, because I never learned. I play by ear, and so does Nick. He's already memorized one Incan song I taught him, so now we can play it together.

I texted Patricia a photo of Nick holding Bonita.

"This is Nick," I wrote. "I hope you can meet him next time you're at Zoo Arroyo. We both love Bonita. Thank you."

She texted me, "I look forward to New Year's Eve!"

I texted her back, "I have started reading the book you gave me and by New Year's Eve I will have finished it. Thanks again."

In the ethics chapter I was struck by this paragraph:

The creation of any animal, whether human or non-human, whether by natural procreation or by laboratory manipulation of embryos, is the creation of consciousness; it is the creation of the ability to suffer. Should not this truth inform our experimentation?

Did I just feel a prick of conscience?

Tuesday, January 1, 2030

New Year's Eve was all a man could wish for.

After a splendid dinner of roasted duckling and plenty of wine, Patricia and I sat on the rug in front of the fireplace, sipped eggnog, listened to Bach's *Christmas Oratorio*, and talked.

She told me that her father had always deprecated her abilities. He said she was not suited to science and should study music instead, never asked her about her PhD research, and did not read her dissertation. She wanted to prove her father wrong. They hadn't spoken for years. Her mother was equally uninterested in her accomplishments. But her uncle Louis Bordeau had shown her affection since she was a little girl. She said he lived in South Carolina and that she would take me to meet him soon. He would be collaborating with us.

"How is your uncle Louis related to you?" I asked.

"Uncle Louis is my mother's brother. My mother's maiden name was Bordeau. That's why my middle name is Bordeau. I also have a cousin on her side, Cousin Willard Tavis. He lives in Charleston."

I asked her if I could read her dissertation. She said sure, and took it from the top bookshelf. "Keep it as long as you like," she said. "It's already out of date."

Her dissertation was on interspecies transplantation.

Patricia asked what my childhood had been like in a small village in Perú.

"Plenty of love," I said. "My mother loved me unconditionally and praised me for whatever little thing I did. And whatever big thing too, like graduating from the University of Lima. She taught me to play the *charango* and the *quena* flute."

I told Patricia how our home was filled with laughter and joy, even after my father had his stroke. I recalled that from his wheelchair my father had coached my friends and me in soccer.

"I'll feel forever fortunate that I grew up in Chasca, where we were all family to each other," I said. "When my father died I was nine years old. I cried and cried, but I gained some new fathers, the fathers of my playmates. My mother and I had little money, but we didn't need much. We had friends."

"How did you learn to speak English?"

"My father grew up in a Peruvian community in Miami. When he finished high school he went to live with his grandfather in Chasca, where he met my mother and stayed. My mother spoke to me in Spanish, but my father spoke to me in English. In college I studied literature as well as biology, and I wrote my literature papers in English."

At midnight we kissed under the mistletoe and went to bed.

"May the year 2030 bring us success," she said.

"May the year 2030 bring us happiness," I said.

When we awoke this morning Patricia asked me whether Jaime would allow us to use the wolves as surrogate mothers for our chimera embryos. I said I was pretty sure Jaime would not. She dropped the subject.

We talked in bed for a half hour.

I asked her why she wanted to create chimeras.

"Because the creation of chimeras is the frontier of biotechnology. If I create animals that once existed only in our imagination I will be as famous as Darwin."

"Darwin showed how nature made humans," I said.

"And I will show how humans make nature," she said. "That's why I will win the Apex Prize."

"Can you imagine creating a human chimera?"

"I've thought about it."

"You have?"

"Don't worry, Marco. You and I are not going in that direction."

"I'm relieved."

"Let's just focus on winning the prize. If we win, you and I will be connected with each other forever. Are you still all in?"

I said Yes.

We made love again.

On my way back to Zoo Arroyo, I imagined a future with Patricia. We could live in her house until I got my PhD at Georgia Tech and she got tenure at Callaghan. If we won the Apex Prize we'd be instantly famous. Universities all over the world would offer us positions. Together.

If we got married, we could have children. I could be a father.

I hope she's having the same thoughts.

This evening I played my *pan* flute, with the window open. Nick must have heard me from his house across the pond, because before long he came over with his *quena* flute. We played together. The music carried, and the wolves started howling.

Andean music is not Bach, but it's my music. It's the music I carry in my soul.

SUNDAY, JANUARY 13, 2030

Patricia invited me to bring something to read while she wrote up some research she had done on reproduction in genetically modified organisms.

So I spent Saturday afternoon on her sofa immersed in Darwin's *Origin of Species*. I was spell-bound. What a thinker Darwin was, and what a writer! When I read his observations on "the mutability of species" I put the book down to collect my thoughts.

I realized that species were not only naturally mutable but also, these days, artificially mutable. That's what modification of an organism's germline could do. That's what Ibarra and Wong had done to create the Ibarra-Wong chimpanzee. That's what they had done to win the Apex Prize.

Over dinner—at Michaelangelo's Italian Café—I asked Patricia if she had read the *Origin of Species*. "It's the most profound book I've ever read," I told her. "Darwin discovered the mechanism for the mutation of species in evolution—natural selection."

"Darwin published the *Origin* in 1859, Marco. That's a hundred and seventy years ago. I'm more interested in what geneticists are discovering today, such as the mutation of species by gene editing."

"Well, you're only thirty-one years old, and you're going to be a leader in the field," I said.

"I'm going to be a leader in the creation of chimeras, dear Marco. And you will be too."

Patricia changed the subject to our future, which I was more than happy to contemplate.

"After you get your PhD, Marco, would you want to live in the United States or go back to Perú?"

"I would want to stay in the States, where the academic jobs are."

"Would you want to have a family?"

"I would. I would very much like to have a family. Would you?"

"Possibly," she said, "depending on what my husband wanted."

After dinner we sat by the fire for a couple of hours talking about zoos. I told her all about Zoo Arroyo.

Little did I know that at that very moment the zoo's Black bear Juliet was giving birth to a female cub. Nick named her Jackie.

SUNDAY, JANUARY 27, 2030

Yesterday afternoon Patricia and I watched the Apex Prize ceremony on television. Dr. Paul Aubert, president of the American Academy of Scientific Research, awarded the prize to Dr. Hernando Ibarra and Dr. Olivia Wong of the Taxon Institute for Advanced Biological Studies. Dr. Aubert commended the scientists for "extending longevity in human beings."

In accepting the prize, Dr. Wong explained how she and Dr. Ibarra are now inserting human genes into the reproductive cells of some thirty adult African chimps in the expectation that their descendants will eventually compose a large and genetically diverse troop of Ibarra-Wong chimpanzees whose vital organs will be available for transplantation into humans. The organs include heart, lungs, liver, pancreas, and kidneys. Within twenty years they expect to have 80-100 Ibarra-Wong chimps who will live "in an undisclosed location" in northern California.

A reporter asked whether the creation of the Ibarra-Wong chimpanzees solely for xenotransplantation was ethical.

Dr. Wong said, "It is as ethical as raising livestock for our consumption."

A second reporter asked whether the Ibarra-Wong chimpanzees were genetically closer to humans than unmodified chimpanzees.

She answered, "Yes. The Ibarra-Wong chimpanzees are more similar to humans genetically than are chimpanzees from Africa."

Dr. Ibarra stood up. "Let me add something, Olivia. The Apex Prize honors us not just for creating one troop of chimps whose organs we humans can use. The Apex Prize recognizes our extraordinary achievement of using germline genetic modification to create a new species. That is the real significance of our project in the history of humankind. Gene editing allows us to create not just new breeds but new species. Where are the limits? I see none."

Another reporter asked, "Do you know about the ARH-GAP11B gene? It's a human gene responsible for brain size. Could it be introduced into the Ibarra-Wong chimpanzees?"

"Of course it could," Ibarra said. "But Olivia and I have no interest in increasing chimp intelligence."

"Right," Wong laughed. "We don't want our chimps to know what we're doing."

Patricia and I went to a Moroccan restaurant for dinner. After a while I said to Patricia, "Hernando Ibarra and Olivia Wong created the Ibarra-Wong chimpanzees to be killed. Does that strike you as genocide?"

"Genocide applies to the mass killing of humans," she said. "Chimpanzees are not humans. They are a lower species."

"But they are primates, like us humans," I said. "And they are highly intelligent. They will be aware that individuals in their troop are disappearing. They will experience fear, maybe terror."

"You're eating lamb, Marco. So why should you be bothered by killing other animals for your survival?"

"The Ibarra-Wong chimpanzees are our genetic cousins," I said. "They are part human."

Patricia did not respond.

I persisted. "Would you be concerned if genetic engineers made a species of smarter chimpanzees? The ARHGAP11B gene distinguished humans from chimpanzees evolutionarily. Genetic engineers could undo the chimpanzee's divergence from humans and create, quote, the missing link."

"That's not our concern, Marco. Let's focus on our project."

I changed the subject. I didn't want to annoy her. My love for her is greater than my desire to win an argument.

This morning, on the road home, I couldn't get the Ibarra-Wong chimpanzees out of my mind. Sure, using chimpanzees' hearts to save individual human lives seems like a good thing from the viewpoint of the person with degenerative heart disease. But from the viewpoint of the chimpanzee, isn't the seizure of his or her heart basically murder?

I remembered a question that Jaime posed when he received the Benningham Prize. "We must always ask ourselves of any of our actions: Who is helped? Who is harmed?"

By honoring Ibarra and Wong with the Apex Prize, the American Academy of Scientific Research conferred legitimacy on the premeditated murder of our fellow primates.

Ibarra's words returned to me: "Where are the limits?"

Where are the limits to gene editing? Where are the limits to the creation of new species? I can't see limits either.

Are there no laws to govern scientific experimentation?

I'd like to talk freely with Patricia about these questions. But I don't want her to think I'm challenging her. She wouldn't enjoy such a conversation. Maybe I'll talk with Jaime and Jorge.

I gave Nick another flute lesson tonight. He is learning quickly. I played him a recording I'd made with some indigenous people near Machu Picchu.

Nick asked me to teach him to carve. Actually he said, "Marco, could you please teach me to whittle?" I said I would, and I gave him a small chisel knife. I told him we'd whittle a bear as soon as I could get some Balsa wood.

TUESDAY, JANUARY 29, 2030

This morning I saw a letter to the editor in the *New York Times* about the Apex Prize.

> *To the editor:*
>
> On Saturday the Apex Prize was bestowed on two scientists for creating a species of primates whose organs the human immune system won't reject. Sick humans will be able to steal from these Ibarra-Wong chimpanzees their hearts, lungs, livers, kidneys, maybe

even their uteruses. Whoopee! Another commodity on the market to enable us humans to live longer!

The Ibarra-Wong chimpanzee, which the scientists named after themselves (surprise, surprise!), will be a medicine cabinet for body parts.

Since Ibarra-Wong chimps are genetically closer to humans than naturally evolved chimps, I would describe the genetically engineered chimps as "humanish."

Here are my questions: How humanish must genetically engineered primates be before we humans decide not to kill them? How humanish must they be to be covered by the Universal Declaration of Human Rights (adopted by the United Nations General Assembly in 1948).

In ten years will the American Academy of Scientific Research honor other scientists for creating a new species of human?

—Carl Walker Conningham
Atlanta

I was about to show the letter to Jorge when a pair of Red foxes designated "A-2029" and "B-2029" arrived at Zoo Arroyo. They were brought down from Blacksburg, Virginia, by two of Jaime's scientific colleagues. Jorge renamed them "Foxy Ann" and "Foxy Belle." Zell and I released them in Sol's Woods.

Snow started falling about 5:00. Jorge invited me over for a glass of California Syrah. So I told him about the Apex Prize ceremony and read him the letter from Carl Walker Conningham.

"I have questions," I asked Jorge. "Have you ever heard of the Apex Prize? And if you have, do you think the prize is reputable?"

"I have not heard of it, but that's not what worries me," Jorge said. "What worries me is the use of genome editing to create new species."

"Is it hard to do?"

"I guess not. For more than a decade scientists have been able modify the germline of an individual to make traits transmissible to the individual's offspring and the offspring's offspring. It's been done to eradicate such maladies as Huntington's Disease. Obviously, if the genetically introduced trait is so significant that the offspring cannot reproduce with unmodified individuals of their original species but can reproduce with each other, they form a new species."

"Scientists will be able to insert human genes into all kinds of hominids to create species that are more and more "humanish," I said. "They've already inserted human genes into mice to make them smarter."

"That's right, Marco. And that project is monstrous."

I agreed. And I accepted Jorge's invitation to share his beef stew. We finished off the bottle of wine.

SUNDAY, FEBRUARY 3, 2030

Yesterday Patricia took me to Columbia, South Carolina, to meet her uncle, Dr. Louis Bordeau, who is on the veterinary staff of the Columbia Zoo.

Louis has restored an old two-story white brick house with a brook running through the front yard. It is five miles from downtown. You can't see it from the highway because of the giant magnolias that surround it. Behind the house he has built a state-of-the-art clinic and lab, as well as a set of enclosures for the Columbia Zoo animals in his care.

He has four purebred dogs, all female: Trudy (a Cocker spaniel), Lassie (a Sheltie), Angel (a Pomeranian), and Sesi (a husky). You can hear them from a hundred yards away. He also has a Siamese cat named Siam.

He lives alone. His wife died of covid-19 ten years ago.

Here's how Louis is collaborating with Patricia and me in our quest to win the Apex Prize. Louis has responsibility for the reproductive health of the Riverbank Zoo's wolverines, jackals, jaguars, cougars, leopards, and pumas. He brings them to his place for their regular checkups, and he delivers their offspring. He gives Patricia embryos and stem cells from any of these animals according to her research needs. He provides sperm to her cousin Willard in Charleston, as well as newborns from large litters.

"What does Willard do with the newborns?" I asked.

"He raises and sells them. There's a lively underground market for hybrid predators," she said. "And for sperm too.

"So Willard is a broker?"

"You might say that. Anyway, it's a lucrative business."

Patricia visits Louis often. They seem personally very close.

We didn't spend the night with Louis. Instead we stayed at the romantic Inn La Rivière. I'd like to stay there again.

We left Columbia early this morning because Patricia had to get back to Atlanta. She stopped at the entrance to Zoo Arroyo to let me off. Before I got out of the car she said that we should keep "our relationship" a secret from Jorge and Jaime. I said that was fine with me. I kissed her goodbye. I was happy that she used the word "relationship."

She gave me one of her notebooks to read before we return to Columbia on February 17.

Sunday, February 10, 2030
On Saturday, just for fun, Patricia and I drove to Chattanooga to see the Tennessee Aquarium. Chattanooga is less than two hours from Atlanta.

We are a couple now.

Wednesday, February 13, 2030
This afternoon Nick came over with his chisel knife ready to carve a Valentine present for his parents. The balsa wood had come in. With my guidance he carved a heart. I carved a standing bear.

"I want to carve a bear next time," Nick said.

"You take my bear home and study it," I said. "And soon you can carve one for yourself."

Sunday, February 17, 2030
Patricia and I spent yesterday afternoon in the lab at Louis's place. *Dios mío.* I had already learned much about creating chimeras from Patricia's notebook, but I hadn't anticipated the excitement of the hands-on experience of transferring a chimera embryo.

Louis provided us with what we needed: embryonic stem cells he had obtained from a pregnant leopard and a three-day-old embryo he had extracted from a pregnant cheetah. Patricia then injected the stem cells into the cheetah embryo to create a leopard-cheetah chimera embryo. We froze the chimera embryo at -321 degrees Fahrenheit. We will transfer it to a pregnant lioness that Louis will bring over from the zoo in a few days.

We stayed at the Inn La Rivière.

At dinner Patricia complimented me.

"You have excellent technical skills," she said, "better

than mine. Next week I want you to transfer the embryo into the lioness."

I gave Patricia a belated Valentine's gift, my mother's silver necklace. I fastened it around her neck and told her I loved her. She said she'd wear it always. She told me she loved me too.

SUNDAY, FEBRUARY 24, 2030

Yesterday we made another trip to Columbia to implant the leopard-cheetah embryo in the pregnant lioness. Patricia had me do the procedure. She took pictures. All went well. The lioness, whose name is Binti, is now carrying a chimera in addition to four lion fetuses.

We have to wait three months for the chimera to be born. Patricia explained the difficulty of determining a due date.

"A leopard gestates for 90-105 days," she said. "A cheetah gestates from 90-98 days. And a lion gestates about 110 days. We don't know how long a leopard-cheetah chimera will gestate in the lioness."

"How many cubs do you think the lion will produce?"

"Normally 3 or 4. But sometimes as few as 2. Anyway, Louis will take the chimera cub and send her to Cousin Willard to raise."

"And Willard will sell her?" I asked.

"Yes, at a high price."

"To a zoo?"

"No, not to a zoo. Cousin Willard will sell the chimera to a private collector."

At cocktail hour Louis fixed us drinks—a bourbon called Cream of Kentucky. Louis likes the finest.

Louis told us that he had a four-year-old wolverine from the Columbia Zoo due to deliver this week and that he was keeping a Grey wolf whom he had inseminated on Thursday. He had the wolf and the wolverine on a wooded acre enclosed by a chain link fence.

"Can you get me an embryo from the wolf, Uncle Louis? And also the umbilical cord of the wolverine?" Patricia asked him.

"How about extracting the wolf embryo tomorrow and vitrifying it?" Louis said. "I'll keep the wolverine's umbilical cord. And you all come back next weekend to make the chimera embryo."

"Sure."

"May I take us to dinner tonight?"

Louis took us to Reginald's Oyster Bar and Grill on the Congaree River.

At one point Louis turned to me and asked, "Will I be seeing more of you, Marco?"

"I hope so," I answered.

"I hope so too," Patricia said.

This morning Patricia employed laparoscopy to remove an embryo from the pregnant wolf, leaving the wolf with three embryos.

I asked Patricia whether we would be writing a paper about our work.

She said, "Sometime. But not yet. Not until we win the prize. And then the world will know what we've done."

I asked her about the research she was conducting in her lab at Callaghan. She said she and a British colleague had a big grant from the National Science Foundation to study the genetics of interspecies organ transplantation and that they would be writing a paper soon.

On the drive back from Columbia we listened to classical music: first Mahler's very long Third symphony, which lasts about an hour and a half, and then Beethoven's Seventh, which I liked better.

Tonight, as I write in my journal, I'm remembering something else Jaime said at the White House: that a scientist makes public his or her findings. I'll be happy when Patricia and I can do that.

SUNDAY, MARCH 3, 2030

Louis, Patricia, and I had an email exchange on Friday. Louis wrote:

> From: Louis Bordeau (LouisBordeau. ColumbiaZoo@zmail.com)
> To: Patricia Maloney (PatriciaBordeauMaloney@ zmail.com),
> Marco Ramos (MarcoRamos2004@zmail.com)
> 11:05 am, Friday, March 1, 2030
> STEM CELLS
> Dear Patricia and Marco,
> At 9:30 am today the wolverine gave birth to two kits.
> I have harvested stem cells from the umbilical cords.
> If you can come to Columbia tonight you can do the procedure tomorrow morning.
> Let me know. I'll make a reservation for you at the Inn La Riviere.
> Louis

Patricia wrote:

From: Patricia Maloney (PatriciaBordeauMaloney@
zmail.com)
To: Louis Bordeau (LouisBordeau.ColumbiaZoo@
zmail.com),
Marco Ramos (MarcoRamos2004@zmail.com)
11:20 am, Friday, March 1, 2030
Re: STEM CELLS
    Hi, Uncle Louis.
    That's terrific news.
    I can pick up Marco at 5:00 pm and we can be
in Columbia by 9:00 pm.
    Thank you for making the reservation for us.
    OK, Marco? I'll pick you up outside Zoo
Arroyo's entrance.
    Love,
    Patricia

How exciting. I replied immediately.

From: Marco Ramos (MarcoRamos2004@zmail.
com)
To: Patricia Maloney (PatriciaBordeauMaloney@
zmail.com),
Louis Bordeau (LouisBordeau.ColumbiaZoo@
zmail.com)
11:29 am, Friday, March 1, 2030
    Hi, Patricia and Louis.
    I'm available.
    Marco

We got to Inn La Rivière at 9:15 pm, ordered dinner through room service, and went to bed.

By 8:00 Saturday morning we were in Louis's lab creating a wolverine-wolf embryo. Patricia had me introduce the wolverine cells into the wolf embryo. I was pleased that she entrusted me with the procedure. She took pictures to document the process.

The pregnant wolf retained her other three embryos.

We vitrified the chimera embryo in Louis's cryopreservation freezer.

For a brief second I thought: What would my dear Catholic mother say? That I have usurped the role of God? That I have violated the laws of nature?

I'm sensing some sort of paradox here. Darwin showed us that we humans were not divinely created, that we evolved just like every other species, that we are not unique. And yet since Darwin, and particularly after the discovery of dna's structure in 1953, we humans have gradually taken greater and greater control over other species. We create gmos—genetically modified organisms—to satisfy the world's hunger. We grow organs in animals to satisfy our desire for long life. And now we—Patricia and I, to be specific—create chimeras.

Are there no ethical constraints on what we humans do to make nature conform to our desires?

Do I dare think Patricia is involved in unethical science?

I would feel better if we published our work and got the benefit of other scientists' opinions. The grand project of science since Francis Bacon has been to understand nature, and scientists advance that understanding by pooling their knowledge. That's why I was attracted to science in the first place.

I will not share my qualms with Patricia. I have discovered that she is emotionally fragile. She needs to win the Apex Prize to show her worth to her father.

Patricia doesn't need to show her worth to me. She is already precious to me.

We won't see each other next weekend because she has a professional meeting in Augusta.

Maybe next weekend I'll have a chance to talk with Jorge about the ethics of bioengineering intelligent animals. I'll tell him about Hernando Ibarra and Olivia Wong bioengineering chimpanzees for their organs. I won't tell him what I'm doing.

SUNDAY, MARCH 10, 2030

I got shot in the shoulder Thursday night, or rather early Friday morning.

I woke up with the thunderstorm and couldn't get back to sleep. About two in the morning I heard a vehicle go up the lane, so I put on my slicker, got a flashlight, and went outside. The rain was pouring down, but I could see a big truck parked near the enclosure for the minks and otters. As I got closer I saw somebody go in. I followed him to the otter pond—I think it was a man, but it could have been a woman. Then the person saw me, and shot me.

I don't remember anything after that. The next thing I knew Zell was waking me up. The rain was gone, and the sun was shining. Zell gave me water, lifted me into his truck, and drove me to the farmhouse. Jorge examined me and said that the bullet lodged in my shoulder, inches away from my heart. An ambulance took me to a hospital in Dahlonega. With its siren on.

At the hospital, a surgeon operated on me, removed the bullet, and put my arm in a sling.

Jorge brought me home yesterday and fixed us dinner— cod and parsley soup and freshly baked bread. He invited me to sleep in his guest room, but I needed my own bed, and my phone and my computer. I didn't get a chance for a conversation about ethics because Nick joined us for dinner. Anyway I was too groggy from the anesthesia to think clearly.

As soon as I got back to my A-frame I texted Patricia that I'd been shot by an intruder but I would be okay. She texted back that she was alarmed and would stop at the zoo on her way back from Augusta.

Patricia arrived at ten today with a bouquet of cherry blossoms and a box of Peruvian chocolate bars. She had found the chocolate at the Augusta farmer's market.

She asked me as many questions about my getting shot as the detective had asked me—more, in fact. I told her about the minks being stolen, which she found disturbing. I was happy that she showed so much concern—both for me and for the minks.

"I love you," I told her. "You have given me joy."

"I love you too," she said.

She left at four thirty. She said she had to prepare for a meeting.

"I'll see you on Friday," she said, "for our trip to Charleston."

"I can hardly wait," I said.

SUNDAY, MARCH 17, 2030

Friday morning Patricia picked me up at 11:30 am. It was an unseasonably warm sunny day. She drove the whole seven hours.

I had asked Jorge if I could work Easter weekend in exchange for taking Friday off. He said, "Good deal!" When I asked Nick if he would take care of Bonita while I was gone, he said, "Do I have to pay you?" We laughed. What a great kid! Eddie told me he was a straight-A student at Witherston Elementary.

Patricia had said Willard was part of our team. I asked her what he did for our team. She said he funded her work as a creator of chimeras, and he would raise any chimera that she, or we, created. He inherited money from his father, but she didn't know how much. He inherited the ranch too, Tavis Ranch. His primary income came from selling sperm and wild animals.

"Why did he start *Wild Beasts Magazine*?" I asked.

"Willard says publicly that he founded the magazine to learn about the preservation of endangered species. But the real reason was to connect with potential buyers."

"So that's why he's funding your work. You're creating chimera he can sell."

"Right. And he's my cousin. We're a team."

I asked how many people were on the team. She said four: Willard, Louis, me, and herself. If we won the $5 million Apex Prize she would get $2 million, and the rest of us would get $1 million each. I said that was fair.

Friday night we stayed at a very fancy hotel, courtesy of Willard, and we ate in the very fancy hotel dining room. We had shrimp scampi. After a couple of glasses of wine I asked Patricia how she imagined our future. She said she expected us to be together for a long time.

"Till death do us part," I said.

"Till death do us part," she repeated.

On Saturday morning we went to Willard's place a few miles outside Charleston. We passed through a gate that said "Tavis Ranch" and drove up a half-mile driveway to a grand antebellum mansion. Right out of *Gone with the Wind*. A tall middle-aged man, very well-groomed, met us at the door and invited us in for Cokes. It was Willard Tavis.

Patricia introduced me as her "partner" and allowed Willard to decide whether that meant boyfriend or scientific colleague or both. Willard was gracious.

"Welcome, Marco," he said. "Any friend of Patricia's is a friend of mine."

Then he said something that puzzled me. "I know a lot about Zoo Arroyo, Marco. I'm making it the feature story in the summer issue of *Wild Beasts*."

"How do you know about it?" I asked.

"I have a photographer who interviewed Dr. Jorge Arroyo last week and took pictures. She sent me the recording and the pictures."

On Saturday night we ate at a seafood restaurant on Sullivan's Island. I asked Patricia what she meant by "partner." She said, "Collaborator, colleague, companion, teammate, co-worker, and lover."

"Does 'partner' mean we get to live together?" I asked.

"What else do you think it means?" she answered. She winked.

Patricia's birthday is Wednesday, March 20. I'm going to surprise her with an engagement ring.

THURSDAY, MARCH 21, 2030

Patricia and I are engaged. I couldn't be happier. I wish my mother were alive to meet her.

At 7:30 last night I knocked on Patricia's front door with a bottle of California Syrah in my hand and an engagement ring in my pocket. I could hear Leonard Bernstein's symphonic dances from "West Side Story" playing at top volume.

"*Feliz cumpleaños, mi amor*," I said. "Happy birthday."

Patricia was surprised to see me—happily surprised. We kissed passionately in the doorway.

I took her to Poseidon's for elegant seafood. Over dinner we talked science. But after dinner, with our coffee and chocolate truffles, I managed to change the subject.

"Do you really think you would like to have children?" I asked her.

"If you would," she said. "Would you?"

"Yes, definitely," I said. "Would having children interfere with your job?"

"Not if I had a good husband," she said.

I brought out the tiny jewelry box containing the ring and wished her happy birthday. I watched her face as she opened it. She smiled.

"Will you marry me?" I asked her.

To my relief she said, "Yes! Of course." And she put the ring on the ring finger of her left hand.

The ring is composed of a blue sapphire solitaire with diamonds on the band. It is unusual, but so is Patricia. I had bought it in Athens, Georgia, using money I'd gotten from the sale of my mother's house.

"Can we get married soon?" Patricia asked, after kissing me.

"Let's figure out who would want to come to the ceremony, and then we can choose a date convenient to everybody," I said.

"I propose we secretly get married in April at Uncle Louis's house and announce it later at a party in the fall. Uncle Louis can give me away. And we can invite Cousin Willard."

I was so thrilled with her enthusiasm that I said Yes. I agreed to getting married by a judge in Columbia on Saturday, April 13. I agreed to keep the marriage secret until the fall. And I agreed to have Willard be the only other guest.

I asked her where she would like to go for a honeymoon. She said she would like to postpone the honeymoon until July 1, after I fulfill my contract with Zoo Arroyo, and then spend two weeks in Perú, so she could see my country.

"Fantastic! Let's go to Machu Picchu!"

"That's a plan," she said. "And after the trip you can move in with me."

"To our marriage," she said, raising her glass of wine. "May we accomplish great things together."

"To our marriage," I said as we clicked glasses. "May we know great joy."

Last night was the happiest night of my life.

I left Patricia at 6:00 this morning to get back to the zoo by 8:00.

Zookeeper Zell informed me that last night Shaggy delivered a 55-pound calf.

Sunday, March 31, 2030

Yesterday I brought my *pan* flute to Patricia's house, and last night I played for her the Andean music I'd loved in my childhood. I revealed to her *mi alma andina*—my Andean soul.

"I want you to know who I am," I told her, "a man born of a hundred generations of Incans. My heart sings to their music."

"I know who you are," she said. "You are the man I chose to marry."

Sunday, April 14, 2030

I am now married to a beautiful and brilliant woman who loves me.

The wedding was perfect. At 2:00 yesterday Louis walked Patricia down the path from the house to the bridge over the brook in Louis's front yard. Patricia wore a beige tight-fitting silk gown. It was low-cut. A probate judge married us on the bridge in front of a bank of flowering pink azaleas. I gave Patricia a wedding ring to wear with the engagement ring.

Willard served Dom Perignon Champagne and wedding cookies.

"Our marriage will be a secret," Patricia said, "for a while."

I said, "You're making me the happiest man on earth."

Willard gave her/us a check for $5,000. Louis gave her/us a portable cryogenic freezer and a set of sterling silver flatware that had been in his family.

By 3:30 we were on our way back to Atlanta as a married couple. I noticed that Patricia plugged the freezer into the car. I asked her if it contained anything.

"Yes," she said. "It contains a small liquid-nitrogen canister with the frozen wolverine-wolf embryo you and I created a couple of weeks ago."

"So it contains a baby," I said.

This morning Patricia fixed us mimosas to drink with the cheese omelette she made. She brought up our project.

"On Friday, April 22, Jaime will implant Red wolf clones in several of your wolves. I need for you—ahead of time—to substitute the frozen embryo of the wolverine-wolf chimera for one of the wolf embryos stored in Jaime's freezer. I marked the canister 'Red wolf clone.' Then Jaime will unknowingly implant the chimera in one of the wolves. Can you do that?"

"Yes, I guess so," I said. "But I hate to deceive Jaime. How did you know the date?"

"Cousin Willard knows everything. Anyway, Jaime will never find out that you made the substitution," she said. "When the surrogate mother whelps, you'll take the chimera before anybody sees the wolf's litter. And the wolf will probably whelp other pups at the same time."

"Okay," I said. "You are sure Jaime will never find out?"

"He will find out when we win the Apex Prize and I give a half million dollars to Zoo Arroyo."

Patricia put the freezer Louis had given us into my Outback.

"Let me get a picture of you. Now keep the freezer plugged into your car on your way home," she said, "and keep it plugged in at your house. Then bring it back to me with the Red wolf embryo."

I agreed to do it. Patricia changed the subject to the children she hoped we would have.

"How many would you like?" she asked.

I said one, maybe two, if she could handle it.

"We'll have two," she said. "Starting soon."

All the way back to the zoo I pondered Patricia's request of me. I am breaking all of Jaime's ethical rules. I am not publishing the results of my research, I am not putting society's benefit over my own, and I am not keeping my emotions out of my science. But after we win the Apex Prize I will get back on track.

Nick spotted me entering the zoo, and within minutes he was at my front door with Bonita and his flute. Nick wanted a lesson. I gave it to him. Afterwards we played Incan tunes together, Nick on his *quena* flute, and I on my *pan* flute. Incan music speaks to my heart.

So does Bonita, who sleeps with me on my bed when I am at the zoo.

At midnight, when the zoo was totally dark and the humans were asleep, I made my way to Jaime's lab and substituted the canister with the chimera embryo for the canister from Jaime's colleagues in North Carolina that contained a Red wolf embryo. Fortunately, the canisters were identical. I texted Patricia that I did what she asked me to do.

She texted me back. "Good work, Marco. I just got back from Columbia, where I spent a couple of days with Uncle Louis. Bring me the Red wolf embryo next weekend."

SUNDAY, APRIL 21, 2030

Friday night I drove into Atlanta through heavy traffic. This is tedious, I thought. I should be living with Patricia, not visiting her.

I took her the Red wolf embryo clone and didn't ask her what she planned to do with it.

On Saturday we cleaned out and painted the spare bedroom—blue, as one might guess—for me to use as my office. Patricia uses the other spare bedroom, which has a big picture window, for her office. Patricia's house is a "bungalow."

At the end of the day we showered—together—and ordered pizza.

Patricia asked me if we could transfer an embryo into Zoo Arroyo's female Black bear. I asked her what kind of embryo.

She said, "A wolf-bear embryo, which I created this past week at Uncle Louis's place. I have it in the cryogenic freezer there."

I must have looked surprised, because she took my hand and said, "Marco, if we are successful in producing a wolf-bear embryo, to be born in late fall, we will win the Apex Prize."

I hesitated. "What do you want me to do?" I asked.

"What I want us to do, together, is implant the embryo in Juliet. Will you agree?"

"Okay," I said.

"When would we be able to do it without anybody else seeing us?"

"May fifth."

I told her that Jorge had asked me to take care of the zoo on May fifth while he and Eddie went to Savannah for a meeting of the Southeastern Zoo and Menagerie Association. She said if I came to Atlanta on Saturday she would follow me to Zoo Arroyo on Sunday.

There was no backing out now. I wondered whether our competing for the Prize would put pressure on our marriage.

We went to bed early.

When I got into my Subaru this morning, Patricia kissed me good-bye and held my hand.

"Thank you, Marco," she said.

On the drive back to the zoo I thought about my mother. Was her marriage to my father perfect? All I could remember was merriment. I never saw any tension between them. Patricia and I love each other, but we don't laugh a lot. I just realized that.

I laugh more with Jorge and Nick. This afternoon Nick came over with his chisel to carve a bear for Jorge. When he finished he got the giggles.

"It looks like a rolling pin with a nose and feet," he said.

I got the giggles too.

"Let's see what Jorge thinks it is," Nick said.

We went over to the farmhouse and showed Nick's carving to Jorge.

"What do you think this is, Jorge?" Nick asked.

"It's a very tall, skinny bear," Jorge said. "Very tall, very skinny. Without arms."

"Oops. I forgot his arms," Nick said.

We could not stop laughing.

Jorge invited me to stay to dinner. We drank a bottle of wine and talked until long after dark. Jorge spoke openly about a woman he had met, but I did not. I have to keep my marriage to Patricia a secret, just as I have to keep our project a secret. So much secrecy.

However, I am married to the woman I love, and some day I will be a father.

Monday, April 22, 2030

Jaime and I implanted female embryos in Faye, Fern, and Luna today. Faye got the chimera. Jaime did not notice anything unusual in the embryo.

Tomorrow we'll implant male embryos in Fran.

Friday, April 26, 2030

I did not go to Atlanta tonight. I told Patricia on the phone that I was too tired.

"Who received the wolverine-wolf chimera?" she asked.

"Faye, the wolf with the yellow collar."

"Sleep well, husband."

"Sleep well, wife."

I will not sleep well. I have committed a crime, or at least a highly unethical act, which I can't undo. My Catholic conscience is in torment. I can't confess without hurting Patricia. I can't extricate myself from the project unless I extricate both of us, and Patricia would hate me if I tried. Patricia and I are married—in everything we do.

I did it for Patricia, whom I love, whom I admire, whom I obey. Did I just write "obey"? I guess I wrote the truth. After we win the Prize I will get my PhD and establish a research program independent of hers, and I will make my discoveries public. I will model my scientist-self after Jaime.

Now I must wait 63 days for Faye to whelp a wolverine-wolf chimera. Then I must take the new-born before anybody discovers what has been done. Another act to be done in secret.

I called Nick and invited him over for a flute lesson. We sat on the front deck and played for the wolves and the owls. By the time Nick left I was at peace.

Sunday, April 28, 2030

Last night we went to a nearby Peruvian restaurant, which I chose. The food made me nostalgic for my homeland. I noticed that Patricia was not wearing her wedding ring. She said she didn't want to elicit questions about our marriage. She said that when we had children she would wear them all the time.

I left Patricia before noon today, with many kisses.

On the way home I listened to Jorge interview somebody named Samantha Wheeling, who wrote a book about animal rights. Her examples of animal abuse got my attention. She mentioned chimpanzees locked up in medical facilities. Was she referring to the chimps being raised for their vital organs?

Then she said something like this: "If you are breeding without regard for their happiness, Green Earth will find you and expose you." She referred to a wild animal trader in South Carolina. I wondered if she was thinking of Willard. I didn't mention the interview to Patricia. I didn't want to worry her.

When I got home, I called Nick. He brought Bonita back to my house. He was full of personal questions, which I answered as honestly as I could. Our conversation went something like this:

Nick: "Where do you go every weekend, Marco?"

Me: "To Atlanta."

Nick: "Do you have a girlfriend?"

Me: "Yes, I do, Nick."

Nick: "Is she pretty?"

Me: "She is very pretty."

Nick: "Do you have a picture of her?"

Me: "I don't."

Nick: "Next time you see her, take her picture. Okay?"

Me: "I will, Nick."

Nick: "And bring her to the zoo some time. Okay?"

Me: "I will, Nick. But probably not soon. She doesn't have much free time."

Nick: "Okay. Can you give me a lesson now? I brought my flute."

I got a recording of Andean flute music out of my desk drawer and gave it to Nick. "Keep this recording, Nick," I said. "And some day you will play as well as these Peruvian musicians."

We played our flutes for more than an hour. Nick has a good ear, and more talent than I have.

As he walked out the door to go home for supper, Nick said, "Some day I would like to play a *pan* flute like yours, Marco."

I said, "Your birthday is July 4th, right? I will get you a *pan* flute for your birthday."

SUNDAY, MAY 5, 2030

I will be a father!

I went to Atlanta Friday night. At the restaurant—La Cantante—I noticed that Patricia did not order wine with dinner. I asked her if she was feeling okay. She reached for my hand.

"We're going to have a baby," she said.

I jumped up and hugged her.

"This is the best day of my life," I said. "I mean, after our wedding day."

She told me she had taken a pregnancy test that morning.

"But don't tell anybody," she said. "And we won't know for sure for a couple of months. I'll go to the doctor next week."

I am so happy. I will be a father. And I will be a good father.

Saturday we talked about our future. We shopped together for groceries, and I grilled steaks for dinner.

Today Patricia followed me to Zoo Arroyo for the transfer of the wolf-bear embryo into Juliet.

I shot Juliet with a tranquilizer dart to sedate her before I entered the bears' enclosure. As she fell to the ground Romeo and Jackie retreated out of sight. Patricia took pictures while I transferred the embryo.

The procedure went smoothly. The only problem was Nick's unexpected appearance. Nick asked what we were doing. I introduced Patricia to Nick as my girlfriend and told him that I was examining Juliet because she was acting sick.

"We'll have to take extra good care of Juliet, Nick," I said, "in case she is pregnant."

Patricia bade us good-bye and departed.

Nick must have called Jorge, because Jorge texted me. I texted Jorge that Juliet had passed a little blood and that I'd tranquilized her in order to conduct an examination. I concluded that she was okay.

Instead of his flute, Nick brought over his chisel knife this evening.

"I need to whittle another bear, Marco. For my mother on Mother's Day."

"Sure, Nick. What a thoughtful present. We have time tonight."

I brought out a chunk of balsa wood and showed Nick the picture I'd taken of Jorge's chainsaw standing bear. By 8:30, as the sun was setting, Nick had completed his bear, complete with arms, which stood 12 inches high.

"Marco," Nick asked, "Are you going to marry your girlfriend?"

"When the time is right, Nick, my girlfriend and I will be living together as husband and wife—and we'll have children."

"I hope that will be soon, Marco."

"I hope so too, Nick," I said. "Anyway, you've carved a really good bear. Tomorrow, if you like, we can stain it black."

After Nick had gone I opened a beer and celebrated my fatherhood alone.

Sunday, May 12, 2030

I got to Patricia's house before lunch on Saturday. Patricia and I both worked all afternoon, I in my newly painted office and she in hers. I built bookcases, portable bookcases in case we ever moved. She completed an article she was writing for the online journal *Stem Cell Frontiers*.

She asked me to read what she had written. I was stuck by the concluding paragraph.

> *The creation of 50/50 mammalian chimeras is revolutionary. Few ideas in human history are comparable. Copernicus discovered that the earth was not the center of the universe. Darwin discovered that humans were not specially created by God. Now in the twenty-first century we humans have discovered how to refashion nature.*

"It's ground-breaking," I told her. "Your argument will get you a lot of attention."

"I hope it gets me tenure. The departmental committee is meeting this week. Is it ready to post?"

"I don't see what you can add."

Patricia clicked send. The article, "Our Chimeric Future," by Patricia B. Maloney, PhD, Assistant Professor of Genetics at the Callaghan Research Institute, appeared on the *Stem Cell Frontiers* website two hours later.

"It will get the attention of the Apex Prize judges," she said. "But I'll write another article for *Nature* when Faye whelps the wolverine-wolf chimera. Do you want to co-author that article?"

"Let me think about it."

Suddenly I had qualms about exposing my dishonesty with Jaime and Jorge.

"Actually, I prefer not to co-author it," I said. "The project was your idea. I want you to take all the credit and win the prize solo."

"Thanks, Marco. But remember that we'll share the award money."

On my way home on Sunday I decided that I did not want to be mentioned in any of my wife's publications. I love her, but I don't love the project, not any more. I don't want any of the award money.

I just realized that I enjoy returning to Zoo Arroyo on Sundays because I get to give Nick a flute lesson.

Why do humans need to refashion nature?

SUNDAY, MAY 19, 2030

The weekend at our home in Atlanta was not as much fun as I had anticipated. Patricia was in a foul mood. I'd never seen her like that.

As soon as I got there Friday night she told me that the Callaghan Research Institute had dismissed her.

"Callaghan fired me!" she said. "My despicable senior colleagues read my article in *Stem Cell Frontiers* and made copies for my department head and my dean. They decided in a tenured faculty meeting on Tuesday that my research was, quote, 'unsound, misguided, hubristic, and unethical.' They recommended dismissal."

Patricia showed me the letter her department head had written to the dean. It said "Dr. Maloney fails to exemplify the ethical values that the Callaghan Research Institute requires in its faculty. She will not be offered a contract for the 2030-2031 academic year."

"I'm so sorry, Patricia."

"I'm not. I don't like my genetics colleagues anyway. They are plodding conformists. I am a non-conforming pioneer. When I win the Apex Prize, I'll be rich and famous, and they will still be low-paid, unknown, plodding conformists."

I asked her where she would go, and whether she would leave Atlanta. I wanted her to remain here.

Patricia told me that we would be together no matter where she took a position. She was morose, and I was subdued. Neither of us felt like going out for dinner.

I made myself a martini and ordered pizza.

We drank our after-dinner espresso on the swing on the front porch. She leaned her head on my shoulder.

"How are you feeling?" I asked her. "Any morning sickness?"

She said, "No morning sickness. But the gynecologist confirmed that I am pregnant."

I kissed her and patted her belly.

"Before our baby is born we should take our honeymoon," I said. "I will take you to Perú."

"Let's wait on that," she said.

Now why would she say that?

Sunday morning as I got ready to leave Patricia asked me what was on my calendar for the week.

I said, "Nothing unusual. I'll help Eddie build a new enclosure."

"For which animals?" she asked.

I said I didn't know. On the spot I decided not to tell her that this Wednesday Jaime and I would transfer Swift fox clone embryos into the Red foxes.

On my way home today I thought more about the genetics department's judgment of Patricia to be unethical. Were her colleagues right?

I found Jaime and Annie and Heather and Holly at the zoo with Jorge when I arrived at noon. Jorge invited me to join them for Sunday dinner. I did, and I had a good time, actually a very good time. We talked about Perú. After our delicious meal of roasted duck I ran to my house to get my *pan* flute and my Andean *bombo*. I gave Jorge the *bombo* to play.

We made music on the front deck for two whole hours. First I played some Andean music, which Nick heard from his house a hundred yards up the lane. Nick came over with his *quena* flute and joined us. Then Annie and Jaime played American popular songs, such as "Puff the Magic Dragon," which Holly and Heather knew by heart, and "Mr. Tambourine Man." Heather and Holly danced. I tried to play along.

About 4:00, Jaime put his guitar back in its case. Heather and Holly said in unison, "Don't stop! Please?"

Annie said, "We'll do this again, children. Okay, Marco?"

"*Por seguro*," I said.

For sure. What could be more satisfying than making music with people I love?

As I sit at my desk, writing in my journal with Bonita purring in my lap, I have a disorienting thought. Did I make a mistake in marrying Patricia?

But she will give me a family.

MONDAY, MAY 20, 2030

I had this odd exchange of texts with Patricia tonight.

> *9:16 pm*
> *Hey, Marco.*
> *Is Jorge interested in buying or selling sperm?*

> *No. Zoo Arroyo does not do that.*
> *Why do you ask?*

> *Cousin Willard wondered.*
> *He asked me to ask you.*
> *Good night, sweet husband.*

> *Good night, sweet wife.*

Now why would she ask that question? Did she want me to get the sperm for her? And why would Willard be asking? How well do I know my wife?

WEDNESDAY, MAY 22, 2030

Today Jaime and I implanted Swift fox embryo clones in Foxy Ann and Foxy Belle—females in Foxy Ann and males in Foxy Belle. Nick watched. The procedure went flawlessly.

The Red foxes should deliver the kits in 50 days or so. The Swift fox gestation period is approximately 52 days.

While the foxes were recovering from their anesthesia I asked Jaime what gave him pleasure as a scientist.

He said, "Knowing that I'm helping make a better world."

I asked him if he considered heart xenotransplantation, such as from chimpanzees to humans, to be a violation of the chimpanzee's rights.

He said that it was. Actually, he said, "Good god, Marco! Of course it is. It's homicide."

I showed him the *New York Times* article about the Apex Prize.

I didn't expect it, but Jaime asked me if I'd like to stay on at the zoo. He offered to extend my contract, presumably for another year. I asked him if I could let him know nearer to the end of June. I hope I showed him sufficient gratitude. I didn't say why I needed time to think it over. My fatherhood is a secret, just like my marriage is a secret, just like my project with Patricia is a secret, and my transplantation of a wolverine-wolf chimera embryo into Faye, and the transplantation of a wolf-bear chimera in Juliet.

And now I have to keep today's procedure a secret from my wife.

Not even a crook would keep so many secrets.

How can I stay on at Zoo Arroyo if I have deceived Jaime and Jorge? Maybe they won't find out.

I think my apprenticeship with Jaime has given me purpose. Now I know why I want a PhD. It is to "save the earth," as the bumper stickers say. I want to do what Jaime is doing. I want to be an honest scientist.

Georgia Tech has a graduate program in reproductive genetics. I'd prefer the program in wildlife genetics at the University of Georgia, but UGA is too far away from Atlanta for commuting. To be a good father I need to stay close to my family.

Sunday, May 26, 2030

Saturday, when nobody was around the Callaghan Research Institute, Patricia and I cleaned out her office and brought home her computer, printer, and paper files. We also brought home her lab equipment, some of which she had bought with grant funds. She left a resignation letter in her department head's mailbox.

"Now I need never step foot on the Callaghan campus again," she said.

We went to a nearby Mexican restaurant for dinner. I ordered a Don Julio tequila on the rocks, and Patricia said, "Make that two."

I must have looked startled, because she changed her order to a Coca-Cola.

"How are you feeling?" I asked. "I mean with regard to your pregnancy."

"Fine," she said. "A little morning sickness, but not much."

I asked whether her pregnancy would limit her chances to get another academic position. She said it shouldn't, that such discrimination was illegal. But she asked what I would do if she got a job outside Georgia.

I said I would go with her, that I would get a job wherever she landed. I wanted to be a good father and a good husband.

She took my hands and said, "You are a good husband, Marco. I do love you. And you will be a good father."

We spent the evening listening to classical music—Sibelius—and cuddling. Our romantic feelings for each other returned. But she said she didn't feel like making love.

This morning before we got out of bed I asked her whether the gynecologist had determined a due date for our baby.

"January," she said. "Some time in January."

I asked her whether I should postpone graduate school, continue at the zoo until the end of the year, and then stay home. I wanted to help with the baby while she was working.

"That would be a good idea, Marco," she said. "Then it won't matter where I get a job."

I wanted to say, "Yes, it will matter where you get a job." But I kept my thoughts to myself.

This morning we both got a text from Louis Bordeau.

> *8:55 am*
> *Hello, Patricia and Marco.*
> *Good news.*
> *Binti the lioness is ready to deliver five cubs, among them the chimera.*
> *Can you all come to Columbia this afternoon?*
> *Willard will be here by 4:00 to take the chimera to Charleston.*
> *But he wants you all to see her first.*
> *Uncle Louis*

Patricia answered for both of us.

> *Hi, Uncle Louis.*
> *That's great news.*
> *Marco has to return to Zoo Arroyo this morning.*
> *But I can be there by 1:00 pm.*
> *Thanks for the heads-up.*
> *Patricia*

I left Patricia shortly thereafter. I would have liked to go with her to Columbia, but I did have to get back to the zoo.

I have conflicting emotions. On the one hand I would really like to stay on at the zoo and learn more from Jaime. On the other hand I want to get a PhD and become a wildlife geneticist. I seem to be following Patricia again, doing what she wants me to do.

But I must accommodate her ambitions. I am committed to helping her win the Apex Prize. I can't abandon that project.

I'm trapped. Patricia is my wife. She will give birth to our baby, to my son or daughter.

On my way back to Zoo Arroyo I listened to Jorge's show "People for the Planet." His guest, a scholar named Garrison Tucker, said something that spooked me. He said if he caught an animal trafficker he would sue him on behalf of the animals and ruin the trafficker financially. He also excoriated Ibarra and Wong for creating the Ibarra-Wong chimpanzee. I texted Patricia and gave her Jorge's website address so she could listen to the whole interview.

Late tonight I got a text from Patricia.

> *10:14 pm*
> *Hi, Marco.*
> *Thanks for the heads-up on Garrison Tucker.*
> *He's not our friend.*
> *I'm happy to announce the birth of Zahara.*
> *She's a healthy 12-ounce leopard-cheetah chimera.*
> *Cousin Willard came and got her.*
> *He will raise her.*
> *He took one of Binti's lion cubs too.*

> *Louis will tell Columbia Zoo officials that Binti gave birth to three cubs.*
> *Your wife*
> *Patricia*

I texted back.

> *10:20 pm*
> *Hi, Patricia.*
> *I'm glad Zahara is healthy.*
> *Please send pix.*
> *Why is Garrison Tucker not our friend?*
> *Your husband*
> *Marco*

She must have gone to bed, because she didn't answer my question and she didn't send me any pictures.

So Louis is stealing cubs from Columbia Zoo animals to give to Willard. And Patricia approves.

Sunday, June 2, 2030

On Friday morning Patricia called me to say that she was going to Charleston for the weekend to see Cousin Willard. She wanted to check on Zahara. I stayed at Zoo Arroyo.

Saturday was great fun. I spent four hours in the petting Zoo talking to children and teaching them about the animals. Blossom was very popular with the six-year-old Girl Scouts, who came here on a field trip.

I told Jorge that I would appreciate very much an extension of my contract until January. He asked me why I shouldn't stay the whole year. I said, "Let's see what the fall brings." I thanked him profusely.

Jorge asked me to give him *bombo* lessons. I said that being able to teach him something would give me great pleasure. I ordered Jorge a *bombo* from Perú.

SUNDAY, JUNE 9, 2030

I went to Atlanta Saturday morning. I'm too tired at the end of the day on Fridays to make the two-hour drive.

I arrived at noon to find Patricia on the phone with Louis Bordeau. She told me that Louis had obtained a position as a research biologist for her at the Columbia Zoo. I asked her when she would start. She said July 8. She would go to Columbia tomorrow to look for a house. She invited me to go with her, but I told her that our staff met on Mondays.

I told Patricia that I had agreed to stay at the zoo until the end of December. She seemed unconcerned.

We picked up boxes at the liquor store and packed up her possessions. Packing was not onerous. Patricia had accumulated surprisingly few personal items in her 32 years of life. And her personal items revealed little about her interests. No art, no collections, no pets.

Nothing like my personal items, which reveal my interests: a closet full of Andean musical instruments, a trunk full of Peruvian ponchos, blankets, boots, and photo books, a cabinet full of wood-carving tools and wind chimes. And Bonita.

We went to a nearby Thai restaurant for dinner. Afterwards we sat on the sofa and watched an old movie with Cary Grant. Patricia likes old movies. I don't, but I'm not about to tell her.

I felt a bit down before we went to bed. But then I looked at her and was struck again by her beauty. How did I win her over? I am indeed a lucky man. She will bear my child.

Tonight I gave Jorge a *bombo* lesson and Nick a *quena* flute lesson. I alternated playing my *pan* flute and my mother's *charango*. I was "in my element," as Americans say.

Monday, June 10, 2030

At our weekly breakfast meeting this morning, Jorge invited us all to a reception sponsored by *Wild Beasts Magazine* on June 24 at the Witherston Inn. Jorge told Eddie to bring Emma and Nick, he told Zell to bring Eve and Abbie, and he told me to bring anybody I liked. He said that Zoo Arroyo was the magazine's cover story for the summer issue, and he hoped we could all come.

Zell reminded us that Luna, Faye, Fern, and Fran were due to whelp in two weeks. I hope nobody noticed that Zell's announcement made me sweat. I sat there filled with guilt over my betrayal of Jaime. I determined to be present at Faye's delivery and to retrieve the chimera before anybody else found her.

Tonight I called Patricia and invited her to go with me to the reception as my date. She declined. I said I would introduce her as a friend, not as my wife. She said she would be busy with the move to Columbia. She asked who else would be going to the reception. I told her. I guess Patricia doesn't want to meet my friends. She was spooked to have met Nick when we were injecting Juliet.

I haven't met any of her friends either. She never mentions anybody.

Thursday, June 13, 2030

I told Patricia over the phone about Garrison Tucker's email to Jorge. And I quoted one sentence: "When I identify the trafficker I will sue him and ruin him financially."

"Could you please forward the email to me," Patricia asked.

"Sure. But keep it confidential." I forwarded it to her.

"I wonder whether Garrison Tucker is talking about Willard," I said. "If so, Willard is in trouble."

"I doubt that Garrison Tucker is talking about Cousin Willard," Patricia said. "Who would be the anonymous tipster?"

"That doesn't matter. Do you think that Willard is breaking any laws?"

"Maybe drug laws. But not any other laws. And we aren't either. Sperm and eggs are traded all the time these days. Sperm, eggs, embryos, dna—all are for sale. So are animals."

"What we are doing is not illegal?"

"No, Marco."

"Okay, Patricia. I trust you."

"See you Saturday, husband."

"See you Saturday, wife."

As write in my journal tonight I listen to the call of a Barred owl. Maybe it's Hoot. I envy owls. The owls don't know the machinations of humans. They don't know the guilt that burdens humans for violating ethical norms. They don't know of our ethical norms, or our laws. They don't know of our motivations, our passions, our hatreds, our fears. They don't know why we drive on the right side of the street, stop at red lights, or put up yard signs. They don't know when it's Monday. Barred owls, who have inhabited these woods for 11,000 years, understand only the need for food, shelter, a mate, and safety from predators. I envy them.

I downloaded *Does Every Species Belong to Us?* so that I could start reading it tonight. OMG. This is the epigraph.

"What will you order today?" said the breeder to the buyer.

"A dozen mink-bears," said the buyer to the breeder, "for my customers want fine fur.

"What will you order today?" said the breeder to the butcher.

"Twenty beefalos," said the butcher to the breeder, "for my customers want lean meat.

"What will you order today?" said the breeder to the doctor.

"Six chimp-humans," said the doctor to the breeder, "for my patients want new hearts.

"What will you order today?" said the breeder to the animal trafficker.

"Jaglions and pumabears, ligers and coydogs," said the trafficker to the breeder,

"for you are the Almighty Breeder and you can breed whatever you like."

"You are mistaken," the breeder said. "I breed whatever you like."

Garrison Tucker is writing about Ibarra and Wong. They are "almighty breeders." Willard is an almighty breeder too. So is Patricia. So am I, if I go whither she goes.

Garrison Tucker opened his introduction with this sentence: "Does nature now belong to almighty breeders? What is nature in the twenty-first century?"

SUNDAY, JUNE 16, 2030

Yesterday my wife was her old self. She looked fantastic in her tight red T-shirt and tight white jeans. She wore her long hair in a braid.

Despite her protests I took her picture.

"You are a beautiful woman," I said. "You don't look like a typical scientist."

"I am not a typical scientist," she said.

Patricia cooked us a gourmet meal of seared scallops and black rice. She poured me a glass of Chardonnay and herself a glass of sparkling water.

"Here's to a new life," she said, raising her glass.

"What are we celebrating?"

"We have a house in Columbia, near the Columbia Zoo."

"And far from Zoo Arroyo."

"Only three hours from Zoo Arroyo. Let me show you pictures," she said.

I thumbed through a dozen or so pictures of a contemporary cedar house with a pasture for a back yard. The interior was all steel and glass. New kitchen. Beige walls. Four bedrooms. Skylights everywhere.

"This is phenomenal," I said. "And the back yard will be great for kids. It looks expensive."

"Uncle Willard bought it for me, with cash," she said. "He closed on it today."

Patricia brought up my future.

"You could enter a PhD program at the University of South Carolina," she said. "Its main campus is in Columbia."

"That depends on what USC offers," I said.

"I checked. It has a PhD program in biomedical engineering. I found the application on the web."

"That might work," I said.

"Try to get a list of the zoo animals. You'll need it for your application to show what you've been doing since you got your master's degree. And email it to me. I'd like to see what you've been doing too."

"Okay. Do you think I could enter the program in January?"

"There's an unexpected opening for a PhD student for this coming fall. You have to apply immediately. I'll be happy to look over your application."

"I'd like that," I said. "Thank you. What will you do in Columbia?"

"Work at the Columbia Zoo and start writing my book 'Nature Is Ours.'"

"Nature is ours to do what with, Patricia?"

She changed the subject.

"I just thought of something, Marco. You're going to be away from the zoo on the night of June 24, right?"

"How did you know?"

"That's the night of the *Wild Beasts Magazine* reception. Faye could whelp our chimera that night. So would you be able to loan me your key to Zoo Arroyo's entrance gate?"

Oh my God. What was she thinking of now?

"Why, Patricia? Are you intending to break into one of the buildings?"

"No, no. I just want to watch Faye while you and your friends are gone. If Faye whelps the little wolverine-wolf I can take her. The chimera, I mean."

That made sense.

"Where will you take her?"

"To Columbia, where I'll hand her off to Cousin Willard. He will raise her."

"When will you move into your new house?"

I didn't say "our" new house. I don't know why I didn't.

"The move is scheduled for Tuesday. I'll come up from Atlanta Monday night, spend a couple hours at your place watching Faye, and then drive on to Columbia. I promised

Uncle Louis to stay in his house all week while he is in Witherston to feed his dogs and take care of a female jackal named Sameera from the Columbia Zoo."

"Okay. Here's my key. I have a spare. Please be careful in Sol's Woods."

"Don't worry. I'll ask an employee of Cousin Willard's, Juan Navarro, to join me. You can call me after the reception, Marco."

Late Saturday evening I received an email from Jorge with an article by Beverly Everett attached. Garrison Tucker was dead, fatally shot. OMG.

Was it coincidence that Garrison Tucker was murdered two days after I asked Patricia if she knew him? Could Patricia have innocently told Willard, and could Willard have sent somebody to shoot him?

I didn't show the article to Patricia.

Sunday, June 23, 2030

On Friday I told Jorge that I might be leaving, that I might be going to graduate school in the fall after all. He said that he and Jaime would be happy to write a joint letter of recommendation for me. I told him I would be grateful. Then, Friday night he emailed me a copy of the letter. I felt shame. It said that I am "intelligent, conscientious, reliable, and, most importantly, honest" and that I "will use science to make life better for humanity." I have betrayed Jorge and Jaime. I have deceived them. What's worse is that I intend to deceive them again. I did not show the letter to Patricia. Another secret from her.

I got to Patricia's house yesterday at 10:00. We spent the day boxing up dishes, silverware, and cooking utensils. The movers will come tomorrow afternoon to haul the furniture to Columbia. They will unload it Tuesday morning, when Patricia is there to tell them where to put things.

Good thing her Atlanta house is a rental, so she doesn't have to sell it.

Last night we ordered pizza for dinner and watched a movie about the COVID-27 pandemic. When Patricia undressed for bed I noticed again that she does not have a baby bump. I asked her if she was sure she was pregnant. She said she was. She initiated the lovemaking this time.

I got up early this morning to return to the zoo. I wanted to go grocery shopping for Jorge and then check on Faye. On my way up to Witherston I listened to Jorge's radio program "People for the Planet." Jorge interviewed a photographer named Lola Montoya, who had come to the zoo a couple of months ago to photograph the wolves. Lola Montoya said on air that she worked for Willard Tavis.

I called Patricia this evening and asked her if she knew a woman named Lola Montoya. She said she did not. I told her of Jorge's interview.

"Should we be worried?" I asked Patricia.

"No," Patricia answered. "Don't give it another thought."

"You might want to listen to it on Jorge's website."

"I will."

I tried not to think about it. But I'm still worried.

I found Faye in good shape, with no indication that she was ready to deliver. But I think Bonita has gotten herself pregnant.

Tonight I played my mother's *charango* while Nick played his *quena* flute. We must have sounded good, because the wolves howled.

After giving Nick a flute lesson, I started worrying about tomorrow night. Patricia will use my key to get into the zoo after 6:30.

Monday, June 24, 2030

At the breakfast meeting for the staff this morning Jorge alerted us again to the imminent delivery of our Red wolf clones. Everybody was excited. I volunteered to be on "wolf-watch," since Zell and Eddie were rebuilding the henhouse.

Faye did not deliver today. Neither did Luna or Fern.

I was excited to be going to the *Wild Beasts* reception. I hadn't been invited to a fancy event in years. I shaved off my beard and trimmed my hair in order to look as nice as possible. I wore my Peruvian *guayabera* shirt. I figured I would see Willard Tavis there.

I did see Willard there, but he pretended to be meeting me for the first time. I guess our acquaintance is a secret. I saw Patricia's uncle Louis Bordeau there too, and he too pretended to be meeting me for the first time. They must not want Jaime and Jorge to know of our relationship. That's okay by me. I don't want to have to explain that they are "my wife's family."

I gave Jorge the Rosewood and Mahogany chessboard that I had carved for him. He seemed very happy with the present.

Lola Montoya said something that puzzled me. She said that Willard had been alerted by "connections" to listen to her "People for the Planet" interview, and that he had not liked it. Of course he didn't. Lola had criticized the breeding of "man-made beasts." Was Patricia his "connection"?

Willard slipped me an envelope full of hundred-dollar bills. "That's for helping Patricia," he said. "Consider it a belated wedding present."

Why would he do that? Was he bribing me for something?

I deposited the $3,000 in my bank account.

I beat Eddie and Jorge back to the zoo. Patricia had left the entrance gate open. I locked it behind me.

I called Patricia, but she didn't answer. She is driving in the dark. She probably doesn't want to be distracted.

Tuesday, June 25, 2030

Que Dios me salve.

A man died last night in Sol's Woods. He had been mutilated by the wolves. And he had been shot. Nick and Abbie found the body.

Who was he? Willard's employee Juan Navarro?

The police can't figure out who killed the man—the wolves or the shooter.

Did Patricia let Juan Navarro into Zoo Arroyo with my key to steal Faye? Was that her plan all along? Did she shoot him? Did she kill him? If so, why? To spare him the misery of being eaten? Or to keep him from talking? She could have called 911. She could have called me.

I phoned her about 11:30 this morning, but she didn't answer. I left a message for her to call me immediately. She didn't.

Just before noon I texted her:

> *11:54 am*
> *Patricia, what happened last night?*
> *A man was killed in Sol's Woods.*
> *He was shot in the head.*
> *Were you with him? Did you shoot him?*
> *Who is he? Juan Navarro?*
> *Were you all trying to steal Faye?*
> *Please text me back.*

She did text me back.

Marco, I'll explain when I see you.
He is not Juan Navarro.
Come to Columbia on Saturday.
My new address is 215 Snapper Drive.

I replied.

The police are here.
Should I be worried?
Do you still have my key?

She didn't respond. I sent her one last text.

Patricia, you are my wife.
I need to know this:
Do you carry a gun?
If so, did you shoot it last night?
Do you still have my key?

She answered.

I do not own a gun.
I am at Uncle Louis's house this week.
Come to Columbia on Saturday.
I'll answer your questions then.

Why didn't she answer my question about the key? If she still has my key why didn't she lock the entrance gate after the shooting? In that case, she was present at the shooting and was possibly the shooter, the murderer. If she no longer has my key, what did she do with it?

The horror of my situation has hit me. I am married to

a woman who probably killed somebody. I helped her do it by giving her a key to Zoo Arroyo.

I don't love that conniving, manipulative, devious woman any more. But I can't divorce her before the baby arrives.

Maybe she'll let me have custody of the baby, so that she won't be burdened by motherhood, so that she can fulfill her extravagant ambitions.

I want the baby.

Despite my inebriation I see our relationship clearly. Patricia dominated me from the night she took me out to dinner and invited me, of all people, to work with her on the Apex project. She captured me with her beauty. She asked me to keep our collaboration secret, and I was happy to do so. At the time I thought she chose me because I was smart, but now I think she chose me because I worked at Zoo Arroyo. She wanted access to the zoo's animals.

I thought that getting married was my idea, but actually it was hers. She put the idea into my head. And she insisted that we do it immediately and keep it secret. Why the secrecy?

She involved me in the creation of the chimeras, and in their transplantation. We are hitched, in marriage and in crime. She took a picture of me transferring the wolf-bear embryo into Juliet. She took lots of pictures of me.

If she gets reprimanded—or worse, arrested—for exploiting Zoo Arroyo's animals, then I lose everything I hold dear for enabling her. I lose my job, my friendship with Jaime and Jorge, my reputation. I won't recover. She will.

If she gets arrested for murder, I am an accessory.

Where did I go wrong?

I want to start over. I want to confess my deception to Jaime and Jorge, beg them for forgiveness, and become an honest man and an ethical scientist.

I have just finished my third beer. I'm looking at a picture I took of Patricia a couple of weeks ago. She looks dazzling. She also looks slender. Way too slender to be two months pregnant. Did she lie about being pregnant so I would stick with her, so I would help her transplant chimeras into Faye and Juliet?

Did she marry me so I could not testify against her?

Perhaps I can avoid getting caught. I must retrieve the wolverine-wolf chimera in Faye before somebody else discovers it. I'll keep a close eye on Faye tomorrow.

WEDNESDAY, JUNE 26, 2030

Today Luna whelped her four pups and Faye whelped one, the wolverine-wolf chimera. Jorge and Jaime spotted Faye before I did. Faye had delivered the chimera, but she did not look normal. She pushed the chimera away from her. Maybe she wasn't producing milk. Jorge and Jaime took Faye and the newborn, whom they named "Sasha," back to the farmhouse.

Faye died. I am responsible. I killed a wolf. Unintentionally. A side effect of another crime.

Now what do I do? Fern has not whelped her pups yet. When she does I can substitute one of her pups for Sasha. I will be stealing Sasha. One more crime. But what's one more crime after becoming a criminal.

Once a man commits one dishonest act he is no longer an honest man. A man can't be ninety percent honest and still be honest. A man who is ninety percent honest is a dishonest man, not to be trusted. A man who is ten percent dishonest is a dishonest man. I am a dishonest man.

Tonight I texted Patricia. I didn't feel like calling her.

9:55 pm

Patricia, did you see the USA Today today?

It has an article about your creating a wolf-bear chimera

and transferring it into a Black bear in a "private zoo."

Now reporters will look at private zoos everywhere.

They'll come here to Zoo Arroyo.

What have you gotten us into?

Faye delivered the wolverine-wolf chimera today.

Faye died. Jorge has the newborn.

I ask you again: What happened Monday night?

She replied.

Marco, don't panic.

I published an article in Reproductive Frontiers about creating the chimera.

I forgot to mention it to you.

We'll talk when you come to Columbia.

Well, I am panicking. And I don't want to go to Columbia on Saturday. I sent another text to her.

Jorge asked me if I knew a Dr. Patricia B. Maloney.

I said that I didn't.

By the way, I am tired of secrets.

Jaime said that the attempt to create chimeras, "freaks of nature," was "unconscionable." Jaime and Jorge would view our Apex project as unconscionable. They would view my contribution to it as unconscionable. They would not understand that I lost my moral compass when I fell under the spell of Patricia. They would not believe that I could ever right myself again.

Thursday, June 27, 2030

I have made a plan.

Tomorrow night Jorge will be in Witherston, and Eddie, Emma, and Nick will be away too. They are all leaving at noon. Jorge asked me to feed Sasha while he was gone. He gave me a key to the clinic. That gave me an idea.

Fern is about to deliver her pups. They will be female Red wolf clones. If she whelps tomorrow after everybody leaves I will take one of her pups and exchange her for Sasha. If Fern doesn't whelp, I'll take one of Luna's pups. And then I'll drive to Columbia and give Sasha to Patricia. Patricia will hand her off to Louis or Willard.

I'll have to see Patricia, but I won't stay with her.

I can't work at the zoo any longer. I can't continue to deceive Jaime and Jorge. I'll text them to say that something has come up and I have to leave. And that I'll be in touch.

After I finish this beer I will pack. My few belongings— my laptop, my clothes, my toiletries, my wood-carving tools, and my musical instruments—will all fit in my Outback.

But where will I take them? I can't take them to Patricia's house in Columbia. I don't want to go to Columbia at all. I don't want to see Patricia. And I don't want to give Sasha to Patricia. I don't trust Patricia to be kind to Sasha. Patricia will just pass her off to Willard. I want to return to Perú. Yes. I will return to Perú as soon as possible. On Saturday. On Saturday I will fly out of Atlanta and not see Patricia at all. That's what I'll do.

But what will I do with Sasha? I am responsible for Sasha. I helped create her, a creature who would live in a cage, who would be a freak, who would be gawked at her entire life. I could not bear the thought of her suffering because of me. Maybe I should euthanize her. Yes, I should. I will euthanize her. That's the kindest thing I can do for her.

So I'll leave most of my stuff here. I'll travel light.

I won't be able to take the coffee table I made, or the floor lamp. I will give them to Jorge. It's the least I can do for all the kindness he has shown me.

I'll give my musical instruments to Jaime. I can buy more in Perú. And I'll give my knives to Eddie and Nick.

Bonita will have to stay here. At least Nick will take care of her.

It's close to midnight now. I have had too many beers, but I'm still thinking clearly.

I like this plan.

I will leave my car at the airport and send Jorge the keys.

I will get a divorce. I will start a new life.

Friday, June 28, 2030

It's almost midnight and I am on a flight to Lima, sipping my second scotch.

Sasha is dead.

Here is what happened.

Fern whelped four pups this afternoon when I was the only person at the zoo. I took the last one without her noticing. Fern will be a good mother. She is a good wolf.

I carried the pup to Jorge's clinic, where I found Sasha in an incubator. I took Sasha out, wrapped her in a towel, and replaced her with Fern's pup. I warmed formula and fed them both.

My heart ached for Sasha. Sasha was born into a world where she would have no companions, no mates, no pack. She would not know freedom. She would spend her life in a zoo or in a menagerie as a lonely, miserable object of scientific curiosity. Patricia designed this creature for one reason only, to win the Apex Prize. And why did Patricia want the creature? To prove to her father she merited his approval. For that reason alone she created Sasha and the wolf-bear chimera Juliet is carrying.

I just wrote, "she created Sasha." That's incorrect. She and I created Sasha.

So I killed her. Yes, I killed her. I murdered her. I destroyed her little wolverine-wolf soul. But she didn't feel any pain. I injected her first with Telazol to sedate her and then with a barbiturate to euthanize her. I buried her in the bison pasture. Wild flowers will cover her grave.

By 3:30 pm I was on the road to Atlanta.

Had I forgotten anything? I locked the clinic door behind me. I put the keys in my mailbox. I labeled my gifts to Jaime, Jorge, Eddie, and Nick. I put food and water on the porch for Bonita. I booked an overnight flight to Lima. When I passed through Witherston I stopped by the bank and emptied my savings account of its $8,983. In the airport parking lot I placed a sign on the dashboard that said, "This car belongs to Jorge Arroyo (JorgeArroyo@zmail.com)." I put the key fob in an envelope and mailed it to Jorge.

I thought about what I would do next. I could apply for admission to vet school. I would never be trusted as a scientist, but I might come to be trusted as a veterinarian.

In the boarding area I texted Cisco.

8: 08 pm
Hola, Cisco.
I am returning to Perú to live.
May I stay with you a few days in Chasca?
I will arrive on Delta #9001 at 6:30 am tomorrow (Sat).
I'll rent a car.
Tu primo,
Marco

To which Cisco replied.

Hola, Marco.
Of course you may stay with me.
I will meet you at the airport in Lima and bring you home.
Hasta pronto!
Un abrazo,
Cisco

Then I texted Patricia, and my plan fell apart.

8:14 pm
Patricia:
Your wolverine-wolf chimera is dead.
I would like a divorce.
You may initiate proceedings.
I want custody of our baby.
Marco

Patricia replied.

Marco:
I will not be having a baby.
We are not getting a divorce.
I presume you killed the chimera.
Where are you now?
Patricia

¡Jolín! Why won't she divorce me?

Patricia:
You misunderstand.
I DEMAND a divorce.
You don't need me anymore.
I don't want to have anything to do with your project.
I am now in the Delta lounge waiting to board a flight to Lima.
I will not return.
Marco

Marco:
You misunderstand.
You need me.
If we are married I can't testify against you.
Patricia

What?

You implanted the wolverine-wolf chimera embryo in Faye.

I have pictures.

You implanted the wolf-bear chimera embryo in Juliet.

I have pictures.

You gave me a key to Zoo Arroyo.

You deceived Jaime.

You withheld information from the police.

You fled.

All for $1 million.

What will the police think?

We will stay married.

I will give up my attempt to win the Prize.

We were once happy. We will be happy again.

Patricia

My phone rang just as the pilot told us to turn off our phones. Jorge was calling. I didn't answer.

SUNDAY, JUNE 30, 2030
Nick texted me today.

3:45 pm

Hi, Marco.

Thank you very very very much for your knives.

And thank you very very very much for teaching me to whittle.

I will take care of Bonita.

I hope you come back to the zoo.

Your friend,

Nick

P.S. Thank you also for teaching me to play the flute.

I texted Nick back.

> *4:49 pm*
> *Hi, Nick.*
> *I am in Perú.*
> *I miss you.*
> *I will send you a pinkillo flute. You can play it with one hand.*
> *Tell Jorge and Jaime I will write to them soon.*
> *Un abrazo,*
> *Marco*

FRIDAY, JULY 5, 2030

This morning, after a week reconnecting with my friends from childhood, I took a bus from Chasca to Lima to look for a place to live. I have an opportunity to try again to do something good with my life.

On July 1, I emailed an application to the vet school of the Universidad Nacional Mayor de San Marcos. Yesterday I got a call from the dean. They have an opening in the department of Small Animal Medicine and a job for me in the clinic. I start on August 4.

I found a nice furnished apartment near the university and near a market. In the market I bought a *pinkillo* flute for Nick and a *pan* flute with 27 pipes for myself.

I was about to forget my serious troubles when I got texts from Jorge and Jaime.

> *6:31 pm*
> *Hola, Marco.*
> *Thanks so much for the key fob to your Subaru Outback.*

And for the Outback. You are generous.

Marco, I still care for you.

Let me know what's going on with you.

One question: Do you know where Dr. Patricia Maloney is?

Jorge

And:

10:15 pm

Hi, Marco.

Jorge just called me.

We both want to know what happened to you.

I attach an article that appeared in Online Witherston today.

Jaime

I read the article.

WITHERSTON POLICE DEPARTMENT RELEASES INFORMATION ON TWO MURDERS
BY BEVERLY EVERETT

11:00 am, July 5, 2030. Detective Mira Dunning of the Witherston Police at a press conference this morning stated that the man who died at Zoo Arroyo on the night of June 24, was murdered.

The victim, Simon Pate of Charleston, South Carolina, had been attacked by wolves but was alive when shot in the back of the head at close range. Medical Examiner Dev Reddy found a 9mm bullet lodged in the deceased man's skull.

The 9mm bullet matched the bullet found in the chest of Professor Garrison Tucker, who was fatally shot in Augusta, Georgia, on June 15.

Detective Dunning has issued an all-points bulletin for a man known as "Gordo," who may have been Simon Pate's accomplice in the Zoo Arroyo murder.

Detective Dunning also seeks to interview Marco Ramos, a former Zoo Arroyo employee; Dr. Patricia Bordeau Maloney, a former member of the Callaghan Research Institute faculty; and Dr. Louis Bordeau, a former employee of the Columbia Zoo in Columbia, South Carolina.

Patricia shot Simon Pate "in the back of the head at close range." She shot him intentionally. She murdered him. Did she also murder Garrison Tucker?

Should I turn myself in? If I tell my story—my whole story, with all the details—I may not be charged as an accessory to murder. That's what I will do.

Tomorrow I will email my journal to Jorge and Jaime.

SATURDAY, JULY 6, 2030

I got a long email from Patricia early this morning.

From: Patricia Maloney (PatriciaBordeauMaloney@zmail.com)
To: MarcoRamos2004@zmail.com
8:09 am, Saturday, July 6, 2030
WHAT HAPPENED
Dear Marco:
I know you are angry. You want never to see me again. You want a divorce. I don't. As I said, a divorce would not benefit either of us.

I am in Lima now. Please contact me.

Wherever you are, you must read the article in today's USA Today titled "Wolf-Bear Chimera Born at Zoo Arroyo: Two Scientists Sought for Questioning." Here's a link. The scientists wanted by the FBI are the two of us.

Now hear my story.

On Monday night, June 24, I was with Gordo, who works for Cousin Willard. I didn't find out that Gordo's real name was Simon Pate till I read the news reports. I thought Juan Navarro was driving up to help me, but Gordo came instead. I picked Gordo up at the Witherston High School parking lot and we drove to Zoo Arroyo in my SUV. I had decided that we needed to capture Faye before she delivered the chimera and take her to Cousin Willard's ranch.

We entered the zoo (with your key) about 8:00 pm and went immediately to Sol's Woods. Gordo gave me his gun and asked me to stay outside the gate. I unlocked the gate (with your key), and Gordo entered Sol's Woods by himself. He carried a dead rabbit to attract the wolves. The pack showed up within minutes. Gordo tried to net Faye (with the yellow collar), and a wolf attacked Gordo. I opened the gate and ran in. The wolf had Gordo by the throat. I shot at him. Then the whole pack assaulted Gordo. I shot at the pack again, and hit Gordo. It was an accident. I was far away from him. The wolves ran off.

I saw that Gordo was dead. Believe me. I didn't mean to kill him. I should have called 911, but what good would that have done? I left the scene and drove to Uncle Louis's house at top speed. I spent the night alone there. And I stayed there all week, even after the movers delivered my furniture to my new house. I apologize for not answering your phone call, but I was in shock.

I no longer have Gordo's gun. I buried it on Uncle Louis's property where no one will ever find it. I still have your key to Zoo Arroyo.

The USA Today article reports the birth of a wolf-bear chimera named Nicky Bear at Zoo Arroyo. Our transplantation of the chimera embryo was successful.

I made another mistake. On Friday, June 28, I accidentally let the jackal from the Columbia Zoo escape from Uncle Louis's clinic. I told you I was supposed to feed a newly pregnant jackal named Sameera that Uncle Louis was keeping. He told me I could take one of her embryos. The day after I arrived I did laparoscopic surgery and extracted an embryo, which I froze and put in Uncle Louis's freezer. On Friday, June 28, I entered Sameera's cage to bring her food. She knocked me down and escaped. I called Uncle Louis, and he got back here as soon as he could. The police recaptured Sameera and took her to the zoo. Columbia Zoo officials fired Uncle Louis on the spot, because Sameera's belly showed surgery they had not authorized. I resigned my new position with the Columbia Zoo.

My relationship with Uncle Louis and Cousin Willard has gotten complicated. Both of them are breaking the law, and they know I know it. Uncle Louis has been stealing sperm and newborns from Columbia Zoo animals to sell to Cousin Willard. He has been stealing embryos from newly pregnant

*zoo animals to give to me. Cousin Willard sells
sperm, hybrid predators, and wild animals he has
raised. He and Gordo sell cocaine on the side.
Both Uncle Louis and Cousin Willard will go to
jail if I talk to the police. I will go to jail if they talk
to the police.*

*They fear me, I fear them, and they fear each
other. And you and I fear each other.*

*I remember from college a philosophical game
called The Prisoner's Dilemma. As I recall it goes
something like this. In a hypothetical situation each
of two prisoners is given the opportunity to convict
the other of a crime to save his own life. If the first
prisoner talks, he goes free and the second prisoner
gets convicted. If the first prisoner remains silent and
the second talks, the first prisoner gets convicted
and the second goes free. If both talk, both get
convicted. If neither talks, both go free.*

*That's the situation that Uncle Louis, Cousin
Willard, you, and I are in. If one of us talks, that
person goes free or gets a light sentence and the
others get heavier sentences. If nobody talks we will
all go free or all get light sentences. I hope that all
of us remember that we're family and that nobody
will talk. The family includes you.*

*Marco, I do love you. And you love me. We need
to be together.*

Your wife Patricia

P.S. I have abandoned the Apex project.

I texted her.

9:31 am
Patricia:
I got your email.
I have questions:
Why did you decide to steal Faye—without even talking to me about it?
Why did you shoot Simon Pate?
I don't believe you shot him accidentally.
I am wondering, Who are you? A murderer?
No, we do not need to be together.
Why did you come to Lima?
I do not want to see you.
Marco

She replied.

I did not murder Simon Pate. I shot him unintentionally.
I came to Lima to find you.
Your wife Patricia

Patricia is a liar.

Tonight I will email Jorge and Jaime my journal entries from October 27, 2029 through today, July 6, 2030. I will include Patricia's letter. I will be the one to talk first.

PART III

The Case

CHAPTER TWENTY-EIGHT

Saturday, July 6, 2030

(continued)

Not until midnight did Jorge did finish reading Marco's journal. For every entry in the journal he had checked his own calendar to correlate what Marco had been doing and thinking with what he had put on his schedule.

On May fifth, Jorge and Eddie went to Savannah. On that day Marco and Patricia had transferred a wolf-bear chimera embryo into Juliet and unexpectedly encountered Nick.

On May nineteenth, Jorge called the number in the *Wild Beasts Magazine* ad, but did not leave a message. The next day Patricia asked Marco, "Is Jorge interested in buying or selling sperm?" She said that her cousin Willard wondered. So the phone number belonged to Willard Tavis. Willard Tavis was trafficking in wild animals, hybrid predators, and sperm. And probably minks.

On May twenty-sixth, Marco told Patricia to listen to Garrison Tucker's WITH-FM interview in which Garrison said he would sue unethical animal traffickers and ruin them financially. Did Patricia alert Willard Tavis? Willard Tavis would have been happy for Garrison to die.

On June thirteenth, Jorge shared Garrison Tucker's email with the Zoo staff. That afternoon Marco shared it with Patricia. Did Patricia share Garrison Tucker's email with Willard Tavis? On June fifteenth, Garrison Tucker was murdered. Did Willard Tavis send Gordo—who was Simon Pate—to Augusta to murder Garrison Tucker before Garrison Tucker could talk with Jorge?

On June twenty-third, Jorge interviewed Lola on "People for the Planet." On June twenty-fourth, at the *Wild Beasts Magazine* reception, Willard Tavis told Lola that he had listened to the program. On June twenty-fifth Willard Tavis fired Lola and Juan Navarro.

Did Patricia Maloney deliberately kill Gordo/Simon Pate to keep him from talking?

Jorge emailed Marco's journal to Mira. On the subject line he wrote, "MUST READ IMMEDIATELY."

He hoped she would read it before her interview with Dr. Louis Bordeau.

CHAPTER TWENTY-NINE

Sunday, July 7, 2030

D etective Mira Dunning met Dr. Louis Bordeau at ten o'clock in the Witherston Police Department's conference room.

"Thank you for talking with us, Dr. Bordeau," Mira said. "This is my colleague from the FBI, Special Agent Troy Washington."

"And this is my lawyer, Carson Morrow."

"Do you solemnly swear to tell the truth, the whole truth, and nothing but the truth?"

"I do," Louis Bordeau said. "Will you permit me to read a statement?"

"Go ahead."

My name is Louis Turner Bordeau. I am a resident of Columbia, South Carolina. I am sixty-one years old, and a widower. I have no children. Until recently I was employed as a veterinarian at the Columbia Zoo.

I have a BS degree in biology from the University of South Carolina and a DVM from the University of California at Davis. I did my residency at the San Diego Zoo, where I specialized in large animal reproduction. I am board certified by the American College of Zoological Medicine.

My responsibilities at the Columbia Zoo fell into the realm of reproduction. I traded sperm with zoos across the country, and I inseminated Columbia Zoo animals. I took females into my clinic when they became pregnant, and I delivered their offspring. I took males into my clinic when other zoos requested their sperm. I treated reproductive problems.

I am Dr. Patricia Bordeau Maloney's uncle and Mr. Willard Tavis's cousin once removed. I am disappointed in both relatives.

This story begins with Patricia's parents, whose love Patricia felt she had never acquired, no matter how high her grades or how numerous her honors, scholarships, academic degrees, and scientific papers. In graduate school she turned to me, her mother's older brother, for approval and for affection. I urged her to leave California and come to the Southeast to live. She got her PhD from Virginia Tech and did a post-doc at Georgia Tech. Then she landed an assistant professorship at Callaghan Research Institute in Atlanta. Her credentials were stellar. I was proud of her, and I told her so.

It was Patricia's cousin Willard who steered her into the world of chimeras. Willard was a dealer, in cocaine on occasion but mostly in rare animal hybrids, sperm, and embryos. Willard persuaded me to give him sperm when I was using artificial insemination to impregnate the zoo's big predators—lions, tigers, leopards, wolverines, wolves, bears, and the like . He used the sperm to breed hybrid predators, such as *pumapards (puma-leopard hybrid) and ligers (lion-tiger hybrid), which he sold for lots of money. Several years ago he got me to give him newborns from large litters without telling Columbia Zoo officials. He never paid me. And I never sold property that was not mine, not to Willard, not to Patricia.*

Willard read about the Apex Prize last fall and told Patricia and me about it. It was Willard who proposed the chimera project. Willard recognized that Patricia's work was at the frontier of reproductive technology and that she could be a pioneer in the creation of 50/50 mammalian chimeras. The three of us would be a team. She had the training. I had a new state-of-the-art lab as well as access to embryos and stem cells. And Willard had whatever money was needed. Willard also had facilities on his ranch to house animals. Patricia would win the $5 million Apex Prize and split it among the three of us. Patricia wanted the fame and fortune the Prize would bring her.

Patricia was self-confident, but not so self-confident that she didn't acknowledge her lack of experience in embryonic transplantation. That's why she brought Marco Ramos onto the team. She had met Marco at Georgia Tech, where he was a graduate student in her lab. She remembered that he had gone to Zoo Arroyo to learn from Jaime Arroyo how to transfer embryos successfully. Patricia seduced Marco. Marco was younger than she by five years, and he fell for her.

Now the $5 million-dollar Apex Prize would be split four ways: Willard, Marco, and I would each get $1 million; Patricia would get $2 million.

Life and Death at Zoo Arroyo   273

Willard benefitted in another way. He would take the new-born chimeras, raise them to adulthood, and sell them. Big animal chimeras, such as wolf-bear chimeras, would fetch a hefty price. I understand he agreed to give Patricia a cut of the chimera sales.

Anyway, Patricia trapped Marco. In January, early on in their relationship, Patricia told Willard, who told me, that she would marry him. "We need Marco's skills, Marco's allegiance to the project, and Marco's commitment to confidentiality," she said. And, according to Willard, she added, "If anything goes wrong, we need Marco in our family."

Patricia betrayed me. I had asked her to feed a newly pregnant jackal named Sameera who was in my charge the week of the *Wild Beasts Magazine* reception in Witherston. Without my permission Patricia operated on Sameera and took one of her embryos. I mean, she stole the embryo from Sameera. Then on Friday she allowed Sameera to escape from my clinic. When the police recaptured Sameera and Columbia Zoo officials saw evidence of the surgery, they fired me. And they fired Patricia from the position they had offered her only days before.

Willard is the wily one. He is smart, handsome, and charming, but ruthless. He is not incapable of murder to protect himself from the law. Let me go no further with this observation.

Patricia is the ambitious one. She is smart and beautiful, but deceitful. She is not troubled by a conscience.

In conclusion, let me reiterate that I never sold anything to Willard or to Patricia. If I broke the law

*in giving them sperm, embryos, and neonates, I did it
out of family loyalty. I hurt nobody.*
—*Louis T. Bordeau, DVM, July 7, 2030*

"That's my confession, Detective Dunning and Agent Washington."

"To what exactly are you confessing, Dr. Bordeau? You have accused Willard Tavis and Patricia Maloney of wrongdoing, but you have not admitted to wrongdoing yourself."

"You are correct, Agent Washington. I plead guilty only to giving my relatives property that belonged to the Columbia Zoo. And I did that for family reasons. I should have said No to my niece and my cousin. I was too kind to them."

"You are less kind to them now."

"I feel obliged to tell the truth."

"You said that Willard Tavis was capable of murder. Did Willard Tavis murder Garrison Tucker?" Troy asked. "Or did he have Garrison Tucker murdered?

"I don't know."

"Why did you visit Zoo Arroyo?" Mira asked. "You told Dr. Jaime Arroyo that you were interested in his reproductive techniques."

"I am a veterinarian, Detective Dunning. A veterinarian on the staff of a first-class zoo, a veterinarian charged with administering first-class treatment of the animals in my care. I wanted to learn the cloning techniques of the famous Dr. Jaime Arroyo."

"Have you ever knowingly broken the law, Dr. Bordeau?"

"Do not answer that question, Louis," Carson Morrow said.

"Do you consider the creation of chimeras to be ethical?" Mira asked.

"I don't consider it unethical. It is scientific investigation."

"Do you see any ethical constraints on scientific investigation?"

"I don't know where you're going with this line of questioning, Agent Dunning. I helped my niece to advance our knowledge of reproductive possibilities."

"Do you remember the veterinarian's oath, Dr. Bordeau?" Mira asked.

"No."

"I'll read it to you."

Being admitted to the profession of veterinary medicine, I solemnly swear to use my scientific knowledge and skills for the benefit of society through the protection of animal health and welfare, the prevention and relief of animal suffering, the conservation of animal resources, the promotion of public health, and the advancement of medical knowledge.

Mira continued. "In enabling your niece to create unnatural chimeras, have you prevented animal suffering, or have you caused it, Dr. Bordeau?"

"I have promoted public health in advancing our scientific knowledge."

"So you consider public health to be human health alone?"

Louis Bordeau did not answer.

"Do you have no empathy for the chimeras you've helped create?"

Louis Bordeau remained silent.

"Can you tell us where Patricia Maloney is now?" Troy asked.

"I don't know for sure, Agent Washington. I suspect Patricia has left the country. She may be in Perú with

Marco. Do you want her contact information?" Louis Bordeau pulled out his phone.

"Yes, Dr. Bordeau. Please forward it to both of us. And please forward Willard Tavis's contact information to us as well."

Louis Bordeau did as requested.

"Thank you, Dr. Bordeau," Mira said. "Do not leave the country. We may want to talk with you further."

LOUIS SHOWED UP AT RHONDA'S MOUNTAIN HOME WITH a bouquet of red carnations, a box of chocolate truffles, and open arms.

Rhonda greeted him without a hug.

"I'm here to apologize, dear Rhonda. I did you wrong."

"Come in, Louis," Rhonda said. "I hope you had a good interview with Detective Dunning. I am having a whiskey sour. Would you like to join me?"

"Actually I'd prefer straight bourbon, please. Make it a double. And yes, I had an excellent meeting with Detective Dunning. I was happy to have the chance to clear my name. Here's a copy of my confession."

Rhonda read the document in its entirety while Louis drank his bourbon.

"You didn't explain why you couldn't come to dinner, Louis. How come? I would have understood."

"I knew that Patricia had operated on Sameera, and I wanted to recapture the jackal before the police got her. I didn't want to tell you what Patricia was doing with Sameera's embryos."

Over spinach-stuffed cannelloni, Louis recounted his meeting with Mira.

"I may move to Witherston," he said, as they opened the chocolates. "I would like us to resume our relationship."

"I hope you don't," Rhonda said. "At least not for my sake. I remember what Maya Angelou said: 'The first time someone shows you who they are, believe them.'"

After Louis had gone Rhonda called the Witherston Police Department and left a voice-message for Detective Dunning. "Detective Dunning. This is Rhonda Rather. Don't put any credence in Dr. Louis Bordeau's confession. Louis gave his niece, Dr. Patricia Maloney, permission to operate on Sameera and take one of her embryos."

Mira emailed Willard Tavis and requested his appearance at the police station at ten o'clock on Tuesday, July ninth. She invited him to prepare a written statement in which he addressed four questions.

1. *What is your personal/professional/financial relationship with Dr. Louis Bordeau and Dr. Patricia Bordeau Maloney?*

2. *What is your relationship with Gordo?*

3. *What do you know about the murders of Garrison Tucker and Simon Pate?*

4. *What is the source of your income?*

She emailed Dr. Patricia Bordeau Maloney and requested her appearance at the police station at ten o'clock on Wednesday, July tenth. She invited her to prepare a written statement as well, addressing four questions.

1. *How are you competing for the Apex Prize for Biological Innovation? Who is funding the project?*

2. *What is your personal/professional/financial relationship with Dr. Louis Bordeau, Willard Tucker, and Marco Ramos?*

3. *Are you aware that Simon Pate, also known as Gordo, is a suspect in the shooting of Garrison Tucker? Did you communicate with Mr. Tavis regarding Garrison Tucker at any time before the shooting?*

4. *Why did you shoot Simon Pate?*

Mira hesitated to summon Marco Ramos. What crime could he have committed? Was it a crime to appropriate an animal's womb for gestation of a chimera? A crime against whom? Against the animal? Was not Jaime also appropriating an animal's womb for a foreign embryo? Was the distinction between a chimera embryo and a clone embryo significant?

However, she needed to compare Marco Ramos's story with Patricia Maloney's.

After consulting with Troy Washington she requested Marco's presence at ten o'clock on Friday, July twelfth. She did not ask him to prepare a written statement. He had already provided his journal.

CHAPTER THIRTY
Tuesday, July 9, 2030

Willard Tavis brought his lawyer, the Charleston defense attorney, Egbert Patten. Special Agent Troy Washington administered the oath.

"Do you solemnly swear to tell the truth, the whole truth, and nothing but the truth?"

"I do," Willard Tavis said.

"You may read your statement, Mr. Tavis," Mira said.

"Thank you."

I am Willard Bordeau Tavis, age 44. My address is 809 Oaks Highway, Charleston, South Carolina. I am divorced with no children. I live on a 200-acre estate, once a Charolais cattle ranch, which I inherited from my father. I am self-employed. I breed, raise, buy, and sell animals, and I trade sperm with other breeders.

I understand that you wish to interview me, my cousin Patricia Bordeau Maloney, and Marco Ramos as persons of interest in the murders of Garrison Tucker and Simon Pate. I suggest you also interview Louis Bordeau.

I shall answer all your questions forthrightly.

Dr. Louis Bordeau is my uncle on my mother's side. My relationship with him is primarily familial, but it is also financial. When Uncle Louis got his job at the Columbia Zoo in 2008 my father had just died and bequeathed me Tavis Ranch. I was twenty-two years old, with a bachelor's degree in history and without a job. However, I did have experience breeding livestock. Uncle Louis approached me with a proposal. He told me that he had access to the offspring of large predatory animals such as lions, tigers, bears, wolves, and wolverines, and that from time to time he could sell me a newborn to raise. Once they reached sexual maturity I could re-sell the animals at high prices.

I was grateful for the opportunity. Eventually, I was also buying sperm from him and either selling it on the black market or inseminating my animals with it to produce unusual hybrids. My first hybrid achievement was a pumapard, which is a cross between a puma and a leopard. Now that Uncle Louis has been fired from the Columbia Zoo, I will have to modify my business plan, so to speak.

Dr. Patricia Bordeau Maloney is my cousin on my mother's side. She is thirteen years younger than I am, but we have been close since she was a teenager. My relationship with her is also both familial and financial. Last fall she came to me with a terrific idea: that we compete for the Apex Prize for Biological Innovation by creating large chimeras, which had never been done before. She said that the prize was worth $5 million. After she explained the process, I said that we needed Uncle Louis to supply the embryos and the stem cells. If he contributed them for free, he *could share the prize with us and get $1 million for himself. She agreed and said that we needed Uncle Louis's high-end lab for creating the chimera embryos.*

A couple of months later she told me that we also needed somebody with technical skill in transferring embryos and that she had somebody in mind. That person turned out to be Marco Ramos, who would also get $1 million of the prize. Patricia managed to get Marco to fall in love with her, which did not surprise me. She's pretty as well as clever, and she can get whatever she wants on the basis of her beauty and her brains. She married him for obvious reasons.

After she left the Callaghan Research Institute, I bought her a house in Columbia so she could continue her work in Uncle Louis's lab. But our quest for the Apex Prize hit a snag. On June 25, Patricia extracted an embryo from a pregnant jackal caged in Uncle Louis's clinic. The jackal survived the operation but escaped three days later and scared pedestrians in downtown Columbia. The Columbia Zoo fired Uncle Louis, and Marco fled the country. Patricia disappeared too.

Gordo worked for me part-time for years. He fed the animals and did whatever needed to be done on the ranch. He asked me to pay him in cash, so I did. I kept him off the books so he could avoid paying income tax. Until I read that Simon Pate had been shot and killed at Zoo Arroyo I didn't know Gordo's last name. He'd earned the nickname "Gordo" for being fat. He said I was better off not knowing it. I assumed he sold drugs because he seemed to have plenty of money.

I know nothing about the murders of Garrison Tucker and Simon Pate. I am aware of Garrison Tucker's advocacy for animal rights, and I admit to being unsympathetic to his cause, but I've never met the man.

What is the source of my income? I am a breeder of large predatory animals, the kind that are coveted by collectors. Lately I've been breeding and selling hybrids. I have been accused of "trafficking in wild animals." That sounds illegal. But I pay taxes, so my business of breeding, raising, buying, and selling animals and sperm is actually legal.

In conclusion: The only illegal part of our family collaboration is Uncle Louis's selling me sperm and new-borns from animals that belong to the Columbia Zoo.
—Willard Bordeau Tavis, July 9, 2030

"That's about it."

"I have a few questions for you, Mr. Tavis."

"And I am happy to answer them, Detective Dunning."

"Why did you connect Simon Pate and Gordo when you read that Simon Pate had been shot at Zoo Arroyo? Were you aware that Gordo was going to the zoo?"

"You don't need to answer that question, Mr. Tavis," Egbert Patten said.

"Okay. I'll continue. What kind of vehicle did Gordo drive?"

"A black Dodge Ram, maybe twenty years old."

"What kind of vehicle do you drive?"

"On the ranch I drive my own black Dodge Ram. When I am out and about I drive a 2029 Escalade."

"Why would a black Dodge Ram be spotted leaving Garrison Tucker's house after the shooting?"

"I have no idea."

"Did you send Gordo to kill Garrison Tucker?"

"No. Why would I do that?"

"Did you pay Gordo, that is, Simon Pate, three thousand dollars near the date of June fifteenth?"

"I don't recall. I may have. I paid him from time to time to help me on the ranch."

"Did you pay Gordo, that is, Simon Pate, two thousand dollars near the date of June twenty-fourth?

"No, I did not."

"Where were you on June fifteenth?"

"Let's see. June fifteenth was a Saturday." Willard Tavis consulted his phone's calendar. "I don't have anything on my calendar for that day. I must have been home."

"Where was Gordo on that day?"

"Probably at the ranch. Gordo works for me on Saturdays."

"Did you know that Dr. Patricia Maloney killed Gordo, that is, Simon Pate?"

"I understood she accidentally shot him."

Troy interrupted, "Dr. Maloney's killing Gordo was convenient for you, especially if you had sent him on the errand to kill Garrison Tucker."

"I did not send him to kill Garrison Tucker."

"Did Dr. Maloney tell you that Garrison Tucker was about to identify you as an illegal trafficker in wild animals?"

"No, she did not, Agent Washington."

Troy turned to Mira. "That's all I need, Detective Dunning."

"Mr. Tavis, I understand you have a license to carry a gun," Mira said.

"I need a gun in case one of the animals gets out of hand. It's a Glock nineteen."

"Where is it now?"

"I have no idea. I can't find it."

"Mr. Tavis, have you ever sold cocaine?"

"I did in my youth, Detective Dunning. I went to prison for three months, but my conviction was overturned. You probably know that. I do not sell cocaine now."

"You have nothing to do with drug trafficking, Mr. Tavis?"

"No, not now."

"Let me ask you a question on another topic. In what kind of enclosures do you keep the animals you raise to adulthood?"

"In normal zoo cages, cages only slightly smaller than the Columbia Zoo cages."

"How many animals per cage?"

"One."

"Do you suppose the animals are unhappy?"

"I don't think about the animals that way. To me they are livestock. Do you think about beef that way?"

"Mr. Tavis, did you have anything to do with stealing the minks from Zoo Arroyo."

"No."

"Did you send Gordo to steal the minks?"

"No, I didn't send him. Gordo stole the minks on his own. He brought them back to the ranch to keep. Minks fetch good money, you know."

Troy broke in again. "And Gordo can't talk—fortunately for you, Mr. Tavis."

"How did Gordo know that Zoo Arroyo had minks?" Mira asked.

"I don't know."

"Did Gordo listen to the recording Lola Montoya sent you of her interview with Dr. Jorge Arroyo?"

Willard Tavis remained silent.

"You don't have to answer the question, Mr. Tavis," his attorney said.

"If Gordo didn't listen to the recording, did you tell him about the minks?"

"You don't have to answer the question," his attorney repeated.

"Okay. Then we may have finished," Mira said. "Do you have any more questions, Agent Washington?"

"That's all for me," Troy said.

"That's all for us too, Mr. Tavis," Mira said. "You may go now. I ask you not to leave the country."

After Willard Tavis had left, Mira said to Troy, "Do you know what most bothers me about this case? It is the insensitivity toward the animals."

"But we can't indict him on the grounds that he doesn't have a heart. We've gotta get him for a crime. I'd bet my paycheck he's guilty of homicide—sending Gordo, aka Simon Pate, to kill Garrison Tucker."

"The question is what Dr. Maloney knew."

"How could Mr. Tavis know that Garrison Tucker was after him?" Troy asked.

"Jorge Arroyo, who operates Zoo Arroyo, shared an email message from Mr. Tucker with his staff. In it Mr. Tucker said, and I quote, 'When I identify the trafficker I will sue him and ruin him financially.' Marco Ramos got the email and shared it with Dr. Maloney, who probably shared it with Mr. Tavis. I know this because I read Mr. Ramos's journal, which he sent to Jorge and asked Jorge to share with law enforcement officials. I will forward it to you this afternoon."

"I will read it tonight."

"When we interview Dr. Maloney tomorrow, remember that she doesn't know we've read it."

CHAPTER THIRTY-ONE

Wednesday, July 10, 2030

"Do you solemnly swear to tell the truth, the whole truth, and nothing but the truth?"

"I do, Detective Dunning."

"Have a seat, Dr. Maloney," Mira said. "You too, Mr. Prichard."

Dr. Patricia B. Maloney wore a black linen pant suit and carried an expensive gray patent leather briefcase. With her hair pulled back in a bun she looked professional. She had hired Atlanta defense attorney Arnold Prichard to represent her.

"May I read a statement?" Patricia asked, reaching into her briefcase for a document.

"Certainly."

I am Dr. Patricia Bordeau Maloney. I am thirty-two years old. I have a PhD in reproductive technology from Virginia Tech. My current address is 215 Snapper Drive, Columbia, South Carolina.

I will do my best to answer your questions fully.

First, I led a team of four people in competing for the 2031 Apex Prize for Biological Innovation. The four people were my uncle Louis Bordeau, my cousin Willard Tavis, my husband Marco Ramos, and myself.

Second, Uncle Louis and Cousin Willard both provided financial and in-kind support for the project in exchange for a cut in the $5,000,000 award. Uncle Louis provided embryos and stem cells from the Columbia Zoo animals, and gave me access to his laboratory. Out of those embryos and stem cells I created chimera embryos. Marco transferred the chimera embryos into surrogate mothers in exchange for $1,000,000 of the award. Marco also identified the candidates for surrogacy at Zoo Arroyo. Cousin Willard took the newborn chimeras to raise on his ranch in Charleston. When we needed money, Cousin Willard supplied it.

Third, I was not aware that Simon Pate, whom I knew as Gordo, was a suspect in the shooting of Garrison Tucker. I don't recall talking with Cousin Willard about Garrison Tucker. But we talk about lots of things.

Fourth, I did not murder Simon Pate. I did not even know Gordo was Simon Pate until I read about his death in the news. Let me be clear: I shot the man accidentally.

This is how it happened. Marco had transferred a female wolverine-wolf chimera embryo into a wolf named Faye at Zoo Arroyo. Marco didn't want the Arroyo twins to discover the chimera when Faye whelped her. Marco told me that the Zoo would be vacated the night of June 24, gave me a key to the Zoo Arroyo entrance gate and the gate to Sol's Woods, told me that Faye wore a yellow collar, and asked me to kidnap Faye. I agreed with the plan. I asked Juan Navarro, who worked for Cousin Willard, to drive *up from Charleston to help me. Juan backed out and sent Gordo in his place. I picked up Gordo in the Witherston High School parking lot, and we took my SUV to the zoo. At the gate to Sol's Woods Gordo gave me his gun and told me to shoot any wolf that got aggressive. He went alone with a net into the enclosure. The wolves attacked him in a frenzy. The biggest wolf sank his teeth into Gordo's neck. I was horrified. I wanted to save Gordo, so I shot at the wolves. I hit the big wolf, and I accidentally hit Gordo in the back of the head. When I realized that Gordo was dead I felt sick to my stomach. I left the zoo and drove at a high speed to Uncle Louis's house in Columbia, where I had promised to stay for the week. I was to take care of his dogs and a jackal named Sameera.*

So the answer to your question of why I shot Simon Pate is this: I shot him unintentionally in my effort to save him from the wolves. The shooting was equivalent to a hunting accident.

In sum, I myself did not break any laws in connection with the Apex project.

If Marco broke any laws, I cannot testify against him, since he is my husband. Nor can he testify against me.

—*Patricia Bordeau Maloney, PhD, July 10, 2030*

"Thank you, Dr. Maloney. Agent Washington and I have a few questions for you. You go first, Agent Washington."

"Thank you for your statement. Dr. Maloney. And thank you for returning from Perú. First, in response to your claim that spouses cannot testify against each other I will clarify the law. According to federal law an individual cannot be required to testify against his or her spouse, but if an individual wishes to testify against his or her spouse, he or she is free to do so."

"Understood."

"Okay. What kind of gun did you use to shoot Gordo?"

"A handgun. I don't know what brand."

"What did you do with it?"

"I buried it on Uncle Louis's property?"

"Where?"

"Under the oak tree in front of his house."

"Why did you bury it? Did you fear getting caught for murder? If you shot Gordo unintentionally, why did you hide the gun?"

"I didn't know who owned it, Agent Washington. I was trying to protect Cousin Willard, in case it was his gun."

"I have a question, Dr. Maloney," Mira said. "Where were you standing when you accidentally shot Gordo?"

"About ten feet away from him. Outside the gate."

"What size shoe do you wear?"

"Size nine narrow. Why?"

"Officer Waters found a size nine shoe print directly behind the site of Simon Pate's body."

"I can explain that. After I accidentally shot Gordo, I went into the enclosure to see whether he was dead."

"When and how did you learn of Garrison Tucker's email to Dr. Jorge Arroyo?" Troy asked.

"What email?"

"Remember that you are under oath, Dr. Maloney. I will ask you again. When did you learn that Garrison Tucker had sent an email to Dr. Jorge Arroyo saying that he was investigating an animal trafficker in the South and asking Dr. Arroyo to call him on Saturday?"

"My husband Marco may have told me. But I don't remember when."

"Did you tell Mr. Tavis?"

"As I said, I don't remember. I may have."

"Did you find out that Mr. Tavis had sent Gordo to kill Garrison Tucker?" Mira asked.

"Mr. Tavis didn't tell me."

"Did Gordo tell you?"

"No."

"And Gordo is dead," Troy said, "so he can't testify. Dr. Maloney, how would you respond to this charge? You learned from Marco that Garrison Tucker was investigating Mr. Tavis. You communicated the information to Mr. Tavis. Mr. Tavis sent Gordo to kill Garrison Tucker. You learned that Gordo had fatally shot Garrison Tucker, so you killed Gordo to keep him from squealing on your cousin. And you buried the gun that killed both Garrison Tucker and Gordo."

"You don't have to answer that question," Patricia's lawyer said.

"Gordo could have confessed to that murder and implicated Mr. Tavis," Troy continued. "If he had survived the attack by the wolves, Gordo could have implicated you in the attempted kidnapping of Faye. It benefitted you and Mr. Tavis for Gordo to be dead."

Patricia stayed silent.

"Dr. Maloney," Troy went on. "Whose idea was it to steal Faye?"

"I said in my statement that the idea was Marco's."

"Are you confident that Mr. Ramos would not dispute your accusation?"

"Yes," Patricia said. "Anyway, it would be his word against mine."

"Dr. Maloney," Mira said, "were you inside or outside the wolves' enclosure when you shot Gordo?"

"Inside. When the wolves attacked him I ran towards Gordo and started shooting."

"I see. And you got very close to Gordo when the biggest wolf held him by the throat."

"I guess so."

"Why did you remove Simon Pate's identification from his body?" Mira asked. "He had no wallet on him, no driver's license."

Patricia looked startled.

"You don't have to answer that question, Dr. Maloney," her lawyer said.

"I want to answer the question. The answer is that I didn't want the police to connect Gordo with my cousin Willard Tavis."

"That's why you shot him," Troy said. "If you had left him alive, or if you had called nine-one-one, he would have explained what he was doing at Zoo Arroyo."

"Why did you not call nine-one-one?" Mira asked.

"Gordo was already dead. What was the point?"

"The police would have wanted to question you," Troy answered.

"Oh."

"On another topic, did you alert Willard Tavis to Lola Montoya's June twenty-third interview on WITH-FM with Jorge?" Mira asked.

"I don't remember. As I said in my statement, we talk almost every day."

"So you are aware of that interview. Did you listen to it?"

"My husband Marco told me about it. Yes, I listened to it."

"Then you knew that Ms. Montoya would disapprove of your chimera project."

"Yes."

Troy interrupted. "Dr. Maloney, did you expect Mr. Tavis to retaliate against Ms. Montoya?"

"No. Obviously not. But I thought he should know his photographer's attitude towards the animals she was photographing."

"Why did you flee to Perú?" Mira asked.

"I didn't flee. I went to be with my husband."

"I am curious, Dr. Maloney," Mira said. "Why do you want to create chimeras? Was it solely to win the Apex Prize?"

"I do, or rather, I did want to win the Apex Prize. No longer. Our team seems to have fallen apart. Winning the Apex Prize was not my sole goal. I wanted to be a scientific pioneer. I still do. I want to show that humans can now mold nature to our wishes. Creating mammalian chimeras that are half one species and half another represents a new scientific revolution, one as consequential as the Copernican revolution and the Darwinian revolution. I plan to write a book called "Nature is Ours.""

"Do you see any ethical implications to creating chimeras, Dr. Maloney?"

"I'm not a philosopher, Detective Dunning. I leave ethics to the philosophers. Science always precedes ethics. Ethicists scramble to make sense out of scientific advances. I want to be in the vanguard of science."

"I see. By the way, Dr. Maloney, have you ever had a pet? A dog, or a cat? Or even a bird?"

"No."

"Is that all?" Arnold Prichard asked. "If so, may we be excused?"

"That's all for me," Troy said.

"I have a few more questions, Dr. Maloney. "First, did Dr. Bordeau give you permission to extract the embryo from Sameera, the jackal?"

"Yes. Of course."

"Did you wear a Georgia Tech baseball cap to the zoo on the night of June twenty-fourth?"

"Yes, I guess I did. I don't know where it is. Why?"

"A Georgia Tech baseball cap was found at the murder site. We would like to compare your DNA to the DNA left on the cap."

"Sure. I'll give you a sample."

"Thank you, Dr. Maloney. Just give us a few hairs and then you may be excused. I ask that you remain in the country until the case is closed."

"My husband is in Perú. Do you plan to subpoena him?"

"Wait and see," Troy said.

Patricia and her lawyer departed.

"She lied," Troy said to Mira. "Marco Ramos recorded in his journal that she initiated the plan to nab Faye. I believe him. His journal is a contemporaneous account of what happened."

"She lied about shooting Simon Pate too. If she shot him in the back of the head at close range it was not an accident."

"We can wrap up the case after talking with Mr. Ramos, I expect."

"I suggest we interview two additional persons. How about Juan Navarro at three o'clock tomorrow, which is Thursday, and Lola Montoya at ten o'clock on Saturday?"

CHAPTER THIRTY-TWO

Thursday, July 11, 2030

"Do you solemnly swear to tell the truth, the whole truth, and nothing but the truth?"

"Yes," Juan Navarro said. "I swear."

"Tell us who you are, Mr. Navarro," Mira said.

"My name is Juan Navarro. I am fifty-five years old. I have lived in Charleston for ten years. I worked for Mr. Willard Tavis until June twenty-fifth."

"Are you related to Lola Montoya?"

"Yes, Lola Montoya is my niece. She is the daughter of my sister Estela Navarro. Her son Benito is my great nephew. I just moved in with them."

"Tell us what you know of Mr. Tavis," Troy said.

"Mr. Tavis is rich. He doesn't have any children, but he has a niece. Her name is Patricia Maloney."

"When did Mr. Tavis hire you?"

"Mr. Tavis hired me in 2026, right after I lost my job as a cook at La Fiesta in Charleston. He found out that I had been arrested for drunk driving, and he paid my bail. I thought he was an angel sent to save my life."

"Did you ever figure out why he bailed you out of jail?"

"Mr. Tavis needed laborers he could control, so he hired men who'd had trouble with the law. I needed the job he offered."

"And what was that job?"

"Caring for his animals. Fierce animals, like lions and tigers and wolverines. I worked with Gordo. Gordo and I lived in the same house on Mr. Tavis's property."

"Specifically, what animals was Mr. Tavis keeping this spring?" Troy asked.

"A newborn lion cub, another cub that Mr. Tavis said was a leopard-cheetah mix, and a pair of minks and their babies."

"Do you know where the minks came from?"

"I learned from my niece that two minks were stolen from Zoo Arroyo in March. So I figured that Gordo stole them from the zoo. He brought them to the ranch in March."

"Did you tell Lola?"

"No. I was afraid of what she might do. And I was afraid of Mr. Tavis. I needed my job."

"The pair of minks are still at the ranch?"

"Yes, with their offspring. The female gave birth to five babies in April. They are very cute."

"How about the cubs?"

"Mr. Tavis brought them to the ranch at the end of May. The leopard-cheetah cub's name is Zahara. The lion cub doesn't have a name."

"I have a question," Mira said. "Did Dr. Patricia Maloney ask you to accompany her on the night of June twenty-fourth to Zoo Arroyo?"

"Yes, she did. But I backed out when she told me we were going to steal a wolf. I asked Gordo to go in my place."

"Why?"

"I knew that Lola liked Jorge Arroyo, and I didn't want to steal a wolf from him. I didn't want to steal anything from anybody."

"Did Gordo object to accompanying Dr. Maloney?"

"No. I gave him the two thousand dollars in cash that Mr. Tavis had given me. He was happy."

"Did Mr. Tavis find out?"

"No, not until after Gordo was killed. Mr. Tavis had already gone to Witherston for the *Wild Beasts* conference. He left Charleston on Sunday."

"What did Mr. Tavis do when he found out about the substitution?"

"He fired me."

"If you had gone with Dr. Maloney that Monday night, you would be dead instead of Gordo."

"*¡Jesús!*"

"Does Lola Montoya know what work you did at the Tavis Ranch?"

"No. Mr. Tavis swore me to secrecy. He swore Gordo to secrecy too."

"Are you aware of Lola Montoya's views on breeding unnatural animals?" Troy asked.

"Yes."

"Do you have anything else that might be helpful to us? We are trying to solve two mysteries: the fatal shooting of Garrison Tucker and the fatal shooting of Simon Pate, whom you know as Gordo."

"Actually, three mysteries," Mira said, "if we include the March shooting of Marco Ramos."

"If Gordo stole the minks, then he's the man who shot Marco," Troy said. "Mr. Navarro, tell us about Gordo."

"Gordo sells drugs. I mean, he sold drugs. Mr. Tavis knew about it, so Gordo had to do everything Mr. Tavis told him to do."

"Mr. Navarro, were you with Gordo on the morning of Saturday, June fifteenth?"

"No. Gordo went out of town that day. So did Mr. Tavis. I remember because I had to feed the animals. Gordo usually fed the animals on Saturdays so I could spend time with Lola and Benito. I was alone at the ranch."

"Do you have any more questions, Agent Washington?" Mira asked Troy.

"No. I'm satisfied."

"You may go, Juan. Thank you very much for coming in. Drive safely back to Charleston."

"Thank you, Detective Dunning. Thank you, Agent Washington." Juan Navarro left.

CHAPTER THIRTY-THREE

Friday, July 12, 2030

"**D**o you solemnly swear to tell the truth, the whole truth, and nothing but the truth?"

"I do," Marco said. Marco was alone. He had not engaged a lawyer.

"When did you get here, Mr. Ramos?" Mira asked him.

"Yesterday. I flew directly from Lima to Atlanta, rented a car, and spent last night at the Witherston Inn."

"We thank you for sharing your journal with Jorge and Jaime Arroyo, who shared it with me," Mira said. "Did you retrospectively modify any entry or any paragraph, sentence, or word in it before emailing it to Jorge and Jaime Arroyo?"

"No, I did not, Detective Dunning."

"Did you delete any entries, Mr. Ramos?"

"No, I did not, Agent Washington. But I didn't include what I wrote before the death of my mother, except for the entry about going to Washington D.C. with Jorge, Jaime, and Annie."

"So I would be accurate in saying that your journal memorializes the evolution of your thoughts and feelings toward Dr. Maloney from the time you first met her?"

"Yes. It memorializes my actions too."

"We intend to ask you about your actions during the past six months, Mr. Ramos. But first, would you like to make a statement?"

"I would, Agent Washington, though not a written statement."

"Please identify yourself."

"My name is Marco Ramos-Martínez. I am twenty-six years old. I come from Perú. I have a BS degree from the University of Lima with a double major in biology and English, and an MS degree in genetic engineering from Georgia Tech. For the last two years I have worked for Dr. Jaime Arroyo and Dr. Jorge Arroyo at Zoo Arroyo. I left suddenly on the night of June twenty-eighth. I fled to Perú."

"Why did you flee?"

"For many reasons. Having been brought up Catholic, I will say that I have sinned. I betrayed the trust of Jaime when I substituted the embryo of a chimera for the embryo of a cloned Red wolf in his freezer. I caused Jaime to implant a chimera embryo in Faye. And Faye died because of me. I betrayed the trust of Jorge when I gave my extra zoo key to my wife Patricia. I betrayed my mother, who believed I would always be truthful and generous. Most importantly, I betrayed myself when I made Patricia Maloney a higher priority than my own conscience."

"You blame yourself for your betrayal of the Arroyos, Marco. Would you assign any blame to Dr. Patricia Maloney?"

"I blame Patricia for seducing me, for steering me into unethical behavior, for lying to me. I blame myself for falling in love with her."

"In your judgment, has Patricia broken any laws?" Mira asked Marco.

"I hesitate to accuse her. But I will say that she must have intended to steal Faye from Zoo Arroyo. I don't know what happened the night her companion was killed in Sol's Woods. She told me she shot him by accident. I do know she manipulated me with her lies. And she conveyed to her cousin Willard Tavis information I gave her in confidence."

"Be specific, Mr. Ramos. What information did you give her in confidence?"

"I told Patricia about Garrison Tucker's email to Jorge and asked her to keep the information confidential. She asked me to forward Mr. Tucker's email to her. When I learned that Mr. Tucker had been shot to death two days later, I wondered whether she had forwarded Mr. Tucker's email to Willard Tavis and whether Willard Tavis had sent somebody to kill Mr. Tucker. I told Patricia about Lola Montoya's interview with Jorge in which Lola expressed her opposition to the kind of breeding that Mr. Tavis does. I think Patricia gave Mr. Tavis the link to the interview. I learned not to trust Patricia."

"Who proposed that you give Patricia a key to Zoo Arroyo?" Mira asked.

"Patricia."

"Why did you give it to her?"

"She told me that she would watch Faye and take the chimera if Faye whelped."

"Did you propose that she kidnap Faye?"

"No!"

"Did you have any idea she would try to steal Faye?"

"Faye was pregnant with the wolverine-wolf chimera."

"What is your view of chimeras now, Marco?"

"I'm horrified that I participated in this Nazi-like experimentation with conscious beings. I will repent for it the rest of my life. I hope to become a veterinarian to atone for my sins."

"Do you have any more questions, Agent Washington?" Mira asked her colleague.

"No, I think not."

"Then we thank you for coming back to Witherston to meet with us, Marco. I must ask you to stay in the area until the case is closed."

"I will."

"I'll contact Jorge and Jaime and tell them we've talked."

"Thank you, Detective Dunning. Thank you, Agent Washington."

After Marco had left the room, Troy Washington said to Mira, "He's telling the truth."

11:45 am

Hola, Marco!

I hear you are in Witherston.

Can you come up to the zoo today?

I invite you to stay here till you return to Perú.

I know that your hotel check-out time is noon, so come now.

Tu amigo Jorge

Hola, Jorge.

I don't deserve such kindness from you, but I accept your offer.

I am eager to see you and to try to make amends.

I will be there by 1:00 today.

I brought my flute.

Please tell Nick.

Muchísimas gracias, amigo mío.

Marco

"Tell me what went wrong, Marco," Jorge said.

Jorge and Marco sat on the back porch swing drinking lemonade. Poe perched on Jorge's shoulder.

"Have you ever been in love, Jorge?"

"I am now."

"Well, I hope you don't lose yourself in your relationship as I did in mine. I had never really fallen in love with anybody before I met Patricia Maloney, the beautiful, intelligent, accomplished Dr. Patricia B. Maloney. I fell for Patricia, and I mean I fell. I was in awe of her. I wanted to do everything in my power to please her. I did whatever she asked me to do, and I followed her wherever she went. I would have followed her through hell. I lost myself."

"Not every romantic relationship leads to self-abandonment, Marco."

"I don't know, Jorge. But I hope I never fall in love again. I'm not strong enough."

"I read your journal. I saw your moral struggle in it. I saw you as a man of conscience who had become enamored of a woman without a conscience."

"By the time I realized she was manipulating me I was trapped. I thought she was carrying our baby. I wanted a family."

"I understand. I do too."

For a few minutes the two men were quiet. They sipped their drinks.

Jorge broke the silence. "I don't blame you, Marco. I blame Patricia. Patricia used you for her purposes. Not all women do that."

"I hate her, Jorge. She stole my soul."

"She did not, Marco. Your journal shows that she did not."

"You read my thoughts about the Apex Prize. I've decided that I don't want to go into genetics. I fear the uses of gene editing."

"What do you want to do? If you want to work for Zoo Arroyo, Jaime and I would welcome you back."

"No, not at this time. I want to go to veterinary school. That will take four years, and then a couple of years in residency. Do you think you might want a partner to help you run the zoo in six years?"

"I would. In six years I most certainly would."

"Will you stay here at the zoo until Detective Dunning releases you to return to Perú?"

"With pleasure, Jorge. I thank you for your kindness."

"You can move back into the A-frame."

Jorge heard Nick run up the front steps.

"Jorge, where are you?" Nick called out.

"I'm on the back porch," Jorge responded. "See who's here!"

Nick appeared with his *quena* flute.

"Hey, Marco!" Nick shouted, bounding up the porch steps. "You came back!"

He ran into Marco's arms.

"Shall we play some music, Nick?"

"Yes, Marco!"

"I'll go get my new *pan* flute and the *pinkillo* flute I bought for you."

"I'll get my *bombo*," Jorge said.

"We'll be a band! The Blue Ridge Mountain Incans!" Nick said.

8:14 pm
Hola, Jorge.

Benito and I have arrived in Witherston.
Detective Mira Dunning will interview me tomorrow.
May we begin our weekend at Zoo Arroyo tonight?
Benito and I have already had dinner.
Un beso,
Lola

Hola, Lola.
Yes, yes, yes!
Your rooms are ready.
So am I.
Dos besos,
Jorge

LOLA AND BENITO ARRIVED AT NINE. BENITO IMMEDI-
ately excused himself and went to bed. Jorge and Lola sat
in the swing on the front porch with a bottle of Cava and
talked until late. They kissed, for the first time.

"*Querida Lola*, can you imagine living with me here at
Zoo Arroyo? With Benito, naturally."

"In my imagination? Yes, Jorge."

"Let me put it a different way. Might you and Benito like
to move in with me sometime?"

"Yes, we might like to, sometime."

"Soon?"

"Let's see." Lola opened her phone. "Benito and I would
be free to move in with you on Saturday, August thirty-first,
at three o'clock in the afternoon."

"Woohoo! Really?"

"Yes, really!"

"Should you ask Benito?"

"Benito has already suggested it."

"So you'll move in with me to please your son. Well, Lola, that's good enough for me. Would you like to join me tonight in my room?"

"I'd like to, Jorge."

"I love you, Lola Montoya."

"I love you, Jorge Arroyo."

CHAPTER THIRTY-FOUR

Saturday, July 13, 2030

"Do you solemnly swear to tell the truth, the whole truth, and nothing but the truth?"

"I do," Lola said.

"Please identify yourself," Troy said.

"I am Lola Montoya, a naturalized American citizen originally from Juárez, México, now living in Charleston, South Carolina. I am thirty-three years old. I am divorced. I have a thirteen-year-old son named Benito. I have a BS degree in ecology from the University of Texas at El Paso, and I will soon have an MFA in photography from the University of Charleston. I am self-employed as a photographer. One of my clients was Mr. Willard Tavis who owns a ranch outside of Charleston."

"I understand you are also an environmental activist, Lola."

"Yes, Detective Dunning. I have been elected president of Green Earth Charleston."

"Please tell us how you know Willard Tavis, Ms. Montoya. And what you know about him."

"I first met Mr. Tavis in 2026, when he bailed my uncle, Juan Navarro, out of jail and gave him a job on his ranch. Mr. Tavis must have liked Tío Juan because a year or so ago he offered me employment as a photographer for *Wild*

Beasts Magazine. He hired me to go to zoos and menageries to photograph their, quote, 'wild beasts' and to record interviews with their owners. That's how I know Mr. Tavis."

"And what do you know about him, Ms. Montoya?"

"I know that he breeds and sells strange hybrid animals to collectors who lock them up in cages. Hybrids such as pumapards, ligers, and coydogs. I consider that business to be unethical. I said as much when Dr. Jorge Arroyo interviewed me on 'People for the Planet.' That was on June twenty-third. Mr. Tavis fired me two days later."

"Can you give us a list of the places Mr. Tavis has sent you as a photographer?"

"Yes. May I email it to you?"

"That would be fine," Troy said. "Do you have questions, Detective Dunning?"

"Yes, I do. Lola, in your opinion why did Mr. Tavis fire you?"

"I think Mr. Tavis viewed me as a threat to his operation. When I was on the radio with Jorge I said that I opposed the breeding and selling of odd hybrids such as pumapards and jackal-dogs. Did you listen to my interview, Detective Dunning?"

"I did. I regularly listen to 'People for the Planet.'"

"I think Mr. Tavis did not want me to give information to Jorge about my photography assignments."

"What kind of vehicle does Mr. Tavis drive?"

"Mr. Tavis owns two vehicles: an old black Dodge Ram and a new silver Cadillac Escalade. He also has a small tractor."

"What kind of vehicle does your uncle Juan Navarro drive?"

"He drives a beat-up old white chevy pick-up."

"Do you know anything about Mr. Tavis's relationship with Gordo, whose real name is Simon Pate?"

"Mr. Tavis employed Gordo to help him with his animals on the ranch, and also to deliver animals to buyers. Until recently I didn't know that Gordo's real name was Simon Pate."

"Does Mr. Tavis sell drugs?"

"I don't know. Gordo sold drugs, according to my uncle."

"Did your uncle tell you that Gordo stole the minks from Zoo Arroyo?"

"No! He did? I mean, did Gordo steal the minks?"

"That will be all. I thank you for coming in today, Lola."

After Lola had left the conference room, Mira said, "Willard Tavis drives a black Dodge Ram. I wonder whether he shot Garrison Tucker himself."

"The same gun was used to shoot Marco, Garrison Tucker, and Simon Pate. Whose gun was it?"

PART IV

Case Closed

CHAPTER THIRTY-FIVE

Saturday, July 13, 2030

(Continued)

"Let's figure out what we've learned from these interviews, Detective Dunning," Troy Washington said. "You dictate. I'll type."

Garrison Tucker Murder

1) Gordo/Simon Pate was absent from the Tavis Ranch on Saturday, June 15, when Garrison Tucker was fatally shot by someone in an old black Dodge Ram.

2) Gordo/Simon Pate drove an old black Dodge Ram.

3) Willard Tavis drives an old black Dodge Ram.

4) Mr. Tavis was absent from the Ranch on Saturday, June 15.

5) Mr. Tavis had motive to kill Garrison Tucker: Garrison Tucker was investigating him for animal trafficking.

6) The same gun that killed Simon Pate had been used to shoot Marco Ramos and to kill Garrison Tucker. Could the gun belong to Mr. Tavis?

Conclusion: Willard Tavis sent Gordo/Simon Pate to kill Garrison Tucker. If this can be proven, Mr. Tavis can be indicted for premeditated murder.

Gordo/Simon Pate Murder

1) Gordo/Simon Pate was shot in the back of the head at close range, indicating the intent to kill.

2) Dr. Patricia Maloney apparently lied when she said she accidentally shot Gordo/Simon Pate at a distance.

3) Dr. Maloney apparently lied when she said Marco proposed that they steal Faye.

4) Dr. Maloney did not call 911 or report the death of Gordo/Simon Pate. Instead, she abandoned his body and fled. She buried the gun. Her actions suggest guilt.

5) Dr. Maloney had motive to kill Gordo/Simon Pate. If he had lived, if he had been given medical attention, if he had been interviewed by the police, he might have fingered Dr. Maloney for initiating the plan to steal Faye. He might have fingered Willard Tavis for sending him to kill Garrison Tucker.

Conclusion: Dr. Maloney can be indicted for either second-degree murder or manslaughter.

Theft from the Columbia Zoo

1) Dr. Louis Bordeau stole sperm and offspring from the Columbia Zoo.

2) Dr. Bordeau provided sperm and offspring that belonged to the Columbia Zoo to Willard Tavis.

3) Dr. Bordeau provided embryos and stem cells from Columbia Zoo animals to Dr. Maloney.

4) Dr. Bordeau gave Dr. Maloney permission to extract an embryo from the jackal Shaheera.

Conclusion: Dr. Bordeau can be indicted for theft.

SHOOTING OF MARCO RAMOS AND *Theft of Minkie and Mickie*

1) Willard Tavis learned from Lola's recorded interview that Zoo Arroyo had young minks.

2) Mr. Tavis informed Gordo of the minks and possibly sent him to Zoo Arroyo.

3) Gordo brought two minks to the ranch in March. Mr. Tavis kept them.

3) Whoever stole the minks shot Marco.

Conclusion: Gordo stole the pair of minks and shot Marco.

"We have enough evidence to indict Willard Tavis and Patricia Maloney for homicide, and Louis Bordeau for theft and possibly Mr. Tavis for theft, Troy. Should we also indict Mr. Travis for 'animal trafficking'?"

"Breeding and selling creepy hybrids and chimeras doesn't violate any laws, Mira."

"Could we indict Dr. Maloney for appropriating uteruses without permission? I'm talking about the clandestine transfer of embryos into the wombs of Faye and Juliet."

"Who are Faye and Juliet?" Troy asked.

"Faye is a wolf and Juliet is a bear."

"I can't think of a law it violates, Mira."

"You live on a farm, Troy. What if I surreptitiously planted kudzu in your wheat field without your permission? Would that be the same as transferring embryos into Zoo Arroyo's animals without Jaime's or Jorge's permission?"

"I can't think of a law it violates."

"That's unfortunate. It violates ethical principles. What about, 'Do unto others as you would have others do unto you.'"

"As Dr. Maloney said, 'science always precedes ethics,'" Troy said.

"So true. Okay. We will arrest Willard Tavis, Patricia Maloney, and Louis Bordeau for committing crimes that are already on the books."

"Jorge, come to the fox pens!" Nick said to Jorge on the phone. "Foxy Belle is in labor. Foxy Ann has already had four babies. Benito is taking pictures."

Nick had invited Benito to tour the zoo while Lola was at the Witherston police station.

"I'll be there in ten minutes," Jorge said.

"Marco is here too," Nick said.

"I'm coming!"

Friday morning Jorge and Zell had put Foxy Ann and Foxy Belle into heavily wooded half-acre pens, each with a small spring-fed pond, each with several options for whelping dens.

Jorge loaded the jeep with a spring scale, towels, his medical bag, and two packages of rabbit meat he had in the clinic's refrigerator. By the time he reached the pens Foxy Belle had whelped her fourth kit.

"Foxy Belle has whelped four male Swift fox clones," Marco said.

"They all look alike," Nick said. "They are perfect!"

"I got pictures of them coming out," Benito said.

Jorge weighed and examined the newborns. "You are right, Nick. They all look alike. They should be genetically identical."

"Jorge, could we name one after Benito?" Nick asked. "We could give the kits all 'B' names."

"Nice idea. How about naming the first one 'Benny,'" Jorge said.

"Yes. And the others could be named 'Barnie,' 'Baxter,' and 'Buddy.'"

"Let's go see Foxy Ann," Nick said. "We can give her kits 'A' names. Let's let Marco name them."

Jorge, Marco, Nick, and Benito entered Foxy Ann's pen. Foxy Ann was nursing four tiny female kits.

"They look healthy," Jorge said. "And identical. Okay, Marco, you name them."

"'Allie,' 'Amy,' 'Annie,' and 'Alicia.'"

"Good names, Marco!"

"As I recall, 'Alicia' was your mother's name, Marco," Jorge said.

"It was."

JORGE AND LOLA WERE ALONE FOR DINNER. AT JORGE'S suggestion, Eddie had invited Benito to eat with his family and to spend the night. He had also invited Marco for dinner.

Jorge poured two glasses of his best Cabernet Sauvignon.

"*Al amor,*" Jorge said. "To love."

"*Y el tiempo para gozarlo.*" Lola responded. "And time to enjoy it."

They went to bed early.

CHAPTER THIRTY-SIX

Saturday, August 24, 2030

"Congratulations to Lola and Benito!" Jorge stood up and raised his glass of Champagne. "Lola has received her MFA from the University of Charleston today, and Benito has won the Southeast Regional Young Photographer's Award with his photograph of two skunks mating.'"

"*Chin chin.*"

"*Chin chin.*"

"*Chin chin.*"

Jorge and Lola, Benito, Estela Navarro, Juan Navarro, Jaime, Annie, and Heather, and Holly all clinked glasses. They were seated at a long table at the Charleston House Restaurant.

"Thank you, Jorge," Benito said. "I used my spy camera. The skunks didn't know they were being photographed. I also have a photograph of chipmunks mating and one of rabbits mating."

"Do we have a theme here, Benito?" Jorge asked.

"Yes, Jorge! Guess what it is."

Lola stood up. "May we raise a glass to my dear mother, Estela Navarro, who came all the way from Juárez, México, to be with us today."

"Chin chin."

"Chin chin."

"Chin chin."

"I have an announcement to make," Jorge said. "Lola has accepted my proposal of marriage. Our wedding will take place on December twenty-first. Lola and Benito are moving in with me one week from today, on August thirty-first."

"At three o'clock," Lola added.

"Hooray," Benito shouted.

"Hallelujah, bro! You're getting married!" Jaime jumped up to hug his brother. "We can have the wedding at my house."

Epilogue

On August twenty-sixth, 2030, Marco Ramos began his first year of vet school at the Universidad Nacional Mayor de San Marcos in Lima. On September twelfth Marco finalized his divorce from Patricia Maloney.

On October sixteenth, 2030, Willard Tavis pleaded guilty to ordering Simon Pate to murder Garrison Tucker. He was sentenced to twenty-five years at the South Carolina State Penitentiary in Columbia, South Carolina. His animals, including the family of minks, were moved to Zoo Arroyo.

On October thirty-first, 2030, Patricia Maloney was convicted of second-degree murder in the case of Simon Pate. She was sentenced to ten years at the Georgia State Penitentiary in Milledgeville, Georgia.

On November eighth, 2030, Louis Bordeau was convicted of larceny. He was sentenced to three years at the Allendale Correctional Institution in Fairfax, South Carolina. His license to practice veterinary medicine was revoked.

On December twenty-first, 2030, Jorge Arroyo and Lola Montoya were married at the home of Jaime and Annie Arroyo. Juan Navarro provided the food. Rhonda Rather provided the wine. Marco Ramos and Nick Crane provided the music.

The End

Photo by Laszlo Soti

Betty Jean Craige retired from the University of Georgia in 2011 as University Professor of Comparative Literature and Director of the Willson Center for Humanities and Arts.

Over four decades Betty Jean wrote numerous books, including the biography of a remarkable human, titled *Eugene Odum: Ecosystem Ecologist and Environmentalist*, and the shorter biography of a remarkable bird, titled *Conversations with Cosmo: At Home with an African Grey Parrot*. She curated museum exhibitions of the lithographs of Alvar Suñol at the Georgia Museum of Art and the Albany (Georgia) Museum of Art, and created the documentary *Alvar: His Vision and His Art* (2006).

For two years Betty Jean wrote a column in the *Athens Banner-Herald* titled "Cosmo Talks," about her parrot Cosmo. Then she turned her attention to fiction and published five Witherston Murder Mysteries—*Downstream, Fairfield's Auction, Dam Witherston, Saxxons in Witherston*, and *Death in Potter's Woods*—and a thriller about genome therapy titled *Aldo*. *Death at Zoo Arroyo* is her sixth Witherston Murder Mystery.

In 2021 she published a collection of essays titled *Ruminations on a Parrot Named Cosmo*.

Betty Jean lives in Athens, Georgia, and enjoys traveling, cooking, entertaining, reading, seeing movies, FaceTiming with friends, and chatting with her beloved Cosmo.

See: http://www.bettyjeancraige.org/

Made in the USA
Coppell, TX
07 January 2023

10650000R00194